Born in Sydney in 1935 of an Irish-Australian family, Thomas Keneally originally studied for the Catholic priesthood but left two weeks before his ordination. He then became a teacher, and studied for the New South Wales Bar. He began writing in 1963. Since then he has been awarded three Australian Literary Fellowships (1966, 1968 and 1973), a Royal Society of Literature Award (1973), and two Miles Franklin Awards (1967 and 1968), among others. His other novels include *Bring Larks and Heroes*, *Three Cheers for the Paraclete* and *The Chant of Jimmie Blacksmith*.

ALSO BY THOMAS KENEALLY
AVAILABLE IN QUARTET EDITIONS

Bring Larks and Heroes

THE FEAR

THOMAS KENEALLY

QUARTET BOOKS LONDON

Published by Quartet Books Limited 1973
27 Goodge Street, London W1P 1FD

First published by Cassell Australia Ltd 1965

ISBN 0 704 31067 8

Printed in Great Britain by
Hunt Barnard Printing Ltd, Aylesbury, Bucks.

To my mother
who was not Stell,
but better.

1

Next door to us, crowded on the east and west by large houses, was the Mantles' narrow little brick place. It seemed to be subsiding crookedly into the earth like an ill-laid tombstone, and was a sunless warren, dim humidity in summer, dim moisture in winter. The laneway to its back door ran flush against our side wall, and beneath the Mantles' lounge-room window, a furze of moss grew a quarter of an inch thick on the mortar.

Len Mantle and Hilda must have been in their early thirties and had two boys to boast of—though *boast* is in this case a cruel word. For the younger one was, physically at least, a slack-mouthed replica of his slack-mouthed father, and *that* was nothing to boast of; while the elder had some congenital disease of the nervous system which was, cell by cell, turning his muscles to jelly and making him walk on the balls of his feet, in what many people who did not know believed to be an insane parody of elegance.

Our old home, my parents' and mine, had been no more than four hundred miles northwards and not even in another state. Still our migration plunged me into shock. The heat was duller. The air was full of sweat. By night I choked with asthma. By day I haunted the yard, not believing that from it you couldn't sight a brown elbow of river, Guernseys cropping an emerald floodplain, the smoke-blue tangle of New England hills. My eyes constantly returned to a galvanized iron fence, and beyond it the brick butt-ends of shop residences. Inevitably, Hilda saw me, and judging me merely lonely, told my mother to send me in to meet the boys.

It wasn't long before I essayed that fungoid lane which led towards the squabbling noise of the Mantles at play with each other in their overgrown backyard. (As Len Mantle was to say, a man with a cause has no time to muck about with lawnmowers.) They sat on flattened grass beneath an old peach tree, arguing over a bow made out of a peach sapling by their almighty father. Their small angry heads nodded polemically. Their hair was straight, fine, Asiatic hair, as if their grandmother had known a Chinaman; and as they spoke, it flopped over their foreheads in wads. There was an Asiatic smoothness and roundness about their faces, and the corners of their eyes were Asiatically taut. No direct acknowledgement of my existence in their own backyard was made, but all the heat went out of their squabble. They began to perform their argument, and I, knowing my place, stood by, showing polite interest as it developed.

'You let the bloody string go loose,' the younger one hissed, pausing for me to marvel at the adjective. 'Comrade Lenin told you not to, he told you how to keep it tight, he told you you could use it even! But off he goes to work and you spoil it on me! Now we have to wait for Comrade Lenin to make us another one, and he might be too busy to make it for years. Comrade, I could kick your guts in!'

The elder brother, Joe, was sitting with his long legs and abnormally arched feet tucked under him. For a while he kept silence for he understood that Lennie, the other one, was just a young buck rattling his spears. What he did not understand, what I did not know, was that he was, in strict truth, sitting on death, that the enemy of his blood and his gens was, at that moment, under the peach tree, seducing his nerves, lulling his muscles to reflexless blubber. He leant across towards Lennie, picked up the bow and flexed it, knobbly elbows splayed out from his sides, for the enemy was in his arms as well.

'Who said *you* owned it?' he asked. 'I remember the day he

made this. He made it for me. I didn't ever say you could use it.'

Lennie leant forward and roared in his brother's face, 'You stinking big liar, Joseph. *I* helped the Comrade make this bloody bow on a day you had the pains. He made it for *me*. Why would he make it for a bloke who can't even walk proper?'

Joseph squinted savagely at the insult, rolled it over on his tongue, spat it out onto the grass. Lennie was wise enough to sit back, waiting for the argument to sprout a new limb.

'The time he made another bow and arrow,' Joseph said at length, 'he let me cut it off the tree with his own knife.' This was answer complete, this was fulfilment, to cut a bough with the Comrade's own knife.

'I was too small to cut it then. That's the only reason. He felt my muscles and said I was a real son to have. He told me he always wants *me* to cut his wood, right until I die.'

Joseph had the calm certitude of mountains and icebergs. His anger was a queer wise anger that gave what he said neither heat nor eloquence but the sting of truth.

'He wouldn't say that. You're six. Who'd talk to a six-year-old as if he was important. I can tell you, Lennie, I'm as good as a grown-up to the Comrade. You're a baby of a six-year-old. Grown-ups tell babies anything. They even tell them Santa Claus.'

Perhaps Lennie *did* lose his self-control there. He yelled and ground his teeth and hurled himself on his brother. Nature had provided for an even fight—Lennie's short strong limbs tangling with Joseph's weak long ones. The two rolled on the crushed yellow grass in what was more like brotherly love than anger.

As they grunted at my feet, and Lennie spat maniac hate through clenched teeth, I saw that I had the balance of power and decided to use it in a statesmanlike manner. To win Lennie, down I dropped on that bundle of melodramatically writhing limbs, that vortex of hisses and threats. Joseph's right arm had been flung wide of the fight and lay along the grass abnormally long, like a pallid eel. On this I knelt. Joseph screamed, and Lennie, about to deal some death blow or other, became immediately still and stared at me.

'Don't touch my brother,' he growled—not forcefully enough to warrant hostilities though, since I was taller than he was. He rose from where he had been sitting on Joseph's diaphragm. 'Don't be so cruel.'

I progressed on my knees off Joseph's arm, embarrassed at the fierce little face glaring at me over Joseph flat on the ground, groaning detachedly.

'The Comrade will belt the tripes out of you for being cruel to Joseph.'

The victim raised himself on his elbows and nodded. Comrade Lenin, about whose exact nature I was still guessing, was something worth placating, said the nod.

'My brother Joseph,' Lennie went on with pride, 'is going to be a cripple. His muscles will squeeze up. And then he's going to die.'

I stared at Joseph's legs, looking for some horrific sign on their lengthy whiteness.

'It won't hurt,' Joseph explained. His face was gratified; his little brother had recognized him as a child of election.

'Are you really going to die?' I asked him.

'Too right!' he said. 'What's your name?'

After a while there was another brawl and I was allowed to join it, fighting at will on both sides.

Sunlight had left the yard and the flaccid grass was cold. Wrestling had overheated me, given me croup, making my underjaw itch in that unscratchable penetrating way that croup does. We were all standing around talking limply when Hilda appeared in the back door, her hair newly combed and her face done up. Her fragrance carried as far as the peach tree.

'Comrade Lenin's train just passed,' she called. It was rarely that she could predict the Comrade's coming, rarely and by a hard road; for only after a furniture-breaking brawl, a bout of repentance, a promise of eternal domesticity by the Comrade, could his wife be sure, for a day or two, of when she would see him and in what state.

Of course, that afternoon I didn't know all this. Lennie and Joseph appeared to me to be people established in their neighbourhood. Out of the peach tree and the rank backyard, out of the *to and fro* of trains, the *to and fro* of Comrade Lenin, they seemed to have compounded for themselves a ritual day. They herded the hours along under firm control. They waved at the trains as if every man and woman on board were their godparents. They didn't blush when the best they earned from any carriage in a long series of dusk electrics was a few half-turned, blank faces. They were happy. Comrade Lenin was on his way home to them.

Out of the last of many vivid knots of people stamping down the street away from the station, he came in a tweedy old sports-coat, grey trousers, and boots. In his breast pocket he wore an enviable blood-red handkerchief embroidered with a white hammer and sickle. He was clearly a relative of theirs; I was still uncertain whether he was their father or not.

Lennie ran to him, Joseph stalked up to him on the balls of those extraordinary feet. As they approached him, he stood still and clenched his fist towards the sky, while a passing typist ducked below the indiscriminate gesture and hurried away.

'Hail Comrades!' he called to the boys.

'Hail Comrade!' they sang.

'Did you have any fights today, Comrades?' he asked, as if training them in the ways of peace were his prime work.

'No fear!' said Lennie.

'Good!' said Comrade Lenin.

As he came through the gateway, I jumped aside, half-hoping he hadn't even seen me.

'And did you behave yourself for the Mother of the People?'

'I did! Not Joseph!'

By now we were trailing the great man down his dim laneway. He reached his hand out onto Lennie's straight hair and lovingly tousled it.

'You're a character, Comrade! You're a heck of a character!'

We walked forward into sunlight. Comrade Lenin met Hilda with suspect ardour. I wondered if he came home daily, for there was something forced and dishonest in their embrace, something feigned like the feigned anger that had flung the boys against each other earlier that afternoon. I can remember now that probably a dozen kitchen windows in flats and cottages looked down on the Mantles' backyard, flats and cottages where rumours of the Comrade's drinking, violence, shiftlessness were harboured. Hilda was a proud girl.

Even now, she looked up at him and murmured, 'You've been having some.'

'Only a nip,' he grunted, and they went inside.

'Why does he wear a red handkerchief?' I asked the boys.

'That's his colour,' said Lennie. 'It's the colour of the Soviet flag.'

'The people's flag is deepest red,' Joseph explained. 'Didn't you know that?'

'Yes!' I lied.

'It's bathed in the blood of the workers.'

'Is his handkerchief bathed in their blood?'

'Yes,' Lennie whispered.

'When did he bathe it in their blood?'

'After they'd been shot in the back by someone. The catilists.' Joseph was bland in his knowledge of whence the workers' blood flowed.

'Why did they shoot them?'

'They were scared of them.'

'Is Comrade Lenin a worker?'

'He's one of the leaders of the workers.'

'Then why didn't they shoot him?'

'He ran away?' Lennie suggested.

Joseph sneered at this. 'He didn't run away. They thought he was dead but he wasn't. There was a soldier like that at the pictures.'

'Soldier like what?' Comrade Lenin had come into the yard in his slippers. He was in his shirtsleeves, the coat and the bloody handkerchief being away somewhere deep in the Mantle house. I could imagine some sort of reliquary, with candles flanking it, for that piece of linen which had been dipped in precious blood.

'You've got a new mate,' he observed. His eyes flapped across my face with gross indifference. There was something about me which made me unfit to pluck a bow, yell or spit, roll and wrestle with his comrades. I was a bit livid and narrow-chested, I admitted to myself, from pneumonia the previous November.

'What's your name, youngster?'

'Daniel Jordan.'

'Well, Daniel Jordan,' he said, slicing my name up with the thin edge of his tongue, 'you'd better go home. I'm taking the boys for a walk. You can come back tomorrow.'

'Yes.'

'Well, be seeing you! Joseph? Lennie?'

They followed him into a kitchen redolent of lamb chop fat. Now I had the whole yard, but mere possession was meaningless without them. Dusk dropped from the peach tree, the lane lay before me like a catacomb. Running its length, I was standing on our veranda in time to see the Comrade usher his sons into the street and take them uphill. Lennie yabbered at his side, Joseph stalked forward as if the ground were strewn with nettles. They reached a point at last where trees and railway embankment, the coming night and steam from a reined-in engine all blended into utter shadow.

2

Then Singapore fell. The very sucklings quaked for its fall. A Cabinet Minister whispered in committee that one armoured division could take Australia. People taped their windows, making them shatterproof, prophesying that the only human factor that could save us was America. Women sought moral guidance on the question of suicide or dishonour. Troops trained with sticks and guarded beachheads with axes.

Bombs homed down on London and corpses were dug out each morning. That was true. Yet no country was ever so naked before invasion as the Australia of 1942.

Civil defence men came to school to teach us to out-hide, out-wriggle, out-delve death from the sky. We were to have white linen bags, to be worn on the hip and to contain a bisected tennis ball (for cupping to your outraged ears as you lay in the gutter during the bombing), a plug of gauze (to bite into), a bandage, and a tin of salve. In answer to the unopposed Japanese armaments, we held up our tins of salve and, since these were primarily suitable for chilblains, ant-bite and minor burns, it was as well for us that they never had to be opened.

Beneath the high altar of the church was the school air-raid shelter. There were two reasons for its location. The playground itself was asphalted and the nuns hesitated to set a pick to its even surface: and then, in that dark hole, we were mantled and protected by the table of God. It was unlikely, the nuns said, that the Sacred Species would be allowed to suffer bombing. In a lavender-painted classroom, with the windows half-open and a yellow surf of boronia breaking on the sills, this reasoning had obvious strength.

We were all sent to the toilets and then lined up in the corridors to practise in our shelter. The entry was a squat green manhole inlaid in the prosperous brick of the apse's outer wall. Sister Eucheria of the Order of Preachers, the ancient Dominicans, smiled plump encouragement back along the flighty column of infants, unlocked the door and stooped down into the darkness within. Sister Stanislaus waited in the sunlight in her supernaturally cream habit to hinder the atavistic panic we all felt in regard to doors you had to bend to enter and beyond which lay what might be the blackness of the pit.

'Keep on coming!' Stanislaus called masterfully, and if that dark cellar had been the foyer of hell, we would have willingly faced its minor terrors rather than oppose her.

Within, the shelter was a place where odd lengths of lumber and camp tables used for Communion breakfasts were kept. There was even an electric bulb which Sister Eucheria had turned on. She ushered me to the far penumbra of its cone of bilious light, and I sat on a stack of tables with some other, mainly solemn, children. From here, the light seemed paltry, the whole place incredibly dim, low-roofed, weighed down. Weighed down by the weight of divinity above our heads, constricted by the acres of darkness on three sides of us, the little pad of daylight which was the doorway seemed furlongs away, and the inpouring bodies of another and another child blotted it out. My chest became tight, whistled with a congestion to match the congestion of this *sub-altare* into which an intolerable stream of children thronged.

'Isn't it cold?' Dolph Conlon whispered, as if we were fleas on the flanks of darkness and didn't want it to scratch itself.

'I'm not going to come in here,' I wheezed, 'even if the Japs bomb the school.'

'Sister Stanislaus'll make you.'

'I'll hide till she comes in here.'

'Then where'll you hide? From all those bombs?'

'I'll hide . . .' If the bombers came languidly across the sky, Eucheria would probably send us to the toilets before consigning us to the abyss. The boys' toilets were corrugated tin and unfit to perish in, being utterly abandoned to the lower uses of what Mother Gonzaga called the *bhoys*. But this austerity outhouse was an apter place to die in than down there choking in the pit. To die in a blitz amongst the corrugated iron, flung across the durable chalk-line which God or, more binding still, Stanislaus had drawn along the floor, and behind which no *bhoy* was to stand while performing a natural function; that would be a joy beside surviving the smallest bombardment vaulted beneath the High Altar.

'Haven't you got any faith?' Dolph asked me. Before I could explain myself, Dolph stood up from our pile of tables and, with a little groan, delivered himself of his lunch.

It was a grey April afternoon for which the air-raid practice was again set down. The glossy reading books were collected by someone who I never was, and, swept along by a tide of blithe colleagues, I drifted into the toilets and out again to find myself, swallowing on a pharynx arid with fear, being marched off to the small green door.

Glossy-leaved eucalypts looked with odious calm at the line of children embarking into the labyrinth. An old lady limped out of the presbytery door and poured a basin of dishwater down a drain. In her warm bubble of domesticity she didn't even bother to glance at us. Low cloud shut mercy out of the sky, and I stared down the nave, begging mercy to turn the corner. Incredibly, it did.

Splendid in her best-wear brown suit came my mother, walking very fast. I pretended not to see her, but a girl at the top of the line touched Stanislaus's cream-serge elbow and pointed towards the splendid apparition. The nun looked up and smiled.

'I've come to get Daniel, Sister,' my mother said. 'I thought you mightn't have heard.'

'Heard, Mrs Jordan?' Without waiting to be answered Stanislaus turned towards the line and called me. As I idled up the side of the ranks, I heard my mother say in a half-whisper, 'There's been a Jap bomber over Sydney. High up. Our grocer's a warden and he was alerted. It's probably gone now, but I'd like to take Daniel if you don't mind.'

Eucheria pushed her head out of the black hole.

'Oh, good afternoon, Mrs Jordan.'

'Sister,' said Stanislaus, 'a Japanese aircraft has been sighted over Sydney. I wish we could send all the children home, but Father's out and we'd have to have his permission. Anyway, their parents wouldn't know what was happening.'

'Oh, I don't think there's any great danger yet,' my mother frowned. 'But, if anything happened, you'd like to have them with you, I mean, parents would, wouldn't they?'

'Yes. By all means, take him. The best we can do, Sister Eucheria, is to go on with our air-raid practice.'

My mother and I walked away and turned for a shy second to wave to the children and Stanislaus. Even to my eyes, Dolph Conlon seemed a small and pale animal, in acute need of a mother. For a moment, I shuddered with the ecstasy of deliverance, the shame of being the only one delivered. Then we began to hurry home.

For every yard of the quiet avenues which separated us from the railway and our place, we searched the shut-in sky. Two American fighters jumped over the western skyline and hummed beneath the dome of cloud—comforting, blood-stirring, silver, blue and red.

'Why didn't they shoot it down?' I asked, and despite the flamboyant Americans holding our attention, my mother didn't mistake whom I meant by *they*.

'They could have been having lunch,' she said, 'or having an hour off. Anyhow, it was a long way up. And it's only one Jap plane. Hardly worth bothering about.'

Since I had begun school, an idea which was probably hereditary had grown to become a premise of life. It was the idea of the large world, the school-world in particular, as a conspiracy to scrape bare all the weaknesses of the soul, to mock the indomitable tenderness of the secret, family world, making them baseless, unmerited and therefore hollow. Only in the thought of my father was I a member of the world, one of the masters. He had been a civilian militiaman who had enlisted just before the New Year. Men with any sort of soldiering in their background were rare. He already had two chevrons to go beneath the divisional patch on his arm. For the past ten days, I had lived on the éclat of those bombardier's stripes (he was an anti-aircraft gunner), had felt a kinship with every two-striped soldier I had seen, even with the Americans who wore theirs upside-down.

Three weeks before, in the Sydney Domain, there had been a display aimed at furbishing the confidence of a city faced by invasion. Since I later discovered that my mother's younger brother, who knew the fulfilment of being a sergeant in the infantry, had all of one subaltern above him and all of two Bren gunners beneath him with whom to hold two suburban beachfronts, this display in the Domain was immorally deceptive. Just at the time, it seemed to make the hundreds who looked on bleary-eyed with pride, and at appropriate times, the warm Saturday morning air thudded with applause. Three truck-drawn anti-aircraft guns careered across the park. On spots marked with lime, as for lawn tennis, they jumped to a halt. From the backs of the trucks poured men in scrubbed webbing and battle order. Some of them set up a screen of Bren guns around the gun positions, jamming in the magazines and tugging in a frenzy at the cocking handles. Behind each truck the crews unhooked their guns, unlimbered them, hauled out the extra limbs which stabilized the gun platforms. Intoning formulae like a horde of frantic monks, they climbed or circulated around the trim altars out of which the blunt barrels grew. Through the horizon and dome of space which they commanded, the guns elevated and traversed in unison. This was for me the embarrassing part of the display. Despite their sleekness, they could have been a string of ancient chorus girls, each flinging one graceless leg into the air. Finally, the barrels lowered towards an imaginary sea to shell an imaginary submarine. Then the men began to limber their guns and package them in their covers. Every soldier in the display was an N.C.O.—no mere gunners allowed. Taking up action stations to the rear of the trucks, they numbered off, reported *gun clear*, *sir*, and saluted the flag. People cheered.

No. 2 on one of those guns was my father, flesh of my flesh, bone of my bone, spinning that barrel and aiming it into the sky by the slightest pressure of his fingers on the controls. Besides which, there were only five such guns in Australia.

There was no doubt that Saturday morning. The Jordans had, to their surprise, joined the masters.

3

It was the Wednesday before Easter. The autumn gales, which used to bring regular floods when we lived on the North Coast, had just struck Sydney. Beneath their violence, the Mantles' place slumped more noticeably into an earth which crawled with rain as if with some sort of organic corruption. From our front bedroom window where I waited to see any stray act of God—a roof blown off, a fence beaten down, a flood at the end of the street—I could survey the flooded approaches of the railway bridge. Earlier that morning, when the local girls, dressed and made up for work, had to take off their shoes and wade to the stairs, there had been some excitement. Now no one came or went except the postman, and I could see, from the way she straightened up from gazing into the letter box, that for my mother and me his coming and going had been quite barren.

She came back into the house and went to the bathroom to hang up the oilskin and dry her hair with a towel. From the slightly opened bathroom window, I could see a little of the Mantles' lighted lounge-room window behind which Lennie and Joseph enjoyed the storm in companionship.

'There's nothing in the box but a big bull-frog,' she smiled. I leant my head on her hip and hung my arm about her thighs.

'Never mind,' I said.

The vista of sub-tropical rain, falling like myopia over a railway embankment, excessive, numbing, the year's most palling bore, washed all life out of the morning. The world was plotting again; the voice of the rain was built of the sizzling voices of a million conspirators, who had managed to prevent a letter from my father that morning, and might manage God knew what that afternoon.

What they *did* manage was a little variety. At two o'clock, the rain stopped instantaneously. Winds, forty miles an hour, which was faster than a car, cleared the streets of rain. The three willows on the embankment groaned like pensioners. My mother got out my gumboots and we went to visit the Mantles.

That afternoon, Hilda had been ironing what was dry in the lounge-room full of half-dried clothing. Lennie and Joseph sat on a rug playing an esoteric game of Monopoly with an incomplete set. Their cosiness, with the wind thudding at their windows, gave us back our spirits. The boys welcomed us absent-mindedly and I sat down smiling, to watch them battle for Pall Mall and Marylebone Station. As for my mother and Hilda, they had talk of ironing and damp clothes to kindle to.

But there was some special excitement to the way that Hilda flipped the clothes about on the ironing table, to the vigour with which she dealt with the iron. Inevitably, she began to talk about her secret.

'Did I tell you about the new doctor?' she asked. 'Well, he's not new, only it's the first I've heard of him. He's in Macquarie Street. Anyhow, the McCalls—you know them, don't you?—they're three up from the bridge—I'll say their backyard'd be flooded—well, they had a grandson, who got rheumatic fever and was just about a cripple, and this man did wonders for him. I'm saving to take Joseph—I never go to a doctor unless I can plonk the money down in front of him.'

My mother said there was no need to worry about that.

'Yes there is. I can't afford to dress as if I had money, so I'd be too ashamed to ask for an account.' Hilda held up one of the Comrade's shirts to the light.

'Besides,' she went on, laying it flat and plying the iron as if she'd been born married, 'I'm never sure about what I'll have in the future. I can only depend on what I've got in hand. I shouldn't say that. Lennie's'—she meant the Comrade—'a good provider, but he's got a cause to finance, and he wouldn't be Lennie if he didn't have the cause. And he's got a weakness for the drink too. But he's a good man really. He lives for the boys and he's really dedicated—to the Future and all that. As far as money's concerned, that's half our problem.'

My mother said nothing, and the wind took her part in the dialogue, butting at the walls, dislodging a rowdy piece of slate from the roof-top. Hilda shook her head over the ironing table.

'Poor old place'll fall apart soon. Anyhow, I can't take Joseph until I've got that three guineas tight in my hand. We've got fifteen quid in the bank of course, but I can't touch that. You've got to leave a little bit in reserve. In case something happens like.'

I saw my mother glance at the mouldering skirting boards, the damp spots on the ceilings, the walls dribbling moisture, the naked fly-blown bulb, Joseph's angular lameness—all this in a second. Her face seemed to say with irrepressible honesty, 'God, in *case* something happens!'

'You wouldn't tell anyone all this?' Hilda asked quickly.

'Of course I wouldn't!"

'Thanks. Glory, they'll all need new shirts before the winter's out.'

It was some time after we were overcoated to leave that the Comrade came home at an hour he was not expected. Someone had knocked so strenuously at the door that the panels creaked. Then the Comrade had come in, helped by an older man with a leathery face in the folds of which large drops of rain glinted. The Comrade carried his coat slung across his shoulders and his injured hand in his good one. Tincture or blood seeped horrendously through the bandages. His lips quivered madly, unable to work together in the making of words. Jagged sound hung from his mouth like icicles.

At last he sat down and managed to smile.

'H—had an ax'dent, Hildie,' he ground out.

The older man waggled his head rabidly.

'Wish I was as keen on the cause as Len,' he breathed.

Hilda ignored him, kneeling to survey the hand. The Comrade held it by the wrist in front of him. It looked like a parcel he would have preferred to leave on a train seat.

'Len, you didn't!' Hilda murmured.

'Brave as the day's long,' the old man butted in. 'They're having a Holy Thursday protest and want someone to give out the literature. So Len ups with a cleaver and whops into his hand. God, he cut down deep. Look, I think he missed his aim a bit, Mrs Mantle. Of course, as far as *they* know' (he thumbed over his right shoulder towards a *they* that was obtuseness and cruelty in a white coat) 'it's accidental like last time. You don't have to worry. He's got a week off on Compo.'

Lennie, Joseph and myself jumped, my mother looked at the floor, when Hilda stood up and whelted the old man across the mouth.

'What in the hell's use is Compo to me? What in the *hell's* use? I've got a cripple of a boy here waiting to go to the doctor. And you offer me Compo as if it were the bloody temple of Solomon.' She bunched her right fist against her forehead and began to cry.

'You encourage him,' she accused the old man, 'to hack away at himself until he's stitches and scars from head to foot. All to hand out dodgers and foul little pieces of paper that don't do a bit of good. You encourage him, but you don't give him anything to make up the difference between Compo and wages! You never do that. You stinking old cesspit of a man.'

The old fellow coughed. 'Well, I apparently don't get much thanks.'

'I'll say you don't!" she hissed. 'I'll say you don't. Your wife dresses better than me. You've got lampshades and curtains. You'll never give a drop of your own blood. What a fool Len is! To try and build a perfect world when there'll always be old pharisees like you.'

'Go easy, girl,' the Comrade managed to say. It was hard to let your eyes leave him. In my mind, shocking ideas on how he got his red handkerchief were galvanizing.

'Go home!' Hilda whispered to the old man. 'Please! Get going!'

You could see she would try to beat him to a mash if he didn't obey.

'Got to go now, old cock,' he called quickly to the Comrade. 'Look after yourself. Afternoon.'

'You know where the front door is,' Hilda prompted; and he showed that he did by slamming it behind him.

Still the Comrade shivered in an ecstasy of shock and cold. Bending over him again, Hilda laid her lips on his forehead.

'It's that Doctor Burnett,' she said. 'He knows what goes on and he never gives Len any pain-killer. As if it should matter to a doctor how a man gets hurt, just as long as he's hurt.'

At the mention of the word 'Burnett', Comrade Lenin gave a small giggle of reflex pain, pain remembered.

'Look, Mrs Jordan,' Hilda called, without turning from her husband, 'I haven't any brandy in the house. But he needs . . . Do you think you could . . . ?'

'Yes,' my mother said. 'I've got a bit inside. Daniel, you can stay here.'

With my mother gone, the boys and I tended to drift in closer to the mystery of the Comrade's blood. Hilda hardly saw us. But the Comrade himself noticed our edging and shuffling. He gazed at us exultantly, eyes distended with opiate pain, yet brighter on the borders of shock than they would ever be in states of undistracted normality.

'Do you Theists,' he asked me, and you could tell he didn't give a damn whether I knew what a Theist was, 'ever suffer like this any more, for what you believe?'

But when my mother brought back the brandy, he drank it as well as any Theist ever did.

4

Wherever we moved together, Lennie Mantle and I saw Joseph as a tithe reserved for death. He merited reverence, for there was something holy about the death of the very young. He was a designated human. The women marked with white crosses in newspaper photographs of crowds were illustrious and lifted out of the masses and designated for £2 by the soap company who ran the whole thing. In a better way than this, Joseph was illustrious and lifted out the mass. Nor did death present for him any mental block. Hilda had decanted the fear of it from his mind but left its mystery; and I believe that when Comrade Lenin was away at night, and Joseph sobbed with the pain in his limbs, she simply took him in her stout arms and promised him an immortality something like the type Stanislaus believed in, but not the Comrade.

The doomed child Joseph therefore saw himself as a sacramental personage to whom apt concessions were due. He brought games to an end on the basis of his vitiated muscles; imminent death was the first claim he dragged into any dispute.

'You'll only go to Limbo anyhow,' I told him, sure of my dogma.

We were lolling in the thick excited sunlight of a Saturday morning. Wartime cars, grunting beneath their bags of gas, drew our lazy eyes; long goods trains set us counting rolling stock. 'The

Charge of the Light Brigade' was on at the *Mercury*, and girls with their hair crimped inside scarves slip-slopped past to make a reservation for the night session.

'What's Limbo?' Lennie asked. It was a joy to pay them back for their *Soviets* and *Sickles*, their *people's blood*, their *red flags*, *Comin terms* and *catilists*.

'It's where you go if you're not baptized but still young—haven't reached the age of reason. Of course,' I conceded lightly to Joseph, 'you'll be perfectly happy. You just won't see God.'

'Oh, I want to see God,' Joseph murmured.

'But there's no God!' said Lennie. His small face was austere and pitying. 'How many times has Comrade Lenin got to tell you there's no God?'

Joseph pumped his shoulders up and down. They were like the shoulders of a hawk.

'Hilda told me there is. She says Comrade Lenin just pretends, that it's just part of his politics. It's part of his game.'

'If he was only mucking about,' Lennie hissed in scandalized certainty, 'he would have told me.'

A local girl went clipping by long-leggedly, our eyes leaving the dumpy sedans and following her lanky elegance.

'Is Heaven better than Limbo?' Joseph asked, like a fancier buying horses.

'It's much better. You've got perfect happiness, for one thing, and you live like a son of God, which is even better than living like a son of the King.'

'Comrade Lenin,' Lennie said loudly, 'reckons the king's just a lazy old German.'

Suddenly Lennie could no longer be suffered. The brat would believe in nothing. He squealed as I sprang on him, sat on his chest, clamped his wrists to the lawn and forced my knee up under his jaw to shut his infidel mouth.

'I bet you want Joseph to be a son of God!' I spat; and when he grunted negatively, I began to twist his left wrist. 'Go on. I bet you do!' He began to pale, to nod his head frenziedly. Having been told by Eucheria that you cannot hurry the things of God, that part of the work must be left to grace, I dismounted from Lennie's unregenerate pot-belly.

'But you'd have to be baptized,' I explained, turning back to Joseph.

Even then, it seemed that there was a speculative light kindled in Joseph's eye. 'If you've got to be baptized,' the light said, 'I'll have five bob of that.'

'How do you get baptized?' he asked.

'Don't think I won't tell Comrade Lenin,' Lennie told his brother.

Joseph's long white arm reached to the back of Lennie's head and clipped it vigorously, sending Lennie hiccuping with sobs to the veranda corner where he draped himself with dramatic feeling against the cold brick.

'It's easy,' I pursued. 'I'd just pour water over your head, all the time saying, "I baptize thee in the name of the Father and of the Son and of the Holy Ghost. Amen."'

As if he were afraid of catching a cold beneath those vivifying waters, Joseph squinted up at the sun.

'How much water?'

'A cupful would do it. I'll get Lennie.'

'Why?'

'He'll have to be your godparent.'

'*Godparent?*' Joseph stared at his brother, looking for some secret dignity hitherto unknown.

'Oh, it just means someone who becomes the mother or father of your soul. It's not particularly important.'

'But why?'

'That's the way we do things.'

Wanting to spread peace in readiness for the Sacrament, I strolled up to the veranda corner to trap Lennie's goodwill with a barrel of honey. He was slumped, choking on tearless grief. I put my hand on his shoulder and he couldn't have shuddered more if I'd touched something flayed.

'Are you all right, Lennie? Do you want to come and see Joseph get baptized?'

Lennie screamed and kicked sideways.

'I'll belt hell out of you if you do that again, Mantle. Now come on, we need a godparent if we can get one. You can be godparent if you like.'

'Don't think I won't tell Comrade Lenin!'

'I'm not scared of damned Comrade Lenin.'

As Joseph and I went off for a bowl of water, and Lennie looked after us with uncontrollable interest, I regretted that the rite I was to perform lacked greater mystery. Yet mystery enough it had to draw Lennie. I was involved with Joseph in an Inquisition of Faith behind the garage when Lennie limped along to give grudging witness to the making of a Christian.

'Do you believe all the Catholic truths, Joseph?'

'What's a Catholic truth?'

I sighed. 'Do you believe Christ is God?'

'The boy in the Christmas Hymns?'

'Yes.'

'All right. I believe in him.'

I paused with the bowl of water in my hands. Could it be as easy as this to send a man to paradise?

'Ready, Lennie?' I asked inconsequentially.

I doused Joseph Stalin Mantle's head and washed him newborn in the name of the Trinity. The heavens did not open up to receive him.

When an American troop-train hove along the outside line at processional pace, the baptismal waters hadn't dried on Joseph's head. From where we stood, we couldn't see the railway for brick garages, but Lennie pointed across country to the street corner where three girls waved in that unique gay manner kept for U.S. personnel. The men in the troop-train were barracking back inimitably. The way they roused a suburban street was also unique.

We swept into the road in time to be seen by the Americans. They seemed to hang from the windows eight at a time. Crisp-shirted, white-toothed, overpaid, flushed with illegal spirits brewed in Woolloomooloo backyards, when they saw us they flung handfuls of His Majesty's coin into the street. There was time to be grateful, to stand in the pinging rain and wave for a second before turning to booty. In that urbane second, from every angle, the railway bridge, the corners, the lanes, ran flurries of children who had heard and recognized the noise of the Yanks coming up the Western line. The leisurely glut, the immense spoils, half-vanished before we could turn to the interlopers. Slower, smaller, fatter children came, grubbing for coin in the gutter, along the embankment fence, on the roadway. There was only a pittance left for us.

Joseph and I *did* see a sleek florin land in the mud below the embankment, but he was still very fast on his spidery legs. Though I pinned him to the dirt, sat across his body, hammered his stomach, he reminded me that he was a new-made saint—if I'd believed what I'd said. He got up from the dirt with that limitlessly negotiable two shillings in his suety hand, and limped across the street in the stilted way his disease imposed on him.

A boy ran past me waving sticks of American gum in my face, that fabled gum whose very wrappings were cherished and gave prestige to their owners. But for my manners, such as they were, it could have been mine.

'You can go to—hell!' I called after him, but he dashed away in his aureole of good fortune which wasn't pierced by the kick I aimed at his backside.

Anyhow, I had done the work of the Lord that morning.

5

I think it was my father's last leave, and we spent the Sunday afternoon watching the Rugby League at Calwell Park. It was a sensible way to use up the last clumsy hours, for we were a family whom, at the best of times, idleness half-killed with melancholy.

There was an ill-controlled rout in the 'A' grade at the Park that day, and Abattoirs United, a team of mighty slaughtermen, reduced the enemy in the first half. It was five minutes before half-time that inspiration died as if by mass consent. The crowd's voice went drab; we could all have been people watching a demonstration of cleaning fluid or margarine; the sublime hysteria was vanished. They became an imposition on us then, all those others, cluttering the time of farewell with stale talk, stirring the lees of evaporated frenzy, pulling their cardigans about them, hitching their cuffless wartime trousers. My father asked if we'd like to go home.

There had been a volcano erupting, everyone knew, on a Japanese-held island in the north. This was why the sunsets were the colour of rust and the afternoon light so bronze. It lay bronze now across the lawns in the reserve outside the Park. It turned to stiff copper the high-up leaves of the blue-gums where, the Mantles said, koalas had once lived. It dashed tawny on us from amongst the grey trunks, and nuzzled the brown flanks of shrubs. It gave the lie to the Andrews sisters who were being pumped through the loud-speakers inside the Park, chortling 'The Best Things in Life Are Free'. We were not its masters, my father even was not its master. Definitively, and not without deep shock, I saw him as much a visitor to the earth as I was, saw the heavy tunic rasping the reddened neck, rubbing away at a crease in the flesh. On the palms of my hand, a sweat of love sprang out.

Comrade Lenin was at a meeting in the Domain that afternoon; we had come across him once in there, handing out handbills, yearning to be called up to the platform to speak. Hilda told us they were training him as an orator, but that it took a long time. In any case, on the strength of the man's absence, I was allowed next door.

It was not too late nor too cold to play *Scorched Earth*, their new game, in the tall yellow grass. This was a confused and riotous form of battle, in which sometimes we would snipe in unison at an enemy advancing from the direction of the Mantles' lavatory, and sometimes we would stalk each other amongst the rank spears of paspalum, sweating, worming, outflanking.

I can remember crawling along the verge of the heavier grass in deep shadow when Comrade Lenin's kick took me at the base of the spine and pitched me into a tousle of buffalo grass that had been three feet away. It didn't particularly hurt to be kicked in that way, it was the unadorned violence that outraged a person. I knew, even before I saw him, that only the Comrade, amongst all people I knew, could see clear to shame me so completely in front of Joseph and Lennie. Their shocked and overheated faces swam now above the tangle of grasses like two ash-grey, daytime moons.

'And while I was playing *his* bloody game!' I thought. 'Comrade almighty Lenin's almighty game!'

'Look at the little Messiah!' he smiled, very genially. He'd been drinking sabbath sly grog in the back of some fruitshop; and he smelt of the over-ripeness of fruit, the woodiness of packing cases, as well as of illegal liquor. Altogether, it seemed that kicking a child hard below the spine was the Comrade's idea of climaxing an elegant afternoon.

'Did anyone ask you to go soul-saving?'

By now I had crawled to my feet. The blunt feel of the Comrade's boot remained, the impact seemed to be fixed in my flesh like a beam of wood. Now I even glanced at his putty eyes, driven to it by the dignity of being right, the immensity of the outrage.

'You're a narrow-chested little runt,' he remarked. 'But you've certainly got a skinful of all sorts of dogmatics and lies. And you go round spewing them all over my boys.'

He had said all this as dispassionately as a judge, but now he grabbed my shoulders and began shaking me.

'Don't you think,' he groaned, 'that it's bad enough the poor little bastard's a cripple without you baptizing him?'

Then he let me go, hiccuped with grief, bit his lip, tears racing down either side of a spongy nose. There was a moisture which was sweat or dribble or tears amongst the bristles of his upper lip.

'Am I supposed to be tickled pink? Joseph's lame, Alleluia? Am I supposed to put up with a little cow like you running around, slopping water over him?'

He began to sway from the waist with grief and anger, which reminded me of the Saturday night two years before in the north when Eve Mulcahy's fiancé had been killed, his truck having stalled straddling the railway line just as the North Coast Mail came galloping up through the dusk. He'd died fiddling with the choke, said one of my uncles who was a shunter. But when my father went in to tell Eve, talcumed and in her slip, getting ready for the dead man to arrive, she had swayed, superbly young white arms raised to her temples, monumentally grieved, just as the Comrade, different creature though he was, quaked with grief now. I expected him, like Eve, to begin kneeling at any second.

Instead, he clouted me on the right cheek as well as, in his awry state, he could. Too mighty a blow to hurt, it swung me back down to his unkept lawn. A sound of frying filled the shell of my head. For a long time nothing, sound or sight, pierced the wadding of numbness that swathed my senses. Then what I heard first was Hilda calling to the boys.

'Joseph, Lennie! Come inside!'

The authoritativeness of hysteria sharpened her voice, and the boys, who'd been standing petrified up to now waist-deep in grass, moved to her, their gaping white faces passing me as I tried to stand up.

'Hurry!' Hilda screamed to them. Before the stridency of the word had ceased thrumming the darkening air, before the people at the dozen kitchen windows around were aware of him, my father came running out of the Mantles' lane.

He was much shorter, much solider than the Comrade. His face was neat, and brown from the sun and temporary fury. He had spent weeks at some jungle-training place where they taught you to throw Japs on their backs, so that the sodden Comrade was scarcely a challenge to him. The people in the windows, hoping to see the living daylights thrashed out of the Comrade, must have laughed cruelly when they saw him arrive. Hilda must have scolded the boys away from the kitchen windows and dragged them into the lounge whence they couldn't see into the yard.

Perhaps it was gratitude that finally turned my stomach over as I reeled to the fence and was sick.

My father was facing the Comrade, looking up into his eyes. A few vague syllables bubbled on his lips before he lashed out at the over-rich lips, the wide, porous nose, the eyebrows hanging like dewlaps. He was terribly merciless, dragging up off the ground again and again a Comrade who in his turn was terribly unresistant. Soon the Comrade was choking on blood, spilling it down his chin as my father stood back to regain breath.

'Come on, you bastard,' the Comrade growled thickly through clogged lips. 'Wallop hell out of me. Maybe you can make me believe in a God who makes cripples out of little children.'

My father pointed to him and said, coolly enough, 'Don't try to make yourself into a bloody atheist martyr, Mantle. You're just scum that tried to bash up a child ten minutes ago.'

The Comrade sagged to the ground, grunted, sighed, shrugged. My mother had arrived, crying without a sound, and was lifting me up. As she cupped my head into her shoulder blade, I released my own tears softly, and in them dissolved the entire shock of the incident. A little retching, a few tears had restored me.

'Come on, Brian! Come home now,' she begged hoarsely.

Hunched on the ground, his long black Chinese hair falling forward into his eyes, the Comrade didn't move.

'Call it a day?' She persisted softly, but as with Hilda earlier, the few words were barbed with a kind of hysteria, and feminine hysteria was something my father, as well as Lennie and Joseph, was in terror of.

'If you go near Stell or Daniel again, I'll kill you,' he said quickly to the Comrade. 'Or if not me, then her father. Or her brother. If you drive her to leave next door, I'll see to it you never get a second's peace till they bury you.'

Still the Comrade didn't move, humped on the ground, a formless organism capable of taking in boundless pain.

'I'll send you back to the slime you rose from,' my father reiterated. 'Do you understand?'

The Comrade said nothing.

So we collected ourselves and went home to tea.

6

It is easy to remember the two distinct armies who mustered on the steam level of Central railway on an autumn night in 1942. There were those who had no families in that city; for whom the shattering business of farewell was over; who could clown by the indicator, buy *Smith's Weekly* at the news-stall, champ down a last pie. For these were the things the excitement of what was merely a train trip provoked you to.

Closer in towards the barrier a more orderly brand of soldier gathered, standing in tight family knots where everyone's eyes were too bright, everyone's laughter too brittle and reverent. Women spoke up shrilly, nursing their duty not to begin weeping at least until the order to board rang out. As if the shelling and privation would begin the moment their train cleared the point which read, 'Unauthorized persons . . .', etc. every man wore webbing and gaiters, waterbottle and rifle. This gave them the look of being soldiers forever, of having taken vows for life in some dubious brotherhood. It made them solemnly gallant for their last moments with their people; but when flurries of steam rose scaldingly from the underbelly of the engine, turning people's heads, the faces above the webbing and accoutrements were drained pale for a second or two.

The train lay empty along the station length; skin-tight with light, waterbottles dusted and full for the trip to the coast. The upholstery was dull and tidy. It was perhaps the cleanest train I have ever seen. But in all its virgin cleanliness, it served merely to emphasize departure. God knew to how many wives and mothers those clean yellow lights were themselves only a leer and a threat.

My father brought us to a stop outside the barrier. In the lee of the indicator we hid, as if we could thus beguile the mechanisms of war, lull the efficiency of battery commanders, render forgetful the train seething beyond the gate.

'Well, plenty of good time!' my mother said. If gaiety were some sort of fever, a rising line on a graph beyond the crest of which were tears, then you could have claimed that she was gay.

'Here comes my troop commander,' my father muttered to her and, as a young officer went by smiling at them, they grinned back strainedly, a glib lie of a smile which gave no light to the wide misery in their eyes, and died on their lips the instant the lieutenant had passed.

'Right at this moment,' said my father through clamped teeth, 'I could kill that bastard Nicholson.'

'That's a flattering thought,' Stell smiled. 'You're leaving us, and all you can think of is Nicholson.' She had reached out and was touching his tunic'd elbow. Perhaps a nerve was there by which he could be soothed.

'But it isn't right, Stell. I could maybe have gotten out of this. That's the thing I won't forget. How in the hell you can forgive me, Stell, is more than I can understand.'

'What about the *kill-me-deads*?' she insisted, pressing a little biscuit tin into his hands. It was full of *kill-me-deads*, which were his name for small fruit cakes.

'I won't forget them.' He stamped his boot on the tarred floor, not hard enough though to make his private anguish public. 'I just had to go to Nicholson and make application. If I had, I might have been allowed to stay with you. Till after Herbie came anyway.' For ten seconds he was quiet. His eyelids seemed to swell and dip in honour of our pitifulness. *Herbie* was his name for his unborn child. He was a great man for names and codes. 'I honestly don't think I would have got away with it, Stell. But I should have tried it. That's where I let you down, girl.'

'I didn't expect you to make any application.' There was a scolding, bright humorousness in her eyes which might soon become unfunny in the extreme. 'I don't want to hear the word again. There are other things to talk about than pink forms in triplicate. Surely there are! Life is more than the filling-out of forms, though that's what they're trying to reduce it to.'

'I'm sorry for the language, Danny boy,' he nodded to me. 'But it's hard to leave the two of you on the one night without swearing.'

Someone blew a whistle blast that cut off all our breaths.

'That's not for me,' my father reassured us.

My mother frowned. 'The thing to do,' she said, 'is to forget all this business about applications and Nicholson.'

'Stell, you should have seen the way he treated the other poor bloke who tried to apply.'

Stell hung her head and bit her lower lip. He took her by the elbows—it was too early yet for a more desperate gesture.

'I'm sorry,' he said. 'I can't help harping on it. It's all I can think of, now that I'm going.'

'Well, I don't want another word,' she decreed in a clear, angry, level, absolving tone. 'When you come home, you'll laugh about men like Nicholson. You'll laugh and toss Herbie on your knee.'

Air Force men who had been summoned by the whistle began to move through the barrier, flanked by women who, besides a few hysterically gay, were erect and pallid, or sobbing and chewing their grief into handkerchiefs.

'Why are they crying?' I asked.

'Those men are mainly airgunners. A lot of them get killed, Danny. That's all there is to it.'

The sling of his rifle had been galling his shoulder and he was tired of it. He dropped the butt on the floor with an unmilitary clatter belying the stripes on his arms. Then he forced a slow, but in the end, authentic smile.

'I'm not very brave,' he said. 'I'm the least brave of the three of us. It's the truth, what you've said, Stell. It's a matter of here we are. We have to live on from here. Look, Stell!'

I could see, in his eyes beneath the substantial shade of the slouch hat, two fierce little squares of light, the reflection of the lights of the station without, but also of a sudden zest within. For, all his life, he shuttled between the utmost borders of fatalism, where all a man could do was comment on his own destiny, and some central temperate zone where the human personality shone unassailably, and the human will rose to heaven like a fortress. Like some angel, he travelled at the speed of light between the two climes, knowing no middle latitudes, dwelling only where either courage or abandonment to the flux of things was the ultimate intelligent virtue. During his time, he practised more than his share of both. But that's another story.

'Never be lonely, Stell,' he persuaded my mother. 'They can't take a man away just by putting him on a damned train and trying to.' The big hat nodded reverently. 'Thank God, I believe in the bloody soul of man. Loneliness is only a feeling. It's what we eat for breakfast. Let's both refuse to tolerate it, Stell.'

He looked down at me and I couldn't help catching the furious excitement in his face. Though he knew as I knew that when the train cleared Central, he would be vanished and lost to us, he seemed to have half-baffled himself, and to be yearning to get aboard and find out for good if loneliness *was* simply what he'd had for breakfast.

'And don't you ever be afraid, Danny boy. Especially not of mongrels like the Comrade. If the sky falls in, it doesn't alter the fact. I'm your father and you're my son. For eternity. Do you know what eternity is?'

Eucheria had told me. 'For ever and ever.'

'I'll say!' he said. 'I'll think of you all the time. We'll never really lose each other.'

But then the bugle began, cackling high over the fruitstalls and refreshment rooms, flushing pigeons out of the sooty dome eighty feet above our heads. He paled, as if already, in the eighth second of eternity, we *were* lost to each other. My mother took him, webbing and rifle too, into her arms. For a second, his forehead came down and, with the brim of his hat pushed back unregimentally, rested on her shoulder.

'Just think of what it'll be like to come home,' she whispered. 'Do you really think you let us down? Just see the way some of these other fellows let their people down, what with booze and gambling and women.'

He lifted his head and frankly crushed her against the unlovely basic pouches which cluttered his chest. They held each other as courting couples do, and made as frantic a leave-taking as any of the desperate couples embracing beneath the great roof.

Already half the regiment was through the barrier. He opened his arms widely enough to take three boys my size, and enclosed me. His webbing crushed my ribs. A few seconds, and he rose, his eye half-taken by the mass of khaki soldiery lunging past the ticket box.

'Got to go, Stell,' he explained. 'Live well, you'll be getting most of the pay. No booze and gambling and women for me. And if anyone gives you trouble, just go back to old Finnie' (old Finnie being an ancestral god who claimed to be my grandfather). 'And God help anyone who gives you trouble then!'

He went and pushed through the barrier with some obscure urgency. On the platform, around the clumps of gunners, Battery sergeant-majors, superb, beefy creatures who had apparently no origins, no wives, no issue, strode around calling, 'Five minute area, M battery.' 'Fall in K battery!' Until the clots of uniforms dissolved and formed a sudden pattern, and a whole regiment was drawn up on the asphalt beside its train. The extravagant noises of the sar-majors had quietened those watching from behind the barrier wire, those whose only claim on the men beyond were the futile ones of blood or eternal love. The R.S.M., against the sole noise of a snuffling steam engine, gave over the parade to Lieutenant-Colonel Nicholson. He was an alien-looking little man, this officer so intolerant of applications for compassionate leave; alien with his weathered, brandy-nobbling grazier's face and his thin moustache the colour of cotton-bush.

Through the grille, we could no longer see my father, already lost somewhere in 'M' battery, all fear, all love, all curses against Nicholson tucked neatly into his tunic and his face unnaturally bland.

I didn't sit still in the train roaring us back to our empty suburb. The pathos of my lonely father set me writhing into the leather of the seat, writhing against my mother's side. There was disapproval on the part of each conscious adult in the carriage. There were a number of unconscious ones—lovers slumped deathly at the end of the corridor, three or four middle-aged men napping in their seats, sated, older than the world, not simply dead but breathing on in the *n*th degree of death. A barrel-chested matron sat up like the wife of Mammon, watching and disliking me. It was an evil night.

When we left the train, a nor'-westerly drove a sharp drizzle into our eyes. I put my face into my mother's hip, against the sight of our street slimy with a compound of sump oil and dew of death, against the long gleam of the eight lines sweeping away to other dead towns.

My mother asked if I'd like cocoa when we got home. I said, oh boy I would, just like a boy in the pictures said it.

'As long as it doesn't keep you awake,' she cautioned.

'No. You wait and see.'

Sleep would be no trouble. In its dark hours, the frazzled pod of the earth would split and a new world spill out. The prospect did not excite, but it managed to provoke a drowsy interest in what might result.

7

'The sunsets are blood-red,' Aunt Verna told me. 'Blood-red with the blood of poor soldiers!'

After a russet winter's day, the sunsets had a right to be blood-red. But the grind of the seasons had little meaning for Aunt Verna beside the drama of the times, the war news, the mashed and bayoneted deaths being died just over the northern horizons. The newspaper tucked high under her left arm, close to her fierce heart, she clutched the door knob, whispered, 'I don't think the little yellow beasts will get here,' and opened the door. There was a job waiting for her in Queensland and she feared to take it.

Behind the door, drawn up to the set table, sat my uncle, he who had the holding of two beaches on his mind. He turned his darkling face to us and smiled his crooked piratical smile. In his eyes was no concern for all that indefensible space which was his to defend. To me he seemed *the* buccaneer, ageless, deathless, of endless resource, fit to stand on the battlefields of the world with Errol Flynn, and match him miracle for miracle.

'G'day, Tiger!' he laughed, shaping up for a fight. I came at him swinging punches, landing them on his khaki arms.

'Hey, wait there, Tiger!' he roared, and holding both my wrists with his right hand, he pulled from his pocket a honeycomb bar available only to H.M. Forces, a treasure, though soggy with body heat. Aunt Verna took it away from me, and before we could start another rough-house, my mother had the meal ready.

Her face was uniformly of a superb pallor since my father had gone. Her brows beneath the hair-line were glossy and hard like celluloid. The swathe of brown hair swaying over her shoulders somehow added to her air of profound fatigue. Matt rose up to take away from her the plate she was carrying. She smiled. There was no doubt, the smile said. She was glad that they were here, that she was entertaining them.

The table talk was a disappointment that night. They were waiting for me to eat up and go, which I did eagerly as the price of hearing something worth-while. I was permitted to leave and slide away into the back bedroom, which I had been sharing with Verna for some weeks. My fort was there, an impregnable little fort of butterboxes being held successfully by two machine-gun crews, left out in the sun last summer and badly contorted, two Royal Household Cavalry with movable lances, a number of kneeling, crouching, grenade-throwing Highlanders, one slouch-hatted Australian, who was my father and commanded the fort, and one Zulu, who was my father's Man Friday. Deployed suicidally in a frontal attack on the place was a haphazard assortment of mercenary elements—three of them headless, most of them lacking paint—and two Germans who were the master spirits of this evil siege, and who would in the end die complex deaths at the hands of my father and the Zulu. But it would be a long battle and ill-fortune would for a long time blunt the arms of the defenders. Not until one of the machine-gun crews lay dead beside their weapon, one of the Household Cavalry went down in blood and a flurry of hoofs, and some of the Highlanders fell back with the grenades still in their hands, would my father lead his men down from the fort and drive the enemy from the plain.

I re-opened battle casually, making intermittent explosive noises to show those at the table that it was now safe to talk.

'Well,' my uncle said, 'I've got it, Verna.'

'How much do I owe you?' Verna asked.

'It's all right. The bloke concerned owes me a favour. Anyhow, I gave him three bottles.'

'Oh, I'll have to pay you for them.'

'Don't carry on, Verna! They were issued to us, and I always save my beer issue. In this country, there's no one from a horse trainer down to a Prime Minister you can't bribe with beer.'

'So you're going, Verna—definitely?' my mother asked.

'Yes,' Verna admitted, ashamed. 'But I feel I should be here for—for Herbie, you know. That's what I worry about. After all, I'm not as stupid or as cruel as the—well, we'll call it *confounded* government. But if I leave you now . . .'

'Don't worry about it, Verna. Pat's coming down from the Cape to look after Daniel. You'd be wrong to stay for that reason. Just the same, you *should* stay. For other reasons.'

No one spoke for five seconds. There was a soft sound such as a canary makes as it squeaks and mumbles amongst the seed. It was Aunt Verna drinking tea. *The herb that cheers but not inebriates*, it had nevertheless lost Verna her job. A floorwalker at Tonkin and Watt had found her sipping it in a fitting-room one Saturday morning. He and the management had treated the affair as an outrage to the war effort, the future of the country being inextricably involved in the future of Tonkin and Watt's corsetry section.

'It's bad when a trained corsetière can't get work,' Verna claimed. 'The fall of Singapore did it.'

'Not only the fall of Singapore,' Matt laughed. 'You should see the Yanks scatter those dollars round up in Kings Cross.'

'But wages don't go up,' Verna said acidly. 'No, not wages!'

Wages *didn't* go up. Women skimped on the grace of the human form and spent their money on food. There were vacancies, the corset factories told her, but they were all above the Brisbane line, and if the country was invaded, the government might abandon the North. There was a job begging in Mackay, a sugar port in the north, offering wages in keeping with a town above an undefended Capricorn. Mackay was a thousand miles away and Verna had no train money.

She finished her cup of tea. 'I'll never forget this, Matt,' she murmured. 'I really will never forget it. I'll never forgive myself for putting you in such danger—a soldier who could be sent off to New Guinea and killed at any time.'

'Don't go putting curses on me, Verna. There wasn't any danger. The return half of a ticket to Mackay that's never been used; a refund's been paid out on it and it was just lying around the Central ticket office doing no good. My mate only had to pick it up.'

'I didn't mean that sort of danger. I mean, I've got you to steal for me. Ten pounds' worth of railway ticket. Grave matter, as the priests say. And I'm supposed to be a Catholic!'

Both Labor people, and bred by old Finnie on a sense of the sacredness of work and protest, my mother and Matt began simultaneously to click their tongues over this scruple of Aunt Verna's. Their God visited the sins of the vested interests only.

'London's being bombed, men are coughing blood in bloody Libya, Russia's in flames. And Verna Jordan thinks God's sitting on her shoulder waiting to see what she's going to do next to offend him. Look, Verna! If he damns anyone, it'll be Tonkin and bloody Watt he damns. Whether you're going or not, keep the ticket. If I was killed tomorrow, I wouldn't want to go to any Heaven they keep you out of for helping your friends.'

'Watch out, Matt!' my mother hushed him. 'Daniel's got ears like an elephant.'

I made more battle noises. The siege sprang alive again, one of the headless mercenaries dying in his own blood on the rim of the drawbridge.

'I wish,' Verna said, 'I had a robust conscience like you, Matt. You're going to be a lucky catch for some girl or other.'

'I'm still hanging around for you to give me the green light, Verna,' he called heartily, and the three of them gave a formal chuckle.

Suddenly, out of the tail-end refuse of the laugh, Verna spoke up in bitterness, regardless of me. I let peace fall on my battlefield and raised my head to miss none of her genuine anguish.

'I'm a poor bloody spinster of a woman.' She was blaming somebody, but neither my mother nor Matt. 'What's a spinster without her job? A little bit of nothing, done up in a black dress and grinning all damn day behind a counter at the best of times. Without the black dress and the counter, she might as well not even exist. And to get a job I have to commit a crime and be the only poor bloody Australian advancing to meet the Japs.'

'That settles it, Verna,' my mother said. A chair groaned. She must have been standing over Verna now. 'We can't let you go.'

'I've got to. A poor spinster's her job. Jobless, she may as well be dead. If the Japs are two miles outside Mackay when I get there, still I'll take the job.'

'Don't make a drama of it, Verna,' my mother persisted with suspect strength of nerve. 'You aren't just *any poor bloody old spinster who may as well be dead.* Not to us.'

Verna sniffed loudly. When she spoke, her voice had a shaky resonance which came of being close to tears.

'The ticket's been stolen.' She laid her tongue down very heavily on each accent. 'I'll have to go now. I can't put Matt to all that trouble without using the ticket.'

'Verna!' said Matt airily. 'It *was* no trouble. I am not sitting in the maw of hell, and the army doctors assure me I'm not possessed of devils. See! And finally, I wouldn't go to Mackay with a whole bloody division of tanks.'

'Since I've got to go anyway,' Verna asked quietly, 'why don't you make the whole thing easier for me? All this pressure on me—'

'I'm sorry, Verna. You're a good woman. Really you are. This is not a brat of a soldier talking now. You're a good woman, so I suppose you'll get looked after. I'll tell you what though. It'll be God or the Yanks who save you, because that part of the country can't be held.'

'Well, don't any of you worry,' Verna all but whispered, and still I was hearing her, I thought in triumph. 'I'll kill myself gladly, joyfully, before any of those little yellow things get their hands on me.'

Then there was silence, such a long one that I became self-conscious about the battle and forgot it. Perhaps the three of them had died in their chairs at table. I rushed out to them, holding my breath, but of course they were all there, Verna and Matt sitting up, my mother slumped, a figure of grief which I did not wish to jolt into tears. It was for her husband sleeping in a transit-camp in Egypt, for her intransigent sister-in-law, for her born and unborn sons that she sat peering down into the black mine of her unmilked tea.

I was still awake, listening for trains, when Verna came to my bedside to attend to my window and perhaps start yarning. Now that the ticket to Mackay was in her handbag, tortuous farewell threatened. She crouched over me in time to see my eyes snap shut too vigorously.

'Daniel!'

'Yes?'

'You haven't made your First Communion yet?'

'No.'

'You haven't got a sin on your soul?'

'No.' It was the theologically based opinion of Eucheria, though I had doubts on the question.

'You'll have to remember your poor Aunt Verna. Especially if anything happens to her.'

'Yes.'

'You'll have to remember me always. Till you're an old man. You'll have to pray for my soul. Will you?'

'Yes.'

'Always?'

'Yes.'

'Promise?'

'Yes.'

'That's the boy.

She stood upright, gazed down at my body, taut with embarrassment, and sighed in the face of the future. Around the room she moved, picking up a toothbrush, plucking her nightgown from beneath the pillow, fumbling for vanishing cream in her handbag. As she went out, I thought, 'I'm glad I'm not alone like that.' By the time she had finished in the bathroom, I was asleep.

Verna could not have been further north than Rockhampton when a Federal Minister announced a marvellous victory in the Coral Sea. The land, the continent, was saved. Eucheria lined us up and took us past the black hole, up the aisle to the sanctuary, to thank the God of triumphs.

8

In the case of the Comrade, one never knew when you would spin round to find him gazing at you. For the Comrade followed out no orbit. A cloven bloody hand, a lightning strike, Party business, even release from Clarence Street lock-up after one of his bad nights; any of these could land him quietly in the corner of one's vision. Such an advent was a peril against which I said a prayer nightly. Yet every month or so, it would happen; and neither the dreamy dislike in his eye nor the vague mockery hanging like lichens on his big lips disturbed me half as much as his sharp interest in me, his clear desire to enter into my mind.

From the cover of their gas meter casing, Joseph and Lennie had me pinned down behind my brick fence by a tempest of fire. There was a bullet in my shoulder. Elegant cords of blood hung like campaign ribbons from the wound. But the essential thing was to be Gene Autry, an honour given according to a rough sort of roster and as the result of an elemental form of collective bargaining. That Friday afternoon, I was Gene Autry and would take many another flesh wound before worming up to the gas box and persuading the two of them to die. Persuasion was necessary. Both of them were liable to lose their dramatic integrity, and while a person performed epics of valour as Gene Autry, they could never be trusted not to turn into some other giant of the West.

In the shade of the wide brick gate post, I lay close for a second, favouring my shoulder wound, ramming ·45-calibre cartridges into the heel of my hand. As I rolled over to fire from the unexpected side of the post, my eyes swept through an arc containing keen blue sky and cirrus-cloud, railway stanchion and the dead-fish eyes of Comrade Lenin, who stood on the footpath as still as a totem. An electric train galloped past, stampeded across the viaduct. By the time it had pounded itself away down the western line, Joseph and Lennie had raced to the Comrade. I stood close to the post and watched a caterpillar unfurl itself along a channel of mortar.

It was Friday afternoon, pay afternoon, and scarcely more than a quarter past four. Yet he seemed to be already something more than half-drunk, which promised a bad weekend for Hilda. Though the lines of his face were soggy, just a little more abstinence and a good shave could have had him looking Messianic. It was a debased air of prophetism which kept the boys subject to his word, loyal to his ideas. To that extent he was a good dialectical materialist, in that to his offspring he seemed to be not a continuous personality but a series of projections; they seemed to be able to believe in him as the seer of this particular hour rather than as the violent drunk of last week, the absentee father of last night.

Now, with his boys beside him, without warning, that flush of rapture he'd shown the afternoon he'd butchered his own hand lit up his cheeks. Today there was no shuddering with ecstasy and pain, but the excitement in his eyes was almost as frightening.

'I could really show you boys something,' he intoned.

'What is it, Comrade?' Lennie asked, but the Comrade looked up and down the railway line, not wanting to shout above the rush of a train.

'We're the blokes who've got the power,' he whispered after a while, 'the *real* power!'

He spat into a handkerchief, staring at me. Then for a time he inspected the spit, perhaps, like old Finnie's sister who seemed to get a lot of sinus, desiring the mucus to be a definite colour.

'It'd be a lesson to you boys,' he said. 'It'd be a better education than anything you've had crammed in so far.'

We did not move, the boys and I; we did not dispute this view on education. But the Comrade was undecided.

'Damn it,' he belched, abandoning himself utterly to his pay-day excitement; to the excitement of sunshine on the embankment, and a roseate gutful of liquor; to the excitement, above all else, of having a momentous secret for the first and last time in his life, and of convincing us that for him such secrets were routine.

'But you'll have to promise to keep quiet about this,' he said, and I realized that he was indeed drunk, expecting Lennie to keep a secret.

'I promise, Comrade,' Lennie whispered, making an extravagant *X* across his chest, wishing his heart, liver and various other organs ripped out if he ever said a word.

'What about you, especially,' the Comrade glowered at me. 'Will you promise by Christ or the Virgin Mary or somebody?'

He mumbled the names as if they were from an electoral roll, which provoked me to look straight into those shallow swamps of eyes and repeat the formula Eucheria had taught us for moments when someone like the Comrade demanded a solemn pledge.

'I promise, as I fear God and honour the King.'

'Well, bugger me!' the Comrade shrugged. 'That'll have to do me, I s'pose.'

You could see that he was a master of some crafts when he turned away, and this time hawked a gob of spittle from his mouth, lofting it into the wind so that it lobbed itself, with a delicacy of a kind, into the gutter.

'Well, come on!' he said.

He led us to the corner a few blocks away which had a tiny, well-tended reserve. Amongst a narrow diagonal path, a bird bath, a bubbler, two benches, a holly (far from home!), a rhododendron or two, and a row of camphor laurels, clogged with railway soot one day, washed clean the next by rain, there was hardly room for any human. Around the reserve was a low brick wall. Across the road were brown flats kept by scraggy ladies whose underwear flapped in the world's sight from bits of cord tied across landings. The brick wall stopped the contagious beauty of the laurels from infecting all this. Most people sat here on the wall at some time or other. It was a good place to rest children on your way to the shopping centre, or to sit and read of the cataclysm in Europe while you waited for the pub to open. An old man was sitting there, eyeing a paper with sad wisdom, as we came up.

'Sit here!' said the Comrade, and so we did. He was more than half-way towards sitting down himself before he realized how hard it is for a tall, sozzled man to sit down on a low brick fence. He straightened rakishly, stretched, put both hands on his hips and groaned fraudulently.

'Lumbago,' he muttered. 'I'll just stand here for a while. They haven't arrived yet anyhow.'

'Who?' Lennie asked quickly.

'Blabbermouth!' the Comrade spat in a rich, savage basso. The old man looked along the fence at us as if we were all part of the futility he'd been just now reading about.

'Blabbermouth,' the Comrade repeated more serenely.

There was nothing in that irksome roadway, except awe for the Comrade, to keep us seated like young gentlemen at his knee. A weary lady with a moustache bore her weekend meat towards us in her graceless arms as if it were a sick child. At the highway end of the street, the yellow-tiled Glasgow Arms had spilt some of its drinkers out into the afternoon sun. Groups of soldiers and workers pecked at their beer and spat into the gutter at moments of either intense humour or intense disgust. Lennie glanced up at his father's straining face and was clearly thinking of asking him once more what we were to look for, and even more clearly thinking the better of it.

We began to talk and nearly forgot the Comrade's presence. Inconsequential traffic rolled by, and the old man folded his paper and jogged away around the corner, while all the time the Comrade said nothing but looked dubiously towards the highway.

Joseph was speaking on the difference between the Australian and American cowboy. The Australian wore no gunbelt but carried his weapons hidden somewhere, or stuck through the belt which merely kept his trousers up. If he took his revolver out, it rarely went back till it spilt blood. (All this, Hilda's father, a genial old fellow who detested the Comrade, had told him.) He was hell with a stock-whip. He could rip a man's head off with it. He was not . . .

'Be quiet!' the Comrade called out. 'Here they come!'

From the highway, three canvas-covered trucks made an entry to the street and parked across from the Glasgow Arms. Nearly army trucks, they lacked the unit flashes above the bumper bars and were driven by civilians. Their shrouded cargoes were a mystery.

'Just watch!' the Comrade advised us urgently, foreseeing questions. 'Watch the men who get down out of those trucks,' he told us, and we studied them as they cuffed the cabin doors closed with that giant-biting-a-biscuit crunch and strolled towards the pub. But there was nothing of consequence about their greasy cardigans and sweaty felt hats. The faces were normal, sunburnt, beer-anxious faces.

'Can you see, Danny Jordan?' asked the Comrade.

'Yes, Mr Mantle,' I concurred, still not knowing what there was to see.

'Good! Get an eyeful! See all you want! Say a word about it and I'll kill you with my own hands.'

'Yes, Mr Mantle.' My stomach lurched with fear of the Comrade, who had a talent for successfully terrorizing me. The street hummed and darkened, blurred and came clear again. Terror had passed like a bubble through my veins. If I had known the depths of the fears in which he threshed and which caused him to plague me, I would have spat at him and run home. But I could not tell then the relative importance of adults, all of whom were kings of the earth.

'Now look!' the Comrade murmured.

From the laneway beside the pub, home of S.P. bookie places, sly-grog shops and worse, six men hurried towards the trucks.

'They're different men,' Joseph breathed.

'That's right,' the Comrade laughed. 'They're *our* men!'

They were not so very different from the six who had recently gone into the public bar, not different at all to the casual eyes of the footpath drinker. Six weathered men had entered the bar, six weathered men slipped from the lane, split into three groups of two, lifted the bonnets in unison, reaching into the bowels of the motors, causing them to growl awake simultaneously. The crews climbed up to their cabins with an air of leisured possession, let their trucks howl for a few seconds at the kerbside, then swung them out evenly and rolled them past us. As they went by, the Comrade held his face away from them, but the men in the cabins were looking to the right, at all costs to avoid an accident a hundred yards from the pub. They turned into Deakin Street, *our* street, yelped into second gear along the railway embankment. Their noise vanished quickly, as if it had been stolen out of the air.

The Comrade stared at us, bright-eyed and triumphant.

'What's in the trucks?' Lennie whispered.

'Something precious, never mind. But it's ours now. My oath it's ours. One day when you're a grown man, Lennie, and everything's ours, you can think back to this Friday afternoon. You've seen the beginning of something very big.

'So've you two!' he added to Joseph and me; *but by the time what I say is consummated*, he implied, *Joseph will have been gathered in to his defective forefathers, and you, Jordan, will have cracked open with the gangrene of dogma*. 'You can see how we get our way in this world.'

Lennie hugged his father's thighs and looked straight up along the line of the Comrade's shirt buttons, across the stubbled chin, around the pits of nostrils to the rims of his father's eyes.

'Comrade,' he begged, 'tell me what was in the trucks. Go on, Comrade. I'd never tell anyone. I'll spit and hope to die.'

'Go on, Comrade!' Joseph chorused, far grimmer in matters of secrets than Lennie because he had only a few years into which to cram the mysteries and whispered things of life.

'When I'm feeling better I might tell you about it, son.' The Comrade spoke softly and compassion curled up the corners of his mouth. 'Now run off home and tell your mother . . .'

'But you . . . !' Lennie began to explain.

'You've already been shown more than you should.' He shook his head wildly like a man who's walked into a tarantula web strung between trees. 'I've got a pain in my head. Can't you get home when I tell you? Can't you, Lennie?'

He took one savage step towards the boy. His sons turned and loped away. I followed them, a little to their rear, to show that I was not bound by the same strong obedience. Their slumped little faces blinked to the afternoon sun as they turned into Deakin Street. The Comrade must have seen their humped shoulders through the rhododendrons, for he called across to them gently, 'Tell Hilda I won't be long!'

An hour later, I was still paddling in the warm lees of daylight at the western end of our veranda, which was bridge and conning tower and centre of command. The Comrade came along. Inebriates fared badly in our street, since it sloped treacherously. Unable to curb their own momentum, they would take longer, wider steps until, opposite the viaduct, they were either trotting or prostrate. There was no doubt today. The Comrade had finished the job and was now quite nastily drunk.

I stiffened against the wall, breathless with chameleon desire. Even the best of drunks I hated, and hell was for me a place full of them. The Comrade's face was the face of drunkenness. There were no sober states for it; it was always at least passively drunk; it was daily more ugly, sad, gorged and incontinent.

He reined himself in at the gate. 'Daniel Jordan!' he called, wavering above the gate-post like a berserk ectoplasm. I didn't move.

'Daniel Jordan, come over here you little bastard when I call you and don't stop there frigging about in the shadows!'

There was something compelling in what I then thought were the ultimates in obscenity. I approached him, thinking of the wrought-iron gate between us.

The Comrade leant on the gate-post. 'D'you know what was in those trucks?' he asked.

'No!'

'You're sure?'

'Yes!'

'D'you want to know?'

I didn't venture to say.

'*D'you want to know?*'

'All right.'

'Then I'll tell you!' He leant across the gate and his breath stung my eyes like the effluvia of Old Finnie's secret beer vats.

'Arms and ammunition!' he hissed. '*Guns* and ammunition from the works up the line. Do you know what ammunition is?'

'Bullets?'

'Yes! Bullets! And there's one for you if you ever tell anyone. One of those in one of the trucks today'll go screaming into your little guts if ever you tell anyone. I'll *blast* it into you. The blood will pour out of you and you'll scream to your mother of course, but it won't be any use. She won't be able to get that bullet out.'

I shuddered for love of the frenzied mother I could see kneeling over a small son retching up blood.

'As long as you understand,' the Comrade said. The words fluttered on his lips together with the constant, small and flatulent noises of a stomach drunk on ale.

I stood crying softly for a while and was shocked to see him gone when I looked up again. The street was empty; no homey train thundered down from Parramatta; the wires above the lines swayed in a dusk westerly. The world was incommunicative on purpose now. It wanted me to go inside; and in view of the travail before her, to treat my mother as a first lady.

9

There was a period of cosmic holiday when the Comrade vanished for a fortnight. Neither early with gory hand, nor on time and pontifical, nor late and screaming drunk did he come back to his people. Apart from his body not having appeared in the morgue nor rolled up goose-fleshed and nibbled from the Harbour's slime, Hilda had no comfort. In the meantime, gossip at the corner, small-talk over the counter were murderous hazards for her pride. The deadly neutral question, 'How's your husband these days?' (*and where the hell is he?*) sliced her soul open like a saveloy.

She was not a good liar. She could not fabricate an iron-bound strand of lies and drag her dignity above the level of the waters. And, even so, her eyes were eternally raw from cupboard crying.

Like the priests of a departed god who honoured their grove no longer, the boys lingered by their peach tree, dazed and obscurely guilty. Their games now were the scanning of train windows for his face, the watching of corners for him to turn them. Hilda had assured them. He would definitely be back.

One afternoon he came down from the station like the best of the bourgeoisie, and hurried down Deakin Street. In the instant Lennie's rapt face squealed, Joseph also sighted him. They ran off, each in his varying style; and the Comrade jolted to a stop as he saw them coming to claim him. He was very pale, I noted as the three came closer. He carried his coat over his elbow and there was a sagging lump in one of his pants pockets. It wasn't as I thought, a bag of gobstoppers. It was the several parts of a Mills hand-grenade.

And don't, Aunt Verna counselled by letter from Mackay, *go loaning money earned by Brian on the field of battle to make up for money not earned by a radical tramp at the abattoirs.*

When the Comrade had first disappeared a few Fridays before, it had been characteristically, with his pay. Hilda had then taken out a third of her savings, and spent three pounds on having Joseph tested by the Macquarie Street specialist who convinced her that the boy was incurable, but promised that if any likely cure were found, he would write and tell her. On the other two, the Mantles lived for ten days. Finally, Hilda approached my mother. She had no right, she admitted, to ask for a loan of money, but she had to keep a tenner in the bank for Joseph's sake. *If a cure were found for Joseph, Stell, and there was no money to pay for it, well,* that would be the ultimate irony. 'How much do you want, Hilda?' asked Stell.

But her eyes hooded with anger when Hilda visited us on the morning after the Comrade's return with two bottles of lemonade and, of course, the boys. She *was* in debt to us, Hilda began. *Indeed*, replied Stell. The word flopped onto the linoleum like a dead fish. But now that the Comrade was repentantly back at work (piece work only, which was all the management would give him any more; wouldn't have got that without the union); now that he had woken up to himself, Hilda was assured of wages at the end of the week when our money would be repaid. Surely no one would begrudge her her little celebration. No one did. We got down five glasses and a plate of drab and circumspect war effort biscuits.

There was only one way to drink aerated waters, and that was as swiftly as, at the far end of the scale of delight, Socrates had drunk the hemlock. The aerated part of the whole thing set off delicious rumblings, starting in the pit of the stomach, thundering up the throat. It was Lennie who gave incipient signs of the Etna in his small, tough bowels. Wherefore we were all sent outside to be pigs beneath an open sky.

'So much for the Sons of Thunder,' said my mother.

There was heavy grass along the galvanized fence where for half an hour we played *Scorched Earth*. Until Lennie called us over to view a green beetle on a paspalum stalk. It looked harmless, he conceded, but it had hidden claws and a sac of poison which could burn through steel. The Comrade had seen an aborigine stung by one of these beetles, and the poor black's veins had knotted and blown up like balloons, until they split and blood gushed out of his ears like water from a burst main. With his limited grasp of words, Lennie dispatched his problematical abo with a fever of pink buboes. Our minds licking around the image of Lennie's fantastic tick, we ambled up to the laundry's blue shadow, reclined on the cement and listened for the venom which might in the next instant dement our hearts and dry our blood to a crust. After a wait of fifteen minutes, there was no palpitation, no scabrous splotch. It was apparent; we would live.

We stirred our limbs, eyed the sun which moved in a slow arc over the highway which was its winter path. But we did not step out to face it. For, unaccountably, there was an alien voice raised high in the kitchen.

I stalked to the wire-gauze door, Gunga Din in the Nabob's camp. With no other noise than air whistling through Joseph's imperfect nose, the Mantle boys crowded beside me, laying their flanks down inch by inch on the concrete step. In turn, we raised an eye above the level of the gauze, glimpsed the cavernous room still warm with the smell of breakfast porridge, surveyed it for a half-blind instant, then snatched our heads down again to the level of the steps.

Inside was some strange woman. Before her strangeness, Hilda and my mother had retreated until they were backed against the dresser with its Coronation of George VI milk-jug. The stranger differed astoundingly from them.

She had wide lips which quivered with a sodden sort of comment on such things as the Coronation milk-jug. Her crooked mouth changed form as often, as irregularly as an amoeba. Her hair fell blonde and stringy, motleyed with dirt or diluted peroxide, on to shoulders motleyed with dirt or sun spots. Her orange crêpe dress began behind her neck, ignored her shoulders, widened down her front in time to clothe her breasts, and cascaded drably from her thighs. The curves of her body sagged fulsomely over her perpendicular lines, flaccid mangoes sagging from the tree. Her legs were bare and she wore open-work shoes. It was summer dress for a pierside heyday; and she must have been cold when she came up against the northerly blowing that day. Not that she lacked climatic sense nor even a sense of clothes. It suited her to be tinsel before Hilda.

'I'm not saying, luv,' she claimed, 'that he's not finished with me. My bloody oath he's finished! I wouldn't let him in the house again. All I'm saying is I kept that gentleman husband of yours for two whole—let's call them damned, luv, there's ladies present—two whole damned weeks. I fed him. I lent him money to gamble with and he went bloody mad at the baccarat last Friday night. I don't know why I financed him. There's a sort of poxy charm about him at first. I s'pose that's what got *you* in, luv!'

She daubed the word *luv* across Hilda's cheeks like slime. I could hear the orange crêpe swish as the lady swung her hips controversially; I could hear Hilda, wifely, plump, tight with rage, grunt at the cruel loose-limbed vulgarity who had barged into her little festival.

'I don't want you in here,' Hilda murmured. Her furry voice came queerly to us, as quiet as the eye of a cyclone sucking in its breath for the purposes of mayhem. 'This is my friend's home. How in the name of Holy Suffering Mike you knew I was here I don't know!'

'A neighbour was passing by when I knocked at your place,' the orange crêpe lady interposed chattily, 'and she said I could try here. Lucky I did, luv. I mightn't never have found you.'

'I don't care how you got *here*. I don't want you in *my* place. And if you don't go now, I'm going straight to the corner and ring for the police.'

The woman laughed. There was no dole in the laugh, but it told us that this lady had found out that the police were a weak and erratic recourse, and that she herself had been unwelcome in innumerable people's kitchens for years. To be unwelcome in Hilda's and ours was for her no new frontier.

'I don't think you would, luv,' she said. 'You're too damned proud. I can tell it. You're fat with bloody pride. And you wouldn't want a couple of constables tramping round in here sneering at the lot of us. And you know, luv, they would sneer. Particularly at you. I mean to say, your husband owes me for more than just food and board and the loan of a few quid. The police'd know all this. They'd say, "Well, the one in the orange might be a fancy lady but that's the last thing the other one is, as far as her husband's concerned. That's the last thing she is, *fancy*." '

Still hunched by the gauze door, we could hear Hilda choking, conjuring up a blow or a word to keep the Comrade's absence simply a dull and faceless loneliness, not a keen, well-detailed shame involving the woman in orange crêpe. Lying on the step, sweating on the side of me which was half-buried in Lennie, and cold on the side pressed hard into the pores of the cement, I could sense that for some reason the orange-crêpe lady was unanswerable.

But before Hilda could spit out a word, it was my mother who spoke up, quite baritone and furious.

'Hilda, get this woman out of my house. She isn't my disgrace. I won't have her in here. I won't have myself and Daniel getting involved in your shame. I won't have a harlot discussing what your husband owes her in my kitchen!'

'Stell,' Hilda protested softly, 'it isn't my fault, Stell!'

'Of course it's your fault! Have you ever thought of leaving him?'

'And you're supposed to be a Catholic!'

'Oh, Hilda! Don't tell me you love him. This whore and God knows how many others and God knows how many in the future . . . he loves them all better than he loves you.'

'Don't say that, Stell! Don't say that sort of thing if you want to keep a friend. It's drink that sends Len astray.'

'Huh!' said the fancy lady. 'He sends drink astray. He's sent a hell of a lot of it astray in the last fortnight.'

'Look at the truth, Hilda! Your marriage is no good. You married the original no-hoper. Get out of it, leave him. If people point at you in the street as a woman whose marriage failed, then let them go to the other place!'

'He's a good weak man,' Hilda claimed frantically. 'You should see that. Surely Brian's got his weaknesses.'

'Dear God, if Brian had the Comrade's vices he wouldn't be a good, weak man. He'd be an evil one, just the same as the Comrade is. I wouldn't be in the same room as the Comrade for two minutes. I don't think I've met a *more* evil man.'

The boys turned pallid faces on me. Blasphemy had left them the bilious tint of young dripping. And yet they did not accuse me, their faces did not purple with rage. The three of us together embarked on a vague hatred of the fancy lady.

'Look, luv,' the lady began again, in the wake of my mother's spoken outrage, 'I don't want to be persistent but he owes me about twelve quid. I'm willing to come to a settlement.' (Here I rose on my haunches to review the room and saw the woman's mouth set in a long crooked grin, the lower lip on one side of her face having fallen away to show a bunch of nicotined teeth. Her shoulders shook satirically.) 'I mean, I don't think you'd want an itemized account.'

While the boys snatched a look each, their mother cursed the lady and wished her to be pickled in the depths of hell. We heard the lady slap some fleshy part of her body and laugh in metallic good humour.

'Get her *out*, Hilda!'

'But part of the twelve quid,' the fancy lady went on as evenly as a politician, 'belongs to a friend of mine he borrowed it from. And with *that* money he bought something from a soldier.'

'I've got nothing to lose, Hilda! I'll soon call the police.'

'Oh, shut up, luv!' the fancy lady groaned. 'This is important. The night before last a soldier came up to my place and gave something to beloved Len. I don't know what it was. It was all done up in a greasy cloth and when I wanted to see it, he yelled at me. "Don't touch that," he said. "It's dangerous." It could've been a gun or something. I mean, I'm not being nasty now, luv, and I've got no money reason like to tell you this. But he could be going to kill you or something.'

The fancy lady was right. For the first time that morning she was not being nasty. We did not therefore anticipate her shriek, or the wide thud of her large unchecked body clopping to the floor. Violence dissolved all necessity for hiding. We tumbled into the kitchen.

The lady was on the floor, her dress up above her knees, one hairless lower leg doubled under her. The right-hand corner of her brow was a mash of bruise and blood, her right eye-pit a well of gore as if the eye itself had been plucked out. My mother knelt listening for the fancy lady's tainted heart and Hilda staggered to a kitchen chair with a bloodied lemonade bottle in her hand, clutched by the neck.

Joseph proud-stepped up to her.

'The Comrade wouldn't kill you,' he murmured, waited, thought all over his brow, and repeated, 'The Comrade wouldn't kill you!'

My mother knelt upright, and glared at Hilda.

'Your husband's lady-friend's alive, Hilda,' she announced. 'What in the name of heaven are you going to do with her?'

'I don't know,' Hilda said reverently, putting down the bottle.

'She'll need stitches.'

'Yes, Stell.'

Stell rose up. 'I don't know how I'll ever forgive you, Hildie.'

Hilda said nothing, running her fingers under the rim of her chair, looking at them for signs of dust.

'Look,' my mother continued, 'we'll put an overcoat on this blasted floozie, and we'll take her around to Dr Slattery.'

'You'll have to wake her up.'

'I'll wake the strumpet up.'

Amongst the soft soap, kerosene, mouse-traps, scouring agents beneath the sink, Stell rummaged for the bottle of ammonia. She dragged the lady's blood-sticky head upright and pushed the opened bottle beneath her nose. The fumes needled at the lady's brain, jolting her head aside as neatly as any flush blow from men-friends of the Comrade's breed. Her shattered eyebrow they sponged with a strong solution of iodine, and when she squealed and rolled her head around, my mother clutched her by the back whisk of strawy hair, fixed the bleeding forehead in space and drenched it in a piercing wash of iodine.

The lady spat out a crisp awesome word I had heard only from a few fishermen at the Cape where old Finnie lived.

'Go and get your overcoat, Hilda.'

Hilda swallowed a sad regurgitating crumb of violence.

'I'm sorry, Stell. I didn't know. I'm sorry. I'm terribly sorry.'

'I'm not worried about that now. Get your overcoat. I'm not taking her half-naked to Dr Slattery. And I don't want *my* overcoat rotten with disease. You clouted her, Hilda. Now you clothe her!'

Lennie hugged Hilda, his arm going hardly more than half-way around her buttocks.

'Stay here with Mrs Jordan!' Hilda said to the boys.

The fancy lady shook her head, spilling dribbles of blood down her cheek.

'Hurry Hilda!' Stell called. 'She's bleeding like a sow. And why not?'

'My overcoat, Stell?'

'Yes. And listen! We'll be all right. Dr Slattery won't find out anything from me. I promise you. And he won't believe this baggage against the word of two of his patients. So calm yourself down, Hilda. And *hurry*!'

'You'll pay, you lousy bitch!' the lady yelled vaguely as Hilda rushed out to find her overcoat. My mother administered again the iodine cure.

'You boys,' she said, 'go into the yard. Joseph and Lennie, don't take any notice of this rotten woman. Do you understand?'

'Yes, Mrs Jordan.'

'And when you go into the yard, stay there, *please*!' The *please* was a quiet but not a soft one. It followed us towards the door like an Arctic, lean and subtle beast. Its ferocity was largely for the fancy lady, but it could not promise that if we vexed it it would not turn on us. The few paternal blasts of temper which had withered me in the past were cosy human weaknesses beside the tigress exasperation in Stell's voice. We walked backwards to the door, and the last thing we saw was Stell picking up a piece of medicated wadding she'd been saving, preparing to lay it like the upper half of a sandwich on the orange-crêpe lady's eye, but waiting a second and laying it down considerably more gently.

'Your mother said a lot of *evil* things about the Comrade,' Joseph commented. You could see that he didn't want to fight over the matter, being so profoundly hurt.

'But the *tart* said a lot of things that were worser.' Lennie accepted insult more vigorously than his brother.

It was best to make conversation. 'Aunt Verna got really mad at me for calling someone a tart,' I said.

We were sitting in a peace-pipe circle on the lawn towards one o'clock. We had heard the ladies leave for Dr Slattery's ten minutes before, but the boys hadn't said much yet, being dazed. The earth was cold after the night before's frost, but the sun was pleasant on Lennie's and my faces and on Joseph's shoulders. A fat magpie had flurried down and gone questing along the galvanized fence, waddling enough to entertain the Mantles for minutes on end.

'Anyhow, what's a tart?' Joseph asked. 'I bet you don't know, Jordan!'

'It's a cake.' I was as prim as Aunt Verna could have wished.

'Don't try to be funny with me, Jordan,' he murmured with a tragic sort of anxiety that I might. 'It's a loose woman. That's what my grandmother told me.'

'Loose woman?'

'That one was loose, all right?' Lennie giggled with enlightenment. 'She had a backside on her like a couple of sugarbags and she wriggled it all over the kitchen.'

We laughed a snide guilty laugh. I glanced a little respectfully at Lennie. No, he wasn't as clever as that. He must have heard that type of talk from the Comrade.

'And she said,' Joseph spat at the memory, 'that the Comrade was going to kill someone.'

'He said he'd kill me!' I told them humourlessly, remembering the afternoon the ammunition trucks had been stolen.

'You know he didn't mean it, Jordan. Grown-ups are always telling kids they'll kill them. My grandfather told us that when we scraped the putty out of the windows at his place. And he wouldn't hurt an ant.'

'The Comrade meant it when he said it,' I insisted, 'and anyhow, why's he bought a gun?'

Joseph ran his fingers over the lawn, picked a plum-pudding, a little sweet green plant that grew melon-shaped amongst the grass. He chewed it in a state of doubt.

'It wasn't a gun, Jordan. That's another lie.'

'What was it then?'

Joseph thought. He had found another plum-pudding, and meditated until it was eaten.

'If you come next door,' he said, 'if you're game enough to come next door, I'll show you.'

The fat magpie bustled into the air, aghast at the suggestion.

'You heard my mother,' I said simply.

'All right then,' Joseph murmured. 'Then if you're too much of a dingo to come and see, then shut up.'

'I'm not a dingo.'

The plum-pudding habit spread. We sought them nervously in the grass and nibbled them down.

'What is it then?' I asked.

'You'll have to come and see, Jordan! Except that you're not game to do that.'

Very pale, I shrugged.

'All right! Will it take long?'

'No!'

'All right! I'll go.'

In the Mantles' kitchen the old table waited for us dimly. The lounge-room was darker still. Slumped by one of the walls, with one leg raised stupidly from the uneven floor, was a long dark-varnished cabinet. Joseph flipped open its doors. Inside were a few dimity table-cloths, some glass-ware and, standing in the centre of the top shelf, upright and substantial like a party of aldermen, five hefty books.

'*Das Kap-it-al*,' I read. '*The Spe-eches of—of Lenin*. Is that Comrade Lenin?'

'Yes,' said Lennie securely.

'It isn't, stupid,' Joseph grunted. 'It's another Lenin.'

'Is this all?' I asked, nodding towards the cabinet.

'No!' said Joseph. 'I just thought I'd show you those books. Not many people've seen them.'

'Well, hurry up! They might be back from the doctor's soon.'

The north wind scuttled down their laneway, mouthing, 'Hurry! Hurry!' Joseph turned to another cabinet, the child of the first, clogged with the same dark varnish, much squatter. He grasped its small white knob and rattled it to show that the cabinet was locked. It was from there on a matter of legerdemain for Joseph. He pulled a penknife from his pocket, gestured it in the air, drew out the blade and opened the door with it. Lennie and I knelt to look inside. But there was yet more to perform. Joseph guarded the entrance with an extended arm.

'Lennie,' he said grandly, 'did the Comrade send us all into the kitchen for a while last night?'

'Yes,' Lennie gurgled. 'He said he wanted us right out of here and don't dare come in till he told us we could.'

'That's right. But *I* didn't stay in the kitchen.'

'You went to the lavatory!' Lennie supplied.

'That's right, only I didn't. I came down the lane and looked in at this window. And that's how I saw what the Comrade was putting in a box. Then he put the box in *this* cabinet.'

'What was in it?' I shrilled.

'Look!' uttered Joseph. And he pulled out a box marked 'Greene's Casuals For Particular Men' and half-full of packing straw. Even Lennie had seen enough Hollywood to tell what it was that sat up on top of the straw like a complacent Easter-egg.

'It's a hand-grenade!' he yelled.

'Yes!'

A green melon with squares cut in its surface lay in the middle of the box. Surrounding it were a few shiny metal rods (one of them with a spring), a lever, a little wick-like fuse, a plug for the bottom of the grenade, and the pin which Clark Gable usually pulled out with his teeth.

'Let me see!' said Lennie, reaching for the grenade. Joseph slapped his hand.

'Get away! This is the Comrade's. I don't know what he wants it for, but he's probably working for the Army or the government or something.'

In the dark room, from the deeps of the cabinet, from the grease caked on the grenade, I could smell death. It was necessary to stand up and back away from the shoebox.

'You aren't going to tell, Jordan, are you?'

'No,' I said, confused, tripping backwards into an easy chair and thinking that it was the grave till its spongy seat sat me up straight in drab spaciousness.

'If it ever got out about this grenade, I'd let the Comrade know it was you who blabbed. You're my friend, but the Comrade's my father.'

I wriggled up out of the puffy arms of the easy chair. It occurred to me that there was no need to maintain a friendship involving terror of the Comrade, secrets of deathly things (ammunition trucks and grenades), and the intrusion of the orange-crêpe lady.

'Who said I want to be your bloody friend?' I roared at them.

They raised their pallid faces to me. The Mantles were notable for their pallor, and when one challenged their fundamental tenets, such as that it is an ultimate honour to be known by the Comrade, they whitened prodigiously.

'Who said I want to be your bloody friend?' I repeated, since it had startled them the first time.

Then I crossed the short darkness to the kitchen door, sped along the lane and within seconds was home again, breathing hard, utterly freed of the Mantles.

Still, at the table at night, in bed, I would hold my breath waiting for the green pod of amatol to blow the roof off the Mantles' place and shock all sense and order out of ours. But the house stood, and after a while I remembered the grenade only when a hearse rolled down the highway or Eucheria led us to pray for the departed.

10

Sister Eucheria looked out on a class in whose souls were crooked ways to be made straight, hills to be made plain, ruts of evil to be levelled. In Dolph Conlon's soul anyway, in each soul there, but not, I feared, in mine. And so did Eucheria fear this.

I was a year younger than the others in the class which she was getting ready for First Confession. She would call me to the front of the class while the others were roaring their spellings, and as every mouth champed away at the letters and every eye consumed us, she would ask me about the faith, try to assure herself that I was at the age of reason, that there was some atom of absolvable guilt in me. For Eucheria was a humanist as well as a theologian, and feared to hurt me by omission from the Penance class as much as she feared to frustrate the Sacrament by presenting to it an innocent.

On a hushed, overcast Thursday morning, Eucheria lined us up in a corridor. A tall girl called Gwen Callan, who wrote the points up on the board for the Greens, who knew the four times tables as if they were the names of her own family, who had led the flower-strewers at Corpus Christi, who was without a doubt ripe for the purifying effects of the confessional, and was in innumerable other ways perfect, strode in queenly fashion down the ranks straightening them, pulling poor Dolph into place by the snot-streaked sleeve of his blazer. The drill of the Sacrament was harboured in our minds; the words of petition, contrition, purpose of amendment marched up and down like brass bands. We scarcely spoke, plodding in strange silence beneath low secretive clouds. Westerlies pushed leaves the size of venial sins around the presbytery backyard, below the presbyteral washing. We had nearly come to the porch when Dolph hissed at me, 'Look,' and turning my head, I saw the priest striding towards the sacristy between drying shirts, a small purple stole in his hand.

Someone tapped my fingers with Holy Water. We were in the nave, where the pews sat up possessively, prejudiced against children. There was an amber, wormwood smell about the dustiness of the place, about the dust which was the bones of martyrs washed to a powder by seas of time and grace.

'In here, Daniel Jordan!' Eucheria whispered. Her face shone, particularly at her coifed cheek-bones. The empty church excited her, as if there were more of the Divine Presence for her to bask in by virtue of the emptiness. She knelt in a state of suppressed exultation. Dolph and I watched her and were astounded. There was in her a genuinely nuptial excitement.

Waiting for the priest, we trundled out varied Acts, Acts of faith, hope, contrition, love. Clause by clause, Eucheria gave us the words which we repeated to the pigeoned clerestories. The priest, who had fine black hair and was built heroically, his cassock binding a barrel-chested frame into the ways of the Lord, came down the aisle. He was not flushed with the glory of his work; he did not look into our faces as if we were all-but-unspotted lambs, cropping the eternal hillsides; his gaze passed us by and focused on the darksome alcove of the baptismal font. Yet I was pleased with the workaday dignity of the man. After all, I knew that most of us could not by the most extreme figure of speech be called *lambs*; and there was an unfussed air of habit about the way the priest pulled shut his confessional door that showed that he knew it too.

'... to love You above all things,' Eucheria prayed, 'even to the shedding of my blood.'

We could hear the blunt noises of the large-framed priest settling into his seat.

'... even to the shedding of my blood,' we roared.

Dolph Conlon recited prayers with a strange fervid mannerism. He held up his head, eyes bright and fixed on the Kingdom. But at every stressed syllable—Eucheria recited prayers in the same way as poetry—he nodded his head profoundly. This peculiarity was laughable in some of the girls, who were merely out to convince Eucheria that they were lilies of Sharon. But Dolph *was* a saint, despite the ragged blazer with the mucus stains on its sleeves. If others had laughed at the way Dolph prayed, I would have tried to throttle them for it. But children are basically fair in these matters. They laughed at the lilies of Sharon, but not at Dolph.

For both Dolph and Sister Eucheria meant that 'shedding of my blood' business. They would, for example, joyously have put their hands beneath a cleaver as Comrade Lenin had, although with them it would not have simply been a selfish craving for the euphoria of agonizing for their cause which led them to it. But Dolph, Eucheria and the Comrade were a kindred to which we others did not belong. They were prodigal of blood, while there was nothing to which we were more firmly attached.

'Now you will examine your consciences,' Eucheria announced, but I had raked mine over before falling to sleep the night before. We knelt in silence, and Dolph, with his nose pressed hard between joined hands, frowned as he lifted enormity after enormity from the black pits of his soul.

In fright, I shuddered upright. The nun was bending over me, smiling, trying to show that she would willingly go into the box with me but that that was not allowed.

'You go into that one, Daniel,' she whispered.

A girl had already risen and swayed into the confessional as if she were Saints Perpetua and Felicity combined, flowing into the arena. Important and terrified, first fruit of Eucheria's corner of the Vineyard, I went into what she called *the tribunal of mercy*, and jammed the ball-bearing door closed behind me. No one must hear my secret shame.

It was a little cell-like place with a high-up beaded window the colour of sago. There was a prie-dieu before the wire grille on which was tied a crucifix. Kneeling, I was just able to rest my nose on the bottom of the grille. During the confession then, I would have to stand, exposed head and shoulders to the terrible absolution of God. Beyond the grille, the sliding cedar shute was closed, but I could hear the girl on the other side of the priest's compartment telling him *fortissimo* that she had called her mother a fat old fool. When that happened, when you overheard another person's guilt, you didn't worry, Eucheria had said, you simply held your hands over your ears. Doing this, I strained forward to kiss Christ's pierced feet, and waited.

The cedar shute opened softly, and the priest held his head sideways to look down at me, for I still had my ears clamped and my eyes half-closed.

'Hello,' he said, as if he were merely a baker or something similiar.

'*Good morn-ing, Fath-er,*' I recited Euphoriesquely.

'You're not worried, are you?' He spoke in the tone doctors adopted when they had the syringe in their hands. It was time for me to bring matters to order.

'Bless me, Father,
For I have sinned.
This is my first
Confession, Father!'

I announced in a flurry of dactyls and iambics.

'Yes,' he said. 'Now you just *softly* tell me of the few little wrongs you've done. And don't be scared, because God is very pleased with you.'

'There is a golden rule when you make a confession,' Eucheria had told us. '*The worst first!*'

'I fight with Joseph Mantle, Father.'

'I see. Well, I think all boys fight.'

I would not have my viciousness minimized.

'But I start fights with him because I like to beat him.'

'I see,' he repeated, no way impressed.

'But Joseph Mantle's half a cripple,' I announced climactically.

'Oh! That's different. Are you going to do your best not to fight him in future then?'

'Yes, Father.'

'Anything else?'

I sucked my breath in, formed my next heinousness on my tongue, and spat it out. 'I hated a man!'

'Oh? Did you really hate him?'

'Yes!'

'Well, you've got to be really mad at a person to hate him, you know. You've got to wish he was dead and in hell. I'm sure you didn't wish this about that man, did you?'

'Yes, Father!'

'You did.' He seemed appropriately interested now. 'Who is the man?'

'Comrade Lenin!'

'Who?'

'Comrade Lenin. He's Joseph Mantle's father. He's a colonist.'

'A colonist? How do you mean?'

'He wears a red handkerchief with a hammer and—I've forgotten what else, Father.'

'He wouldn't be a member of the Colonist Party?' the priest asked with quick insight.

'Yes!' I said.

'And is that the only reason you hate him?'

'No, Father. He punched me. He said he'd kill me.'

The purple stole rose and fell as the priest shrugged. 'First of all, are you going to forgive him?'

'Yes.'

'Good boy. Now next, have you told your father about this Comrade fellow?'

'My father's in Egypt, Father.'

'Well, have you told your mother?'

'No! I didn't tell her—he said he'd kill me.'

'Well, he might have been joking anyhow. But tell her anyway. Will you do that?'

'Yes, Father!'

'Now make sure you tell her. Right?'

'Yes, Father!'

The priest half-stood up to stretch. Then he hid a yawn and began again.

'Now, I am going to ask you a very important question. I'm only asking you this so that we can stop this Comrade bloke if he's doing you harm. You tell me the truth, because I'm your friend. Now the question is, has the Comrade ever tried to do anything dirty and evil to you?'

'No, Father.' I told him that the Comrade had threatened to shoot me if I ever told about the ammunition trucks.

'You see, my little friend,' the priest went on, 'if you tell your mother about all this, she can get the police to stop him if he tries to scare you again.'

'Yes, Father!'

'And tell your mother, if he ever troubles you, she can get help from me. My name is *Father Peters. Peters.* Will you remember that?'

'Yes, Father!'

'Yes. Just ask for Father Peters at the presbytery. Now, anything else?'

'Sometimes I hide in the long grass when my mother wants me to go and get the milk. And I tell lies.'

'All right! I think that will do you. Have you had a happy First Confession?'

'Yes, thank you, Father. Oh, and Comrade Lenin cuts himself up with a meat cleaver. He goes out on constipation from the meat works and hands out newspapers for the . . .'

'For the Colonists?' the priest asked intelligently.

'Yes!'

'You keep well away from this Comrade Lenin fellow, won't you? And remember, Father Peters. As soon as he tries anything, come to me! Now, for your penance . . .'

I held the door open for Dolph, conscious for the first time of the notoriously long session I had had in the confessional. Three seatfuls of gaping uninitiates watched Dolph go in and me come out. Their large eyes washed me up and down, saying, 'There goes a sinner and a half.' Then, on the strength of my new innocence, I plodded up to the Lady Altar to speak with the Virgin Mother.

The sun had rolled between two cloud-banks, and lit up with a quick, invigorating fervour, the *St Paul-without-the-Walls* façade of the church, and the line of children standing below it. Intense was the gaiety of those thirty-five infants as they waited for the priest and Sister Eucheria to finish talking, in so far as the Seal of the Confessional allowed, of the morning's work. Dolph and I, at the back of the column, could hear fragments of what was said.

'Definitely very young, Sister,' the priest murmured. 'I wouldn't recommend that they make their Communion until towards the end of the year.'

Sister Eucheria's reply was blown away as the wind rose again and the cloud-banks moved in on our brief sun.

'Well, to tell you the truth,' the priest pursued, 'there were a few I couldn't absolve even with the most conditional of absolutions. You can't absolve the utterly innocent, you know, Sister. There were a few of them I simply blessed. That satisfied them. They thought they'd been to Confession.'

This statement of priestly policy I did not clearly understand, and Dolph, with his native decency, did not listen to. Yet I *did* understand that some of us had acted in a tableau but no sacrament. I kicked at the pathway, loosing an ankle-high spray of gravel. Here, as in other fields, was the same daunting incompleteness that afflicted everything in which I was concerned. I had, for example, won a card for being champion speller a few weeks before, but champion speller of rows three and four, the ungifted, unelect half of the class. I had been given charge of children at the bubblers one day—but kindergarten children. People from my own class would have squirted me with supreme irreverence. And today, I could say I had confessed, but whether I had been to Confession or not, that only the priest knew.

Dolph, hazed with glory, and myself with a bone of disappointment lodged in my throat, gave no trouble to Eucheria as back we marched to class.

11

In June, talk of the Comrade's galloping degeneration followed us around like a condition of existence. We did not go out often, since the much pre-figured Herbie was to be born in July. Wherever we did go, people wanted to ask us about the Comrade and the way he was treating Hilda, about the eye-patch she'd been wearing which they were willing to bet covered no sty, about Lennie falling to sleep at school because of the yelling of abuse and hurling of cups and clothes-brushes which went with the Comrade's irregular homecomings. Where did he get all that drink from? the women on the corners wanted to know. They would have hated to see how bare *her* cupboard was, they all nodded.

It was true that, drunk, the Comrade was becoming a consistent wife-beater. Hilda would be thugged by him once, maybe twice, or even three times a week. She knew that we could hear the din of these beatings and, on the mornings after, would stagger into our place to tell us how contrite the Comrade was. And each time, my mother would give her tea and beg her to leave the brute but for heaven's sake, don't tell him she said so.

At the end of June, a week early, Stell gave birth to a baby son. Aunt Pat, down from the Cape, took me up to the small maternity hospital, away from the soot of the railway and with young pines in its garden, and we visited the crowded little ward where the babies, with huge labels pinned on their gowns, lay three to a cot, indulging the shortages of a war of which they had little part. Some nurse with a decorative taste had put Herbie, black-polled and resolutely serene, in the middle of two bald girls who were bunching their minute fists and wailing with what was partly grief but mainly annoyance straight up into our faces. Pat laughed and said that they'd expected a cradle of their own and wouldn't have come had they known the accommodation was so lacking.

Through short, veering corridors we searched for my mother's room. The door of the labour ward was partly open and screams from inside sent us pale. A nurse came along, said 'Those Italian women always panic!' and closed the door fully. She led us to my mother in a room dominated by snapdragons, roses and dahlias, rather than by the five quiet women lying there. Stell's cheeks and brow were white and half-transparent like polished soap. She had ribbons in her hair and seemed invincibly happy.

A day later, Herbie was named. Father Peters had come to the hospital to anoint a woman who had lost her child and was now dying herself. After the rites, he visited my mother to congratulate her.

'What are you going to call him?' he asked her.

'I'd like to call him after my father,' Stell said. 'But that's impossible. He's an Irishman and his name's Finbar. People call him Old Finnie.'

'But Finbar's just Irish for Brian,' the priest told her. 'My name's Brian and whenever I was called to Holy Orders, they'd announce me as Finbarrus Peters.'

My mother quoted a Latin tag Old Finnie had taught her. 'Roma locuta est, causa finita est,' she said. 'And my husband, who's in Egypt, his name is Brian too.'

One morning Pat, who was staying in Sydney for a while to be the baby's godmother, opened the door to get the milk and found her boy-friend, out of his God-abandoned training camp in the bush for the weekend, sitting on the back steps with his tunic collar up around his ears and dew on his hat. Although there seemed nothing delectable about Pat, her eyes swollen from sleep and her dress not yet properly settled on her loping country-girl body, her soldier beamed at her and managed to kiss her obliquely on the forehead before she told him to wake up Australia and come inside, he must be frozen to death.

'It's been a bit cold out there,' he admitted. 'My great-coat's in at the railway.' He thought it gallant to have a great-coat. 'Goodday, Dig!' he called to me where I sat spooning over an unmilked bowl of rolled oats. My mother was home and my new brother. It was Saturday and a Saturday I didn't want to share with a young soldier when soldiers were tuppence a dozen and one no longer accepted them on the basis of their uniform alone. As well, he had caught me with my pyjama top on. It was an unheroic beginning! I elected not to cultivate this nineteen-year-old man who stood across the table rubbing his hands and saying, 'You wouldn't have another bowl of that, Pat?'

'This is Noel,' Pat told me. 'You remember Noel. He's from the Cape. He knew you when you were a baby. Say *hello*, *Noel*!'

'Hello, Noel!' I said challengingly, implying that he'd find it insufficient *now* simply to tickle me under the chin, implying that anyhow I didn't give a damn about the pyjama coat. When my mother appeared and made him welcome, I could foresee a spoilt Saturday with Pat's soldier around the place washing his socks and getting Pat to sew on his buttons. It was too late to sit up and look receptive of an invitation when Noel unexpectedly offered her a morning in the shops, lunch somewhere, and after that the pictures or the races or fabled Luna Park or the Zoo. They rollicked off to the station together before nine. From next door, the Mantle boys saw them and waved them on their way, being born wavers, having waved the comings and goings of the Comrade since before they could walk.

They hadn't gone long, Pat and her trooper, when the door bell rang. We approached it trying to guess whose silhouette it was on the other side of the wrinkled glass, wanting to be sure it wasn't the Comrade's before we opened it. When my mother did, it was Mr Conlon, Dolph's father, a wiry little man with large hoary eyebrows and straight grey hair. He had a box of vegetables on his shoulder.

'Mrs Jordan,' he said softly, lifting the brim of his Akubra with one knotty finger. 'I met you and your husband at the football once. I'm Greg Conlon. The wife sent me down with some vegetables for you.'

Invited in, he stood in the hall, a very unassertive little man. I had always thought of him as a large, square man, for he was a famed anti-Communist organizer at the abattoirs, and often Sister Eucheria asked the class to pray for him in his dangerous task.

'Come right through, Mr Conlon,' my mother said, 'and have a cup of tea.'

Mr Conlon lumped his box down on a kitchen chair and began to empty it.

'There's a few pounds of peas,' he mumbled, 'and potatoes have been a ridiculous price. And I hope you like the peach conserve. Jean—that's the wife—makes enough of it each summer to drown in.'

'How can I thank you?'

'Better if you didn't. Excuse me.'

He walked across the room and pulled aside the curtains with green hillsides and bunches of bananas on them. His nose close up to the glass, he smiled. 'Old Comrade Mantle. Your husband told me he lived beside you.'

I looked but was not tall enough to see past the Mantles' side wall and lavatory at the same slant angle at which Mr Conlon eyed the Comrade leaning against his far fence in the morning sun.

'Do you know him?' my mother asked.

'I'll say I do, Mrs Jordan. I never met a dirtier moron. He's getting to be an embarrassment to the other Reds even.'

'How's that?'

'Well, if he keeps skipping work much longer, they'll just have to let the management sack him. Which'd mean they'd lose a very handy *robot*. That's a fellow who does exactly what he's told. I suppose you know, Mrs Jordan, that he often slices himself up with a cleaver to get time off for Party work.'

Mrs Jordan told him that we did certainly know this.

'Apart from that too many of the true Reds detest him. It's hard even for them to admire such a momumental bludger. I mean, if they're pretending to be the Party of the workers, the upholders of the rights of the proletariat, well, they can't very well use blokes like that as the symbol of the Party.'

Mr Conlon stayed at the window, grinning at the unaware Comrade.

'He's given me a lot of worry,' my mother said, and she and Mr Conlon swapped a glance which told that he knew exactly what she meant and that I didn't.

'Besides that, he has a bad effect on Daniel. He seems to disturb him.'

'That'd be just about up to his weight,' Mr Conlon nodded. 'Well, let's not waste the morning on that brand of vermin.' And he pulled the banana curtains together.

Having viewed the baby and played with its incredible little hands, Mr Conlon declared he'd have to go; he had to take the boys for a haircut. I thought warmly of my friend Dolph having his angular head barbered, and helped my mother convoy Mr Conlon to the door. There we discovered that he was yet another of those Irishmen who talk best on a doorstep when, threatened with the likelihood of departure, they have not so definitely departed that they cannot spare you an extra ten or so thousand words.

He was propped sideways to the door, speaking of the war, the Labor Party, the Communist Party, the Church, education, when the Comrade issued from the Mantle place, bound for the paper-shop or for that sly-grog lane beside the Glasgow Arms. Whatever it was that turned the Comrade slowly out of his gate and brought him ambling by our place, it was an eventuality which both he and Mr Conlon would mourn for the rest of their lives.

'I've spoken to a heck of a lot of American soldiers,' Mr Conlon was saying at the time, 'and they say that MacArthur has so many enemies in the Democratic Party, that he's being starved of men and supplies.'

'Thank God he was supplied with enough to save us!' my mother responded with nervous piety. But she gave up all show of normal conversation when the Comrade halted before the gate and leant his folded arms along the gate-post. For a while he eyed us, one eyebrow down, one up, an aspect of him which recalled the smile of the orange-crêpe lady. He grinned in his languid, boozy way. By then, Mr Conlon had become conscious of him.

'Well,' murmured Mr Conlon, 'some people are lucky!' Irony, however trite, became the hour. 'Mornin', Comrade!' he called lustily.

'Dear Mrs Jordan!' The Comrade wagged his head in burlesque civility. 'You've had a man in to fix the sewers. I seem to remember that man, Mrs Jordan. He was a shop steward once. A big unionist. A friend of the workers. He used to be a puppet of Archbishop Kelly. But he's changed now. Now he's a puppet of Archbishop Gilroy.'

'None of that's too original,' Mr Conlon whispered proudly. 'The Reds have been saying that sort of thing about me for years.'

He spoke up to the Comrade.

'Whose puppet are you, Mr Red? Report in to Mr Engels and get him to renew your strings! You look a wreck!'

'I have a hard life,' the Comrade called back. 'We all do. We all have to work too damned hard.'

'Never mind, Saint Molotov. There's always heaven to look forward to.'

'Fat consolation!' the Comrade grimaced.

Both men fell quiet while an old couple tottered past in their best, the lady with an extravagant collar of broad lace, and her small husband jiggling a watch chain across the most bourgeois of little bellies.

'Yes, a fat consolation!' the Comrade repeated when the old people had gone.

In return, Mr Conlon became whimsical. 'I don't know, Comrade! An eternal meat-cleaver, an infinity of fingers to whack away at, an infinity of blood to bleed away with, an infinity of Compensation schemes to cover the whacking and the bleeding. I think you'd enjoy it, Len.'

Our visitor smiled broadly, and my mother, led to it perhaps by mere politeness to a guest, made the same mistake. It came to the Comrade that he was being ridiculed. He straightened and pulled his arms to his sides. His face became blue. He spat.

'Are you laughing there, Mrs Jordan?'

My mother, in an instant, swallowed her smile.

'Are you laughing there?'

'Why not?' Mr Conlon yelled. 'Why shouldn't she laugh? Perhaps you think she should be reverent. Or perhaps she should be afraid. Like the boy here.' He designated me by clamping a bony hand down on my scalp. 'Listen, Comrade! You're laughable! That's all! Laughable!'

But the Comrade's fury was not diverted. He stood immobile, totally absorbed in Stell's having smiled in ridicule of him.

'Would your husband laugh, Mrs Jordan, if I write to him and tell him that you're mucking around with our brave unionist?'

'He'd laugh all right! Do I look like a lady's man, Comrade?' Mr Conlon asked. His tongue rolled wryly within his cheeks. His wiry little body seemed on the verge of pouncing into the garden and thence at the Comrade's throat.

'I don't know what you look like, Conlon. You look like some sort of bloody fawning insect to me.'

His grease-grey cardigan flying with passion and the morning breeze, the Comrade stepped back from the post. Seer-like, he stretched his right hand in front of him, and one damaged finger quivered at Mr Conlon on the veranda.

'I'll bring your house down around your damned ears, you clerical arse-licker.'

'Go back home, Comrade! I've been threatened by experts. Go and have a blasted shave! You look as if you crawled out of a rusty tin.'

A volley of sneezes shook the Comrade's dissolute shoulders in proof of Mr Conlon's insult. Three or four times he had to swallow before he could say, 'I'm not threatening, you whore of bishops and monsignors. But when you go up in a great red blast, you just think that it was *me* who sent you. I want you to know that Len Mantle sent you hurtling into the Garden of Eden. And all the Garden of Eden is, Mr Shop Steward, is a bloody great brick wall the dead crash into. I'll hurl you at it so hard and fast you'll be in bits. The almighty union man'll be dead, and his great God won't stop him from turning into a stew of putrid muck.'

He bit at the air, breathless from his pell-mell jeremiad.

'I'll send you all up!' he concluded, and his mind dressed the image of the grenade in coatings of lustre and secrecy and valour. An honest-enough-looking smile settled on his face, and we could barely hear him whisper, 'So go to hell!' Remembering the morning paper and the sly grog or whatever it was, he jerked around and made his fugged way up Deakin Street. The faces on the veranda followed him.

'There goes a sweet one,' said Mr Conlon.

Unnoticed, I put my head down on the door-jamb and closed

my eyes. There was an instant's blackness, but in its centre a mote of yellow flame sprang up and spread, eating the dark away, opening up a blue abyss. I held my breath and waited to hit the Comrade's brick wall. But my mother's hand went around my neck and pulled my head up.

'See, Mr Conlon?' she murmured, cupping me by the ear against her hip. 'See what I mean about Daniel and the Comrade?'

12

'Why do you want to know?' Uncle Matt asked me.

'I had an argument with a boy in my class.' I paused on the lie, considered it, set it aside for Father Peters' absolution, another item amongst the assembled data which would prove to him that I was as maliciously evil as any other human.

'About grenades?'

'About how they work.'

He rolled his eyes at the ceiling and whistled. 'Kids these days!' he groaned.

It was the mid-afternoon of the same Saturday. We had entertained Pat's trooper for breakfast, Mr Conlon for morning tea, though he wouldn't have any, and now Matt had come, to lunch with his sister and see the new baby. Though it had squeaked at him irritably and once only, wrinkled the corners of its ancient little eyes, and slept again, Matt seemed well satisfied. As we talked, the baby was still sleeping, slung in his lambswool snuggery in the lounge-room, his lilliputian hands either side of his chin, palms up, clenched, paw-like. My mother had gone for a walk in the sun to the chemist's.

I fetched the writing pad and a blunt pencil.

'There's this big green thing,' I said, drawing an egg-shape, 'and it's got these markings on it.' I drew squares over the surface of the egg. It looked unjustifiably like a grenade when I'd finished. I was certain that I could draw the contents of the Comrade's shoebox with passable craftsmanship.

'That *big green thing*,' Matt smiled, 'is fat with amatol. It goes off like judgement day. Everyone of those things costs the government ten quid.'

'Why's it got marks like a pineapple on it?'

'To help it explode into fragments. You know, little bits. The government's got to get its ten quids' worth.'

I sketched the pin.

'What does it do?' I asked.

He laughed in a superior way, as if I were simple enough to think that the egg and the pin were the total secret of a hand grenade. Without looking at him, I drew the shaft with its spring, the striker, the plug, the little fuse.

'Whoo there, Nana!' he grinned. 'Where in the hell did you see all this?'

'I saw it—oh, a lot of places.'

'Where, for example?'

'At the Easter Show they had one in a glass case.'

He wrinkled his chin in comment on the wisdom of the people who ran the Easter Show.

'You've got a heck of a memory, Danny-boy!'

'How does it all work?'

The chair squealed as he leant back, wooing memory with his tongue in his cheek.

'Give me a look at what you've drawn, please. You'd better give me the pencil too.'

For a long time he stared at my diagrams, until I began to believe that he knew nothing about grenades. Once or twice he made a slow amendment to my work without any sign of confidence.

'That's more or less it,' he mumbled at last. 'Look here! This little fuse thing they call the detonator. And it's got a little metal cap on it, like this.'

'How does it work?' I persisted humourlessly.

'Well professor, I know! Doesn't that amaze you, you bloody little smart alec?'

He slapped me across the shoulders then, and we wrestled for a while.

'But aren't you going to show me?'

'All right, damn it all.'

With the pencil in his clenched fist, he demonstrated how the sprung shaft fitted down the centre of the grenade and was held by the lever which was held by the pin. He showed how the striker fitted into the base and how the detonator was inserted.

'Then all you do is screw in the plug.'

If you pulled the pin, then threw the grenade, the lever fell free, the shaft plunged and hit the striker, which set off the detonator, which detonated the high explosive, which blew every bloody thing around to pieces, or so Uncle Matt said.

'From the time you pull that pin, Danny-boy, you've got four seconds.'

'In the pictures they've got seven seconds.'

'Yes, but they're bloody wonders, those Yanks. Why, if you had seven seconds, the Japs'd throw it right back at you. Then you'd be up—up a certain street.'

I stared at the diagram which Matt had now laid down. There was a lack of most adult brands of concentration in him, and it had him instantly on his feet, sparring at the banana bunch curtains.

'If you look at the bottom of the grenade there are two holes, aren't there?' I asked.

'Yes.' The curtains sighed beneath his volley of punches.

'And you put the top of the det—you know, the fuse thing, in the hole that doesn't go right through,' I recited.

The jabbing fists stilled. He leaned back from the window and thought.

'You put the top of the detonator in the hole . . . that's right. Listen, you haven't found any of these grenade things, have you?'

'No!' A lie, once out, might as well be workmanlike. 'No! There's a boy in my class thinks he knows everything!'

The fists remained frozen, the head statuesquely cocked.

'Well,' I ventured, 'he gave a talk on guns yesterday. You know, big guns. He had pictures and everything. I want to give a talk on grenades.'

The concept of Eucheria admitting the roar of artillery into her pretty class-room was in itself such an unconscionable lie that I felt my eyes bulging with fright. If Matt forced me into the truth and stormed next door to pulp the Comrade for terrorizing us with a piece of His Majesty's most deadly equipment, it would make a sweet Saturday. But when Matt went back to camp, there would be pitch nights and wet Tuesdays and doldrum Wednesdays when the Comrade could have his way with us. *Mary, Mother of God, make him believe this lie which will be my last lie ever.* In the prayer were palpably involved far more layers of mind and appetite and animal apprehension than in the easy gabble of contrition I had recited to Father Peters. *If you make him believe this last untruth, I will love my neighbour the Comrade, I will convert Lennie, I will never again get new boys to wet from the far side of the boys' line.*

Matt nodded.

'D'you want to see your damned old uncle fight?' he asked.

'Where?'

'In a stadium, boy. Blast it all! In Leichhardt bloody Stadium. A four-round semi-final. Army versus Navy. The divisional champ gets sick. So who does the whole bloody Seventh Division want to fight for them? Why, that veteran of the Syrian campaign, the hero of Bardia, Sergeant Matthew Jordan.'

I couldn't understand him but clapped lightly. He received the applause with a wide gesture of his hand.

'And I'm going to take *you*! I'll tell you, we'll get this youngster, what's his name? Noel! We'll get him to go with us and see you don't clear out with the prize money.'

Quickly I reviewed the half-forgotten diagrams, tore them up and put the pieces in the waste box near the sink. Memorizing what I had just destroyed, I walked back towards Matt. I could feel the memory of the Stadium slackening what I believed were most practical and vital fears. The mothering noise, the high-up secretive lights, the nervy wanness of fighters became in a few seconds keenly desirable as symptoms of a large mannish sanity which would, however, like Matt's protection, prevail only for an hour or two.

'Don't you want to come?'

'Yes!' I said. 'How do you throw it?'

'Throw what?'

'A grenade.'

'Oh hell!' he said.

13

I can remember the fight night as a sharp spell of joy. We cut importantly through queues with our free tickets. We loped through entrances which no one else could use. We waited in a yellow corridor beneath the bleachers while Matt consulted no one but the manager of the Army boxing troupe. We strolled into the bar where the belts of old champions, barnacled with metal work and imitation rubies, hung sterile of cut, contusion and brain bruise above the bottles.

Matt sat me on the counter and the barman whistled and said, 'You're starting him on it young, Dig!' Noel had a beer. I had lemon squash. 'I'm fighting,' said Matt.

Noel and I took to our seats in the front about eight. A man in a bow tie, whom everybody whistled, climbed into the ring and welcomed the members of H.M. Forces. The proceeds of the night, he said, would go to the British Empire Fund. A sailor in the front called to the man in the bow tie to go and do something or other—I couldn't hear precisely—to the British Empire Fund. There were cheers and uproar. Thank you, said the man in the bow tie. Again, there were cheers and uproar. The first bout, the man persisted, was a bantam-weight quarter-final.

A small sailor crawled into the ring and faced a small airman. Around us, bets and flasks of spirits were passed with speed and a modicum of secrecy. The bell tolled tinnily, cheaply, joyously. The little men eyed each other for a short second, pounced in and began a breathless rough-house. In round four, the little airman simply fell over and didn't have the strength to get up.

To begin with there were four such fights, superb grudge fights; and the referee had to put forward all his strength, and military police had to hover up to the corners, before the fighters could be pulled apart at the end of each round. A spirit of delicious, just-legal mayhem pervaded the tiers of beery faces stretching up towards quarter-lit bleachers.

'The next bout is a semi-final of the middle-weight division,' the man in the bow tie said at last. It would be over four rounds between Sergeant Matt Jordan and some sailor or other. Very soon, we knew that Matt was bound to lose. The sailor was intent within his large white stoker's body. Even beside Matt's Cape-bred olive trunk, he seemed savagely Italianate. And he clearly desired to win, a purpose not prominent in Matt's motives for becoming involved in the Service championships.

The sailor was a nimble man, nimbler than Matt, who stood by sponging in blow after blow without reeling. At the flurry of dance-steps and trim jabs which was his enemy, Matt gazed and concentrated for an opening, seeing one through the pain and sweat in his eyes and jolt of his head, and unleashing too-late punches which would have felled a telegraph pole. In my mind frolicked the stubborn image of Matt sparing with the banana bunch curtains.

Towards the end of the first round, he lost his temper. He dropped his guard and seethed at the sailor, while the sailor had his way with Matt's eyes and ears, nose and jaw. When the round ended, the referee managed to persuade Matt to sit down.

'If he gets one of those hay-makers of his on that sailor's chin,' Noel said, 'it'll be goodnight, sailor!'

But defeat sat heavily on my stomach like a surfeit of something sticky.

To begin the second round, Matt hared out across the ring before the sailor had properly left his corner and was standing pushing at his mouth-guard with a gloved hand, and thwacked him across the jaws. The sailor tottered, the referee let the fight continue, the sailor's friends wished multiplex obscenities on Matt's head, and the troops roared, 'Rip it into him, Dig!'

The sailor shook his head and Matt clouted him above the eye. In that second the bout became a brawl, for the sailor survived Matt's foray, but lost precision and self-control as well as a drop or two of blood. 'He's opened the bastard's eye up,' a soldier screamed. 'You'll do us, Dig!' For three short uproarious minutes, the sailor and Matt hailed on each other a series of goliath clouts. One possessed, barbaric yell hung and shifted like a haze in the lighted space between dome and ring. The bell clanged dimly, making continued fighting an assault in law. The referee, trying to part the two, was clearly explaining that no one could win if both men ignored the bell. He waddled around them, pleading in one ear, then in the other. Moustachioed with blood, his back brilliantined with sweat, Matt's gothic figure had regressed from all human reasoning. Military police tried to mount the ring, but a cordon of sailors blocked them, roaring, 'Give 'em a go!' The military police began to twirl their truncheons. We could all but hear the referee begging the sailor, mouthing each word for its long journey to the half-drowned mind. We could see the sailor's partly turned head, the cleft eyebrow seeping meatily down one side of his face. A few seconds before the military police threatened their way into the ring, the sailor stood back from Matt and crashed his fist into the referee's mouth. The referee reeled to the ropes and fell across them, while the people on that side of the ring whistled cruelly at his face crumpled with shock, and his lips mouthing blood.

Two provosts dragged Matt from the sailor, dressed him in his gown and escorted him along the aisle. He walked like a drunkard, his head was down, but we cheered him and wept with pride.

'That's my brother-in-law,' Noel told the soldier next to him, a presumptuousness which in the éclat of that moment was easy to forgive.

'You'll do us, Dig!' the soldiers roared.

Later in the night, the loudspeaker called Private Noel Dalton to the Army dressing-room. We rose immediately, obviously initiates, obviously essential people. Speculative eyes followed us, but it was below us to glance back at them. We carried our mystery lightly away on our shoulders.

Matt lay on a table in the dressing-room, a medical orderly sitting beside him, sponging the viscid gore away from his nose.

He just wanted, he said quietly, to make sure Noel would take me home. He had to go to hospital. They thought he had a broken nose. He seemed very sick.

We both told him what a tremendous fighter he was.

Sydney is a rainy city, I was to learn years later from a geography text. Twice as sunny as London, twice as rainy. Rain poured down with sub-tropical ardour, but not in any rainy season. Out of ash-grey thunderheads massing in from the beaches to the mountains after a day of sweat, out of ochre-fringed cumuli sitting up like judges where the winter sun went down, rain fell decisively if at all, with deliberate intent, its eye on the chance of washaway and flood and the dousing of best clothes.

It was such rain that woke me later in the night; certainly it was not Joseph with a coin in his fingers, tapping at the window. I turned on the pillow and saw him beyond the glass, staring like a runny oil portrait, his hair washed down into his eyes. 'Let me in!' he mouthed as laboriously, as soundlessly as that piteous referee earlier in the night.

I stood upright, tottering on the new springy mattress, to feel behind the blind for the window catch. All our windows were locked now of a night. Though I couldn't see cause for it, I knew it had reference to the Comrade, to his always looking sly and speaking in a low voice to Stell whenever they met in the street. Even on the mildest of nights my mother locked up completely, grunting with anger when the catches were hard to force. And then, in secrecy, apart from the one time I had seen her do it, she would put a claw-hammer under her pillow.

Whenever it rained, the catches were stiff. I laboured with the window while Joseph's patient, frightened, soft-boiled eyes bleared up at me through the glass. When the catch gave, it gave with a rush. I swayed and the bed groaned like a bass violin. My shoulder pushed at the frame; the window went up with a series of short gasps. Joseph slithered into the room head-first, wheezing and in sodden pyjamas. He righted himself and waited shivering, dripping rain into a small, gleaming pool at his feet. His ankles were caught in the rectangle of moist light from the railway.

'It's cold,' he grunted, smothering a sneeze in his pyjama sleeve.

'I went to the fights,' I told him.

He shuddered. 'Why don't you close the window, Jordan?'

'All right. And you should have seen what Matt did to a sailor . . .!'

He glanced at the other bed. 'Is your uncle here tonight?'

'No!' I explained. 'He's in hospital. Hey, I've got some clean singlets and you can have my dressing-gown.'

I slid across the room and got them while Joseph peeled away his pyjama jacket and high-stepped out of the pants. In a short time he was sitting on my bed still shivering but mainly from the deliciousness of new warmth and the sound of the rain. His head was bowed, and he knotted and unknotted the tassels on the rug so raptly that it was clear he would not be diverted by Leichhardt Stadium and the sailor's eyebrow.

'Why did you want to see me?' I asked him. 'It's raining like—like hell.'

He sneezed again, wearily, without resistance.

'Hey, watch out! You'll have my mother out here seeing if I'm uncovered.'

'That bur-luddy grenade!' he moaned.

'The grenade?'

'Yes.'

'What's happened?'

A truck whined into Deakin Street. Its unhooded lights raked the ceiling and drenched Joseph with light. We listened to it shuffling up through the rain, an oil drum or two bumping on the back of it.

'He's put it all together!'

'The Comrade?'

'Yes. He came home tonight and Hilda and him were fighting. It woke me up. Then it woke Lennie. Hilda was crying so we went out into the lounge-room and he had the grenade sitting up on a dinner-plate, all put together.'

'The pin and all?'

'Yes.'

'Is it still all together?'

'Yes.'

I could feel some terror nerve thudding in my throat.

'He said that he might as well pull out the pin and blow us all up because no one loved him and we were poor and I was a cripple. We were all crying and asking him not to. I sort of knew he wouldn't blow us up but I couldn't help crying. All he had to do was pull out that little pin.'

'What happened then?'

But for that everlasting light from the railway, it was very dark now. All I could see of Joseph was the shape of his head. I heard him swallowing and sobbing intermittently.

'He just fell asleep. And Hilda took him to bed and we went back to bed too. But I was scared. I don't like thinking about that grenade all put together. I'd rather be in here.'

It was easy to imagine the Comrade, wandering through the night, bound for the lavatory, pausing at the grenade, drawing the pin, leering for four fretful seconds, then dying of perversity. I could picture as well, my hands writhing to do it, how easily that small white detonator could be plucked out and the grenade rendered safe.

'And where did he leave that grenade when he went to bed?'

'It's still on the cabinet. I'm not game to touch it. It's on the dinner plate on the cabinet.'

We listened. Perhaps through the dark walls and the rain we could hear its deadly little heart-beat.

'The trouble is,' Joseph continued, 'he'll wake up in the morning and blame me or Lennie or Hilda for putting it there.'

'Why?'

'He doesn't remember. He doesn't remember what happens of a night.' Joseph punched once sharply at the mattress. 'That burluddy grenade,' he whispered again, convinced that it was the inanimate mechanism of rods and levers and metal and amatol which had corrupted the animate Comrade.

'I know how to make it safe,' I promised him. 'It's easy if the Comrade really doesn't remember anything in the morning. I'd just have to take out that little white thing.'

I blinked at the glittering simplicity of a new idea.

'I could just throw away the fuse. And then the grenade'd never be any good.'

Joseph wagged his head very irritably, being a boy who needed sleep to loosen those diseased and gangling limbs and who was now close to exhaustion.

'No! That won't work. He'll raise old Harry in the morning if any part of that grenade is missing.'

I nodded, sad at a world where simple saving ideas were blocked by equally simple damning ones. Yet it was still an achingly easy thing to creep down the Mantles' lane, with Joseph's help to make safe the grenade, the Mantles' place, our place. Then one could run back through the rain and sleep in genuinely secure warmth.

'As long as the Comrade won't remember!' I repeated.

'As long as everything's still there in the morning!' Joseph countered reverently. 'As long as when he asks me, Joseph Mantle, where's that damn whadyacallit fuse, I can say, over there on that dresser. I wouldn't mind you pulling out that fuse, Jordan. But how do I know you won't blow up the whole damned street?'

'Matt taught me grenades backwards!' Getting peevish too, I defied him to believe otherwise. 'Look, you start off with a pair of tweezers—you know, bathroom tweezers. Blow it all, we've got a pair in the bathroom. Then you unscrew the plug at the bottom' (if the Comrade hadn't wound it in too tightly) 'and pull out the fuse with the tweezers. Even if the Comrade does pull out the pin then, it won't go off if the fuse is out. And he'll be too groggy to know what's happened.'

'What do you mean groggy?' Joseph growled, but there was something merely habitual in the protest.

'What do you think I mean? I'm not going to have a blue with you over that now. He'll be too blasted groggy and you know it. He'll be too groggy to look for the fuse in the dark. So he'll just go back to bed. And then, in the morning, when he's sober, he won't want to blow himself up anyhow.'

I waited as the rain cut its voice by half in the space of a second, and stopped altogether in the next two or three. There was left a gaping silence into which somebody's faulty guttering dripped resoundingly. If Joseph left me, I thought, I might lie down in the silence, whisper the Acts Eucheria had taught us, wait for the judgement day boom of the grenade. It might not kill the Jordans with any sort of pity; it might merely shatter all our windows, and start a fire in the ruins of the Mantles' place, and throw up their sundered bodies in our sight. If he left me, I might go bawling the truth to Stell. But if he wanted me to, I would go with him, balancing terror against the exultation of controlling death by means of a pair of tweezers and a twist of the hand.

'As long as you're sure the Comrade won't remember,' I said once again.

'Come on!' He jumped off the bed and sought on the floor for his soaked pyjamas. Some unlikely stimulant had stirred him in the darkness. Now he wanted to rush through the whole affair and get at last to bed.

'Wait there a bit. We've got to get those tweezers. And I nearly forgot. We'll need a torch.'

'Bloody oath!' Joseph murmured, a small prayer that courage and colour might be added to our perils now.

From the bathroom, I could hear the mingled breathing of Pat and my mother sleeping in the front room. I stood on the bath tub and with one knee on the wash basin, opened the shaving cabinet. Taught by the occasions when I'd come to the bathroom to have splinters pulled from various parts of me, I knew that the tweezers were on the bottom shelf. I had them in my hand and was jumping down when my knee knocked into the sink my father's shaving mug, kept there as a memorial. It spun and clattered on the porcelain. It had been made for such times, made not to break.

'Who's there?' Stell called.

'I'm just going to the toilet, love.' It flattered her to call her *love*.

'Oh!'

I pushed back the toilet seat, stood straining my stomach muscles with audible success.

'I'll come and tuck you in,' she offered.

'No, it's all right.'

'Urrh!' said Pat, turning over.

'See you!' I whispered and returned to Joseph.

It was hard to get the window up without the covering noise of the rain. Only the slightest of winds spun along the embankment, yet the cold sawed through the place where my pyjama coat was done up, and nuzzled at my ankles. I had gumboots on, but Joseph's feet, bare on the cement paths of Deakin Street, must have been throbbing with cold.

We could not safely open the Mantles' raucous gate. Instead there was the fence. Joseph, stuffing his pyjamas into my dressing-gown pockets, slid over it head first, dropping on to his hands and knees on the wet grass quite soundlessly. I vaulted it, coming down on one leg, jolting my lower and upper jaws together with an explosive snap.

'Cut it out!' Joseph grunted.

The Mantle laneway was navigable enough. There were pools of water and rowdy little pieces of gravel, but the Comrade and Hilda had no window opening on it. In the lane was utter night. We found Joseph's window, which was Lennie's also, by feel. Joseph pushed open a small fly-window that gave on to his bed.

'Oh, hell!' I stamped.

'What's the matter?'

'I didn't bring a torch!'

'I'll get you one. Do you want to come in?'

'No. You go in and you can pass things to me through the window.'

'You're windy, Danny!'

'Hurry up!'

'You're windy! Give me a lift!'

I cupped my hands above my knee, and into them he put his clammy foot and slid through the window. Within the limits of his fate he was very lithe.

'Won't be long,' he called, and his bed creaked. Back in his own home, he was savouring the occasion. The fly-window whispered forward a few inches. By now I could just make it out.

'Are you still there?' I whispered to it, and it withdrew and no one answered.

'Oh, angel of God my guardian dear,' I said. It was the bluer darkness at the end of the lane which I could not stop myself from looking at. 'What side of you is your guardian angel on?' some girl in row one had asked Eucheria. And Eucheria had answered, 'Your guardian angel is not on your left or on your right. He is always with you, but he does not take up earthly space as you and I do, as your mother and father and all your friends do.' As the Comrade might do in the next instant at the end of the lane, giving it its fourth wall of blackness beneath a moonless heaven.

Rain scampered once like mice across the roof, then slanted down in earnest. But in the narrow lane you could keep dry by pressing up against the brick, forgetting the caterpillars and the enamelled black heads of scorpions you'd seen poking out of holes in the mortar in summertime.

'To whom God's love commits me here, ever this night . . .'

'Hey, Jordan, where are you?' Joseph called lightly from the window.

'Here! Got a torch?'

'Yes. Hang on! First of all . . .'

Through the window his hands sought mine and dropped into them the grenade, greasy, cold, very heavy. The little finger of my right hand could feel the edge of the plug, and I arranged my hands around the surface and tried to unscrew it. As I ground my teeth, Joseph turned a very sick torchlight on my efforts.

For over a minute I strained at the plug, in darkness again because Joseph had decided that even that sparse light was unnecessary. Without my even knowing that he had gone, he came back from the kitchen where the Comrade kept, hung from the gas-pipe as if he were a most avid handyman, a hammer, a wrench, a spirit level, and a few other basic tools.

'Here are some pliers,' he whispered, shining the torch on them.

Within a short time the pliers had done their work, Joseph grasping the grenade, the torch tucked under his arm and spraying the lane with dim drunken light as we writhed over the plug. When we had it out, I dropped it into my pyjama coat pocket and drew out the tweezers.

Their silver arms were on the belly of the fuse as Joseph's torch snapped off.

'Don't move!' he said.

From the front of the house came a wail that might have been a motorbike far up Deakin Street at first, but mounted to become the shriek of a man falling down some chasm. The grenade flew from my hands like a frog. I did not hear it fall, my ears drenched with that unchecked screeching. At length, we could hear Hilda's voice, hushing, dissipating the noise.

'It's all right. It's all right, dear. Settle down now. Nothing's happening. I'm with you.'

'It's just the Comrade,' Joseph explained. 'He has nightmares.'

I knelt immediately among the puddles, seeking the grenade with my hands before Azrail, angel of death, could plummet down and give it a final explosive kick. The knees of my pyjamas became wet and muddied. It would be the morning's job to explain that to Stell, as, if morning ever came, I'd be willing to.

'Give us a bit of torch!' I begged Joseph.

He swept the floor of the lane with light. Lolled in a quarter of an inch of slush was the grenade. Since it was best to deal with it where it lay, I remained kneeling, tilting it towards me, and did as I had promised Joseph—plucked out the detonator. When I had the plug back in, I wiped the whole thing clean with my pyjama coat.

'Here you are!'

I pushed grenade and detonator at him through the window.

'Come on, give me back my dressing-gown.'

'You're in a blasted hurry,' he commented, but eventually he passed it out to me. I made a cape of it around my shoulders.

'Goodnight!'

I ran off lightly, all but blind in the rain. Let the Comrade hear a gumboot squash into a puddle! My cold joints worked like a racehorse's. Over the Comrade's fence, and I was thinking of the pyjamas. I could postpone discovery of them until the next washing day by putting them deep into the dirty clothes bag and dressing in my other pair.

It seemed that the drugged sleepiness of the bedroom returned instantly to me, with the window locked and the rain gurgling beyond it. The pyjamas managed to get themselves changed; and since I was convinced in an obscure way that I had offended someone of importance, I made an act of contrition. That and a luxurious instant or two of warmth are my last memories of an improperly long night.

14

Sunday had been a depressing, safe day, padded in on all sides by soaking rain. No sound, not even of a raised voice, came from the Mantles'. Traffic on the highway hummed on a long uniform note which became a mere refinement of silence, and most of the day's trains, with their airbrakes on, seethed past dully on the wet rails.

Pat made no concession to the weather. Like a demoniac Judy Garland, she waltzed from chore to chore. She was a loud, gay girl as she peeled the spuds, for Noel had been asked to dinner.

For me it was a limp, vaguely guilty day, and every old idea I picked up and fingered flashed back its agate edge of guilt. Provoked by the rain, I thought of sleep and warmth, the times I had felt them advancing like companionable mists filling up the valley bottoms. But uneasiness for last night's lack of them prevailed. I thought of escapade, of Sundays at the old wharf on our river up north. We would sway on it until its rotten timbers swayed also. At one time, one of my friends crashed through its planking (cut by men dead fifty years before) and dropped into waist-deep silt across which a panic-ridden black snake slithered for the bank. But last night's humourless sabotage had soured all that.

In the afternoon we visited Matt in hospital. He snuffled at us unfamiliarly through a white mask which covered half his face.

He was well enough though, pinching all the nurses' backsides for our scandal and amusement. But not even Matt could make it a day worth the living.

Beneath Monday's honest sun sopping up the dew, I crossed the railway bridge to the bus. It seemed that above us was a new universe dwelt in by homelier fates. Under them, I was confident that normality could be conjured back to Deakin Street. I yearned to get to Eucheria and become involved in the endless Monday lessons, to utter them as a propitiation. For there were omens and prodigies beginning to unhinge my life, and the repetition of ordinary things would be a spell against them.

For most of the morning, I managed to be half-happy and welcomed tedium as an opiate. The hours washed over me like the tide over the home of a shell-fish who feels that if he can keep his purchase on the sand for a small while longer, he will be secure for ever.

Eucheria herself destroyed the oblivion of the morning by telling at half past eleven a story which, considering that memorable day as a whole, it has always been impossible to forget. Years afterwards, in a classical Greek class, I recognized the names of the two lovers of Eucheria's story with the same thrill an Englishman in the Siberian *taiga* might feel if he came on an inn owned by a Brown or an O'Toole.

There was a prince called Soter, Eucheria told us, who had always lived in his father the King's citadel built of the world's best cedar, marble and gold on a hill above an ancient town. Soter had never left this home, had never needed or wished to. He could remember no other life.

When he was still a young man, he heard one evening, drifting up the hill with the smoke from the town's fires, the spell-binding voice of a young lady singing for the townspeople after their day's work. From the time he first heard the voice, Soter knew that he could not leave this young woman to perish amongst the diseases and poverty which had spoilt the beauty of the town.

One twilight when he waited on the walls listening to her, he filled his lungs with the evening air, and himself began to sing. His voice spread over the town like a honey-brown cloud, fell on its roofs like a sweet rain. In his song, the prince pleaded with the girl to leave the squalid streets and climb the narrow ridge to the palace gate, where they could, for the first time and for at least a few seconds, see each other's splendour.

For a long time there was silence in the town which had heard its prince and the princely power of his voice. The girl was the first to speak, in an undertone, asking some of the townsmen to lead her up the defile to her lord. One by one, in voices coarser by the second, they refused. They would not give up their songstress even to Soter. She would have to stay below the hill like themselves, suffering the same ugliness, hunger, fatigue and death as they would. On the wall, the sense of loss shook Soter's body.

In the town, the crowds broke up. The girl limped home, no spirit left for singing. Soter, who could see the whole town laid out below him like a map, thought that there was something questing and wary about her as she moved along the streets, her hands stretched a little way ahead of her. He watched each step she took, so closely, so affectionately, that it was some time before he saw that she had come to the edge of the town. With an early moon glittering on the outline of her hair, she had begun to mount the hill. Some of the people saw this from their windows and ran out to stop her, but when they saw their prince on the walls, they went back home.

Yet the girl seemed unable to deal with that steep climb in the quarter-light. Soon she fell over a boulder and lay weeping. Blood flowed from a gash on her forehead. Weak with pity, Soter clutched the cold stone of the ramparts.

'Tell me what your name is,' he called to her, 'and why you cannot climb this hill.'

'My name is Pneuma,' she called back. 'And I cannot climb this hill because I am blind.'

Soter staggered back from the walls. Except for his father, he had never known such love as he knew then. For no one had he ever known such tenderness.

'Go back to your home for this short night, Pneuma,' he said. 'Tomorrow I shall send a palace guard to guide you along the ridge. From tomorrow's dawn you will live in my house and be the glory of the King's family.'

Soter stood on the wall all through the night with the dew on his hair and mists gathering around him. At dawn he sent the Captain of the Guard down into the town to find Pneuma. But when the royal officer asked the townspeople where she lived, they stoned him, and drove him back up the ridge. It was a sick and bleeding Captain of the Guard who reported to Soter without having even seen the girl.

Beneath the morning sun, Soter gazed down on the stirring town and yearned to see Pneuma. From a palace window came the moans of the Captain as the King's physicians tended him. It was no use sending soldiers for the girl, Soter decided. He would go himself. The idea came to him with a rush, and he ran to tell the King.

The King listened to him and approved the project. 'But,' he said, 'as long as she is blind, how can she choose between the squalor of the town and the grandeur of the palace? In this small casket'—and he drew from a pocket within his royal robes a box cut from a single lump of onyx—'is the gift of sight. Its casket might as well be onyx as gold, for there is no fit home for it on this earth other than the kingly head of man. Give this gift to Pneuma in the hope that she will climb this mountain to reign with us of her own free accord. Only then will she be welcome at my court.'

In the town, carrying the casket concealed, Soter was not recognized. The people did not expect him to have come down to them, to be walking the littered, ill-drained streets. Within a short time, he reached Pneuma's home and saw her rise swaying with delight at the sound of his voice.

'Pneuma, I have not come to take you to my father's house,' he told her. 'I have come to give you the gift of sight so that whenever you wish you can freely come to me, and just as freely leave again.'

'If I could see all the kingdoms,' she told him, 'and all the towns that have been and will be, I would still never leave you for an instant.'

He took out the gift, and Pneuma waited, breathless in the darkness which she had known from her first baby breath. But the onyx box could not be opened, though Soter pulled at it from every side and hurled it against the walls of Pneuma's home in the hope of breaking it and dashing the gift into the girl's eyes. In the end, Pneuma wept softly and slumped to the dirt floor, crippled with despair.

The townspeople, hearing Soter's frenzied efforts to crack the onyx box, collected before the girl's house, and at last recognized the prince. In the crowd was a young labourer who would not give up his hopes of Pneuma's love, not even for the King's son. He inflamed this crowd of people who did not want to lose their songstress, inflamed them to such a fury of resentment against Soter that they crowded into Pneuma's hovel screaming their hate in Soter's face, ripping the royal emblems from his clothing, spitting on his noble brow, flinging at him blow after blow until he fell, and kicking his royal body until he was on the edge of death. Then the young labourer came forward to Soter and, with his knife, dug out the prince's eyes.

When the crowd saw this last enormity, they rushed away to their homes. Their shame they hid behind locked doors and boarded windows; but there was no way to block their ears against the wailing of Pneuma bent across the shattered body of her prince.

Yet, in her blindness, her hand stumbled on the onyx box. Now she tried to open it and give him the benefit of whatever lay inside. Soter's blood had drenched it, and now it opened to a flick of her hand. She felt for the gift, lifting it out of the casket. It was a real thing but neither round nor square, soft nor hard, heavy nor light. It had the feel of being infinitely precious, and when she had lifted it a little way, it melted through her hands like water. In the following instant, she knew for the first time what it was to see, for she saw the bloodied face of her lord, and, even as it was, it was the most piteous and beautiful thing she was ever to see. In the strength of her love, in the clearness of her vision, no one daring to stand in her way, the young labourer having darkened his house and locked himself in raving with guilt, she carried Soter back to his father's house, where her love and the King's power restored his sight and his strength completely.

In their kingdom on the hill, Pneuma became Soter's queen.

Of course, said Sister Eucheria, Soter is the Saviour and Pneuma is the Soul of Man, blinded by the Fall, unable to find its way to the Kingdom, until the Saviour came down from His Father's House to give it the chance of returning freely with him. But the gift he brought could be opened only by his blood, just as the onyx box was opened by Soter's blood. And as by that gift Pneuma was strong and able to carry Soter's bleeding body, the Soul of Man became strong, became pure, pure enough to carry the bleeding body of the Lord in his own body. As we would soon do, said Eucheria, when we approached the mystery of Christ's Body and Blood.

In the classroom there was only the sound of breathing, every mind dabbling for implications in Eucheria's story. Yet allegories are, in more than one way, delusive. Even on that Monday I sensed this, that in Eucheria's class, beneath the smooth faces were personalities already jagged and motives already intricate. The grand simplicity, the single purposeness of people like Soter and Pneuma had almost vanished even here. Except in the cases of Dolph Conlon and Sister Eucheria. But these were rarities; and Eucheria was the story-teller and therefore, in some strange way, did not come into account.

So, as I listened to the story, unaware as yet of what it symbolized, I found myself gazing across at Dolph. He was sniffling sadly with his head sideways on his blazer shoulder, and only his fear that he would not be able to pull out his handkerchief in time holding him back from complete absorption. Gwen Callan and the Lilies of Sharon did not glance in his humble direction—four seats down in row four. Each of them confidently saw herself as Pneuma. But I stared at Dolph, not because he was identifiable in the story, but because, take away his leaky nose, he was simply straightforward enough to inhabit the same honest world as Soter.

It *was* an honest world, I thought, in a multiplicity of ways. It was a grandly untechnical world. To have his way with Pneuma, the young labourer had to win a crowd. To crush Soter's bones he had to wield his own fist, ply his own boot. To blind Soter he had to clutch his own knife, and suffer the guilty mess on his own hands. He could not destroy his enemy from an antiseptic distance. In that world you had to do your own searing, rending, breaking, blinding. You could not simply draw a pin, hurl a mechanism, pull down your hat and walk away.

A small girl from third class tottered down the corridor jangling the dinnertime handbell. We said grace and stood like statues, the row that most successfully stood like statues being let out first. One row held their breaths for so long and hunched up their shoulders so crookedly that no sculptor would have admitted to them. Yet Eucheria usually let them go first.

When I intercepted Dolph, he was dawdling across the asphalt on his own. I led him away to the bench furthest from the incinerator, where all the master spirits seemed to be. We sat and opened our bundles of sandwiches in that quiet corner where the sun had shone all morning. The brick wall warmed our backs through our clothes. Dolph bent his pale, freckled face to his food, ruminated on it with his thick Irish eyebrows. A face of no great account, I thought, but brave enough and definitely stubborn. Eucheria didn't send him on messages to other nuns, but that was probably because she didn't want mucus all over her envelopes. Anyhow, I told him the entire history of the Comrade's grenade.

I told him how it had been, according to the state of the Comrade's liver, set aside for the Conlons' destruction, for the destruction of the Mantles themselves, and might, next time the Comrade was drunk or angry, be dedicated to anyone, even to the Jordans. At first, Dolph cried very quietly to avoid drawing the attention of one of those ten-year-old girl prefects. He could see that if the Comrade could abstain from pulling the pin on his own family while suicidal with booze, the night would come when he'd pull it on the Conlons and fling it through their lounge-room windows.

My friend composed himself by taking a few fierce bites from his sandwich. Now he began to threaten that he'd tell his father who'd tell the police. But the Comrade would blame it all on me, I protested. Dolph swore that my name as the source of the story would be kept a secret; and one promise of Dolph's would outlast a gross of Lennie's. My underlids quivered with joy. From under my eyeballs a few warm tears rolled up. I was aware of the sun glinting on them. Now all the weight of the business was on the Conlons.

But Dolph had entered a third stage of defiance.

'If you know how grenades work,' he said, 'then why don't we blow it up ourselves?' His face had already pinkened with rage. He was consumed with a mature anger at the Comrade's having introduced such an untoward element into our lives; an anger which I felt only hazily and at times, since I still thought that adults, guided by esoteric motives, had the right to be as inhuman as they liked.

'I'd rather do that,' Dolph growled. 'I'd rather blow up that old dill's bomb all by myself. Will you, Danny?'

'We wouldn't be able to get it. Listen, Dolph, how would we get it? We can't steal it out of his place.' I still felt securer than I had been for days, but Dolph's features were bunched in the most intractable of frowns.

'You'd better just tell your father about it,' I prompted.

'I'd rather blow it up myself. To pay him back quits. Anyhow, can't you ask Joseph to get it for you?'

It was true that Joseph would be willing to be rid of the grenade which had had malicious influence on his father.

'What if we just got it and threw it in the Parramatta River?' I suggested.

Dolph shook his head over some minute point of honour.

'That wouldn't be paying him back quits.'

I began to dislike the term.

'The Comrade would *pay me back quits* if he found his grenade was gone.'

As an expression of anguish, I re-wrapped my lunch. In a world of want, we were forbidden to throw food away in the playground. I would have to take it home with me or fling it into some vacant allotment between school and the railway.

'I'll tell you what,' Dolph said. 'My father comes home from work about the middle of the night. They call his shift the middle shift. Then he has a bath. You ought to hear our bath-heater going. It wakes Robert up.' (Robert was his elder brother.) 'A lot of the time it wakes me up. I'll make sure it wakes me up tonight.'

'How can you be sure something'll wake you up?' I asked irritably.

'I'll make sure. Look, Danny, let's show him! Let's show him we think he's an old fool!'

Some years later, when Dolph's father came to sue a national trade union before the High Court of Australia, it was demonstrated even once more that out of a strange, doomed perversity, Conlons would bow only to an enemy smaller, more defenceless than themselves. For a little time, no more than fifteen seconds, Dolph's wish to *show* the Comrade presented itself to me as what decency irresistibly demanded.

'But the Comrade,' I whispered. 'If he ever found out!'

Dolph was eating quickly, his perturbation no longer fear but something healthier. It demanded that he should be nourished.

'I'll tell you what!' he said. You could see that he was trying to balance sense and honour, if sense is the word for my side of the argument. As he spoke, he gauged me from under his thick farmer-like eyebrows. When the bath-heater woke him that night, he would come and wake me. We would then get the grenade . . .

'How?'

'Can't you work it out with Joseph?' He spoke patiently, yet as if he had every right to be impatient. I too felt that he did. 'Didn't you say he hated that grenade?' he asked.

Therefore we would wake Joseph, take the grenade to the swamps, a partly reclaimed wasteland by the river, and explode the thing. There was no other possible way to *show* the Comrade. Dolph was profoundly convinced of that. Whenever it was that we got back from the swamps, that was time to tell Mr Conlon or the police or any other adult agency; and Dolph promised to call on all of them as soon as we did return.

'It'd be the bravest adventure of all,' Dolph decided. 'It'd be marvellous!

It would be the sort of endeavour that justified the food a person ate. In the dark with Dolph, to hurl that detested thing away. Far away in Deakin Street, the Comrade might hear it in his sleep and stir screaming.

'It'd certainly show him,' I conceded.

15

With a feeling that I had come a great way towards spiting the Comrade, I made my arrangements with Joseph. But when night came, the dream of defiance sufficed, as I believed it would suffice for Dolph and Joseph. I was gay at table, and Stell, who had looked sideways at my recent pale cast of thought, sent me to bed with a lot of hugging.

When Dolph knocked on my window, as on a front door, I woke choleric, muttering uselessly at the closed pane. The air was full of a seething which at first I thought was a locomotive sidling along the embankment. It was in fact a great wind, and Deakin Street, which was a street of few trees, seemed that night to be raving with leaves. Wind cuffed brick corners, and chased its tail on little landings and in the courtyards of flats. The world was unreasonably cold, unreasonably late, unreasonably stubborn in the wispy figure of Dolph who could be barely seen, waiting for me beneath a lemon tree which overhung our place on the east.

When I'd asked him about the grenade that afternoon, Joseph had been very sanguine. To him, the films were an infinite source of useful expedients. Abandoned in any part of the earth and in any circumstances, he would never have despaired until he had tried the last item in his sizeable corpus of Hollywood veldtcraft. All that was needed tonight was a quick, quiet means of waking him, but whatever it was, it would have to be based on something he'd seen at the Mercury on Saturday afternoons. Finally, he decided to knot lengths of string together, tie one end around his thumb, have the other end trailing free from his bedroom window.

The Mantles' side gate was open for us, and grinding softly in the wind. The lane was not as black as it had been two nights before, and we found the string swaying through the barely opened window and pulled it. There was a soft unprotesting gurgle. Within seconds the grenade was handed through to us, followed by the detonator, followed by Joseph's long legs questing firm ground.

In Deakin Street it was dark but for the few hooded lights from the signal box and station. In the north-east was a nearly full moon, but the wind seemed to blur its influence. The time was probably after one o'clock. The houses mouldered dully, tucked away behind their gardens like the handicraft of people long since called away. The highway was empty. On our way back there might be fruit shop people driving in early to the city markets. But this was too early even for them.

Dolph and Joseph seemed to move together very companionably for people who had scarcely met before. 'You didn't take long to get ready,' Dolph complimented Joseph. 'I slept in my clothes,' Joseph explained, pulling his crumpled collar up around his ears. His pants hung crookedly, over one hip, under the other.

As for the grenade, which I was bearing clutched in against my stomach, it had for two days sat up on the dinner plate where it had been left on Saturday night. Joseph had put the detonator behind some letters on the smaller cabinet but, as far as the Comrade knew, his little green pudding of death had been fully primed all Sunday and Monday. A significant listlessness had overcome the Comrade since his return. Or perhaps he had brought it home with him from his sojourn with the orange-crêpe lady. Neighbours had been outraged on two occasions to see him slumped against his far fence, not bothering at need to move the five yards to his lavatory, but urinating in full sight of them. They had reported the fact to each other as if it were proof of ultimate decay. They did not know about the grenade.

Just off the highway, the Meatpackers, the Glasgow Arms' rival, waited in dim green tile, humping a long and shaky upstairs veranda. It was a sad, amicable old pub with suspect refrigeration.

Bred in the days of blither licensing laws, the few mad hours of dyspeptic carouse allowed in 1942 tired it. It had that same air you saw in matrons nodding their heads over coupon-books. The Meatpackers knew what it was to suffer the whimsies of legislators.

We were nearly past it when someone called to Joseph from the other side of the highway. The wind distorted the call, enough to justify us in hiding in the Saloon Bar entrance. Against the cold bitter smell of disinfected steps, we held our breath. Now that we had begun our undertaking, we wanted it attended by the conventional hazards and alarms. Yet before we even glanced into the open street, we knew that it was merely Lennie pursuing us.

I had never felt such pity for him as then. He was scampering over the highway, chased by all the phantoms of his six and a half years on this earth. He did not look back over his shoulder at them, but from side to side, seeming embarrassed, not wanting to be seen by anyone but us. He considered himself unmanfully dressed. As the three of us moved spontaneously out of the shadows to show him where we were, he hurried up carrying his short pants by their firemen's braces and with his sandshoes in his other hand. His feet were bare beneath his pyjama trousers and he had a cardigan on over his pyjama coat.

'Wait till *you* want to go somewhere!' he threatened Joseph.

'This is very dangerous,' Joseph explained calmly. 'I didn't want you to get killed.'

'Well, wait for me now!' he demanded.

He changed in the doorway of the Meatpackers and Joseph did up his shoe-laces. Benumbed that our enterprise had brought us as far as the far side of the highway, we accepted Lennie as a partner to it. For who could drag him caterwauling round to Deakin Street and put him back to bed? Sitting on the steps, he sneezed three joyous, abandoned sneezes.

'My colonial!' he told us sunnily. 'I'm glad I caught up to you.'

We went on. The wind kept us quiet, blowing what we said down the road as irretrievably as a fat man's bowler. The grenade was warm on the side against my stomach while my fingers, cupped around its outer side, were numbed so that it felt strangely unequal in shape. When the cement footpaths gave way to grass we walked processionally. Beyond the last house, on the edge of the swamp, Joseph demanded a rest. We sat in a circle on the damp earth while he took off his shoes and massaged the balls of his feet.

'Does it hurt much?' Dolph asked.

'Not too much,' Joseph sighed.

His little brother spat or made the noise of spitting. 'He's only going to die of it, that's all!'

'When?'

'Hilda . . . she's my mother,' Joseph told Dolph, 'her young brother died of it when he was sixteen.'

'That's not too bad,' Dolph said. 'That's a long while yet. You can have a lot of . . . of fun . . . before then.'

Lennie persisted. 'He gets terrible pains.'

'I had a cousin called Peewee Conlon. Everyone called him Peewee. He drank kerosene and died when he was four. That was unlucky. Anyhow, you might live longer than all of us.'

Dolph was not a liar, even by intonation. He was giving comfort, and you could tell he was merely giving comfort. On the damp verge of the swamp our foal blood stirred against the worm of death even as he spoke. No merely doctrinal training could convince us that it was a blessed thing to die young. Only Joseph, who had always carried his doom intravenously, was unaffected by the sharp taste of death which alighted for a second on our lips like a fly, and was then blown away. Joseph gave his feet a final knead and put his shoes back on.

We went on for over a mile along a gravel road lined by briary scrub. This hissed and crackled like a brush fire as the wind combed it about. A few miles away, across the darkling salt flats, two radio towers rose iridescent to the moon. Joseph pointed to them.

'The one closest to us has *Rip Ramrod and the Plainsman*.'

'Boy, did he fix the Cattle Baron!' breathed Lennie.

'And that other one is the one *Guns Gatsby*'s on.'

'We're allowed to listen to *Guns Gatsby*,' Dolph said. 'But *Rip Ramrod*'s on at the same time as the A.B.C. news.'

'Urrh!' we grunted.

Now there was an embankment on our left, and beyond it a gradual basin where antique bedsteads, depleted batteries, cracked cylinder-heads, disembowelled mattresses, corroding chamber pots decayed in a tangle.

'Where are we going to blow the thing up?' Joseph asked,

implying that this was the place. I agreed. We could hurl the grenade into the tip and shelter beneath the embankment. Lennie nodded. 'Yes!' said Dolph.

At my shoulder, Lennie sniffled heavily while, with Dolph playing torchlight on my hands, and Joseph holding the grenade, I performed the insertion of the detonator. Someone whistled at my adroitness and I poked at the small white fuse once again, frowning at the same doubt which I had suffered at Joseph's baptism. This purely adult thing, a special weapon of destruction, seemed improperly easy of operation. I screwed in the plug and we all in turn gave it a final tightening. I smiled.

'Rightoh! It's ready. Don't worry if I drop it. We dropped it the other night, didn't we, Joseph? And it didn't go off.'

We climbed the bank. Below us in a jumbled mess whose silhouette we could hardly make out were the mean relics of a thousand lives, soon to be joined by a relic of the frenzies and fears of the Comrade. We were exposed now from head to heels to the wind, from the quarter of the Tower which broadcast *Rip Ramrod and the Plainsman*. It butted us in the small of our backs. It boxed our ears and made as if to scalp us.

'When I pull this out'—and I pointed to the pin—'and let the grenade go, we've got four seconds.' They would have to hug the embankment with their hands over their ears.

'Can you throw it far enough?' Dolph asked mildly.

'Of course I can.'

'I think the one who can throw the furthest ought to throw it.' Joseph dropped on his haunches and searched the ground. 'Why don't we have a try-out with a goolie?'

So we had a confused throwing trial along the length of the embankment which Dolph won. Throughout the contest the grenade had lain beside the torch on top of Lennie's pyjama pants. Now I picked it up and tipped it into Dolph's cupped hands.

'It's heavy,' he whispered in reverence. 'I can't throw this far enough.'

'Then why in the hell did you kick up a fuss in the first place?'

Dolph shrugged. 'I didn't want to start a blasted fight.'

'We should have stayed at home in bed.' As a comment on our indecision, Joseph sat down on a nearby kerosene drum.

'Why don't we throw it in this can,' he said without warning, 'and roll the can down the slope? It'd go further than we can ever fling it.'

I grunted at his typically exotic idea. 'Give the damn thing to me. I'll hoy it far enough for you.'

'Wait a bit!' Lennie said. 'It's the Mantles' grenade. Don't forget that!'

It was a point. On its basis, Joseph reiterated, 'I reckon chuck the grenade in the can and roll the can down to all that rubbish.'

Dolph noddely urbanely. 'I reckon that's a good idea. Here you are, Danny.'

My hands received the grenade again and Dolph went and dragged the drum into place. As he turned it, the wind bassooned against its lip. Lennie giggled at the sound. We waited while Joseph tried to argue his brother into taking shelter behind the mound. But Lennie claimed he had come especially to see the pin drawn. His small face, blue under the moon, opposed us like a shut fist. Not that there was cause for argument. A few strides would take us all into safety.

Dolph bent to the can, ready to roll it downhill.

'Ready?' he said as if the word were a large lie or a sacrament, whose effects would never be wiped out.

I clutched the orb with both hands and Joseph pulled the pin. We loitered in that awesome moment when death had only the sinews of my thumbs to beat.

'When I throw this in the can, run!'

It was thrown and the can began to roll, but not one of them ran. We were hip to hip with death, yet so safe; and the rareness of our situation imposed on us its own inertia. The can rolled smoothly for a second, but snagged to a stop on a half-buried beer-bottle or a contrary scrub root. Moving to it, Dolph tried to kick it along with the sole of his foot. There was an echo of heroism to the metal clip of his shoe striking the metal of the drum. Lennie did not resist rushing forward and lunging with his sandshoe.

'Come on,' I yelled, and turning, careered into Joseph. We dragged each other down into safety, but the Comrade's grenade went off before we got our hands to our ears. The noise snatched the breath out of our mouths. Air gathered, bulged, cracked open like a water-melon. Reverberations wailed away down the road, stumbled off through the scrub. Silence came when the embankment fell in and half-buried us.

We struggled out of the damp soil and ran through a hardly altered landscape to Dolph and Lennie. Dolph was on his stomach, with his head towards us, his backside in the air and his knees pushed hard up under his stomach. His body seemed whole until I laid my ear down on his back to listen for his heart or the rattle of breath. I found myself staring into a large irregular wound in the back of his head and, at the same instant, tepid blood welled from a place between his shoulders and wet the side of my face. It was useless to listen for a noise in his body, what with ringing ears and the wind yelling at my shoulder.

Lennie was on his back, with his head closer to the place of the blast. Joseph knelt over him silently, and it was Lennie who sobbed briefly, so softly that you couldn't swear to it. Some sizable piece, perhaps the plug, had shorn away the left side of his face from the eye down. My head was clearer now and I put my ear to his heart. There was no sound.

'Hell, Joseph,' I moaned. 'Hell, we've killed the two of them.'

Joseph looked up from the hideous face, and then slumped to lie beside his brother.

'That bur-luddy grenade!' he told me. 'That bur-luddy grenade!'

16

Dr Slattery injected something into Joseph's hip and mine, and whatever it was, it held me for seven or eight hours a whit below the surface of sleep. Here imagination and memory moiled imperfectly around the images of Lennie and Dolph. There was daylight on my eyelids, but Dr Slattery's alchemy kept them shut, and in the funereal yellowness of that morning sleep, I spoke freely with both the boys. Intermittently one of us would remember that they were dead, but the fact could not destroy our familiarity, and very soon we would be yarning again in the way we were used to.

'Victims!' said the Comrade, full of doleful reasonableness in the kitchen. The boys melted at that word. They would never be back. My eyes opened to drawn curtains and a closed door. Light like a brown light of mortuaries was in the room. Traffic was in full voice both in Deakin Street and on the highway. In the kitchen my mother and the Comrade were engaged in a dialogue amazingly temperate on the Comrade's side, amazingly frank on my mother's. It was probably the longest conversation they were ever to have with each other.

'Let me speak to you as to a reasonable man,' my mother said. 'You haven't been reasonable in the past. You try to get away from things by drink or bullying.'

It was strange, waking to hear people talking in their wide-awake mid-morning voices.

'Hell, have you got to bully a man? I've lost my son. My only healthy son. I don't blame anyone. If kids find something like that in the swamps, they'd want to blow it up. I just came in here in sorrow, to see if Daniel said anything yet.'

My mother laughed at him, as mockingly as she liked. For some reason he was no more than a bad joke to her now.

'You're a poor, miserable lump. Yes, and you needn't glower at me in *my* house. You've had too free a run, Mr Red. I know about your grenade. And I know how you got it. On the black with money borrowed from a fancy lady.'

The Comrade rumbled out a spiritless protest. A chair grated briefly along the floor and I realized that the Comrade was seated at the table like the best of neighbours exchanging sympathy the morning after a disaster.

'I've been in contact with my father at the Cape. Trunkline to the fishing co-op. He knows all about it now. I've posted a letter to Brian. It'll take a week or so to get there. When it arrives, Brian will know who's to blame, too.'

'Why in the hell did you want to . . . ?' the Comrade asked quietly.

'Because I didn't want to be found strangled in a stormwater canal. I know you, Mr Lenin. You'd end my happy life without a qualm. Just to keep on with your miserable one.'

A kettle squealed. Stell called above it.

'You couldn't take a week's imprisonment, locked up from your pleasures. If ever a man needed his coarse little pleasures . . . !'

The kettle was silenced. It was probably the water for young Brian's noon-day bath.

'Your liberty depends on me now, Comrade.'

'For God's sake,' he grunted, 'you could stop calling me *Comrade* and *Mr Red*.'

'Perhaps,' my mother speculated. 'Anyhow, I promise you nothing. Except I swear to you, before the God who brought you out of nothing—why, only He knows—that if I see you even look in Daniel's direction in the days to come, you're a finished man.'

There was a slack sound of the Comrade flopping his head down on the table.

'I don't know,' he groaned. 'You'd never talk to me like this if I wasn't buggered with grief. And buggered with something else too. I don't know.' It was a voice that longed for sleep.

'All right, then,' said Stell, hard as flint. 'I don't want to even lay eyes on you again. You will not look sideways. Or speak or act sideways. If I come down Deakin Street and you want to walk up it, wait till I've gone, turn back inside. No more foul eyes, Comrade, no sort of eyes at all. Remember all this, Comrade! Remember it so well that no matter how drunk you are, you'll still realize that if you come near us it's the end of you. I want you to understand too. You might be the People's fool, but I'm not the People's woman.'

'All right, all right, all right!' he growled. 'I'll be an angel. All I care about anyhow is Lennie. If I began to cry, if I could start crying for him, I'd never stop. But why don't you think of Joseph? Don't you think his life's been bad enough? Say there was an inquest. And then a trial. Him being asked questions that'd put his father in jail. Think of that.'

'Joseph is all I do think of. Joseph and Hilda. I think of them more than you do.'

'I must have a tumour on the brain,' the Comrade claimed very softly.

'Have you ever thought you might be just rotten?' Stell had spoken breathlessly this time, as if every word were a risk. But the Comrade sighed and waited for her to go on.

'Hilda has lost her son,' she said. 'It was a horrible way to lose a boy. Instead of staying with her, you're roaming around trying to organize people into keeping you out of trouble. Why don't you just go home and spend the day in honest grief?'

After this, they were quiet for a long time. I feared that they had been swept away by one of those cross-currents of sorcery which derange human affairs. We had had such matters read to us, by Eucheria for instance. However, it appears that the Comrade was merely slumped over the table. At last the chair rasped as he got up.

'I think I'll go,' he sighed. 'I can't be bothered going and I can't be bothered staying. But a bloke has to move or they'd think he was dead. I should be angry at someone. I don't know. I saw Lennie this morning. His face was awful. Even what was left. But I can't be bothered being angry. And, don't worry, I can't be bothered bothering you. And don't be scared even if I do. I'm just a poor bastard.'

He pushed out the back door and it flopped loosely shut behind him, a dead and disenchanted sound. Almost immediately, Stell opened my door and, seeing that I was awake, stumbled to me and cupped my head against her chest. She shivered for the Arctic closeness of death.

The old red-headed police sergeant grunted at Stell's question.

'It's no use asking me to be lenient for the sake of his wife. If your story's true, he's an irresponsible maniac. Nothing can save him from prosecution.'

The sergeant stared into his drained tea cup. He had confessed earlier to having grandchildren, and you could see past the blue serge, nickel badges, silver braid, to the freckled semi-baldness, the scraggy neck and flabby shoulders of a grandfather.

'No,' he said, 'you can't save him, but let him go on thinking you might. He's pathetic as long as you've got the whiphand. But if he realized you didn't have it, well . . .'

My mother said, 'Sergeant, Daniel seems to think it's his fault.'

The sergeant turned to me, wrinkling his kindly freckles.

'It wasn't your fault, cobber. It was this Mantle bloke's.'

He glared at me with terrible conviction, and then cast about for his hat.

The red-headed sergeant had pity on Joseph and Hilda. He could have pestered the truth from them. But he accepted the boy's statement that he had found the grenade himself, and Hilda's claim that she had heard or seen nothing about her husband's obtaining anything lethal.

The sergeant was wise in a fashion. Grief had bewildered Hilda, and she numbly pursued her habit of loyalty to the Comrade. After a week or two, she would wake in the morning and know from head to heel that Lennie her son's familiar body was definitely below the ground, that for it there would never again be hugs and pay-day ice-cream and bread and treacle at half past three. That would be enough to crack any habit.

* * *

'This boy,' Sister Stanislaus told her third grade, 'this boy went off playing with explosives in the middle of the night. Didn't you, sir?'

I agreed with her, eyes down. Someone had spilt a great quantity of ink on the floor. The stain spread on the amber lacquered boards like a continent of night, as irregular as the continents of the earth. In one of its wider gulfs I landed an invading force with my eye. It edged inland from the beaches.

'And because of this foolishness there was an accident. Wasn't there, sir? Tell the class!'

I didn't want to tell them. I dug my chin into my chest instead.

'Dolph Conlon blew himself up. Didn't he, sir?'

'Yes.'

I turned my head to glance at the class. Through the mist of tears, their eyes homing on my face were enormous, but their faces no more rapt than if I'd broken a window. I felt with great joy that I had returned to them, that in weeks past or to come many of them, who had never seen or touched a grenade, had been or would be stood above that little island of ink to be intimidated by Stanislaus.

'Why did you do what you did, sir? Why did you go out in the night with a bomb in your hands?'

'Dolph wanted me to.'

'Don't hide behind Dolph, sir. Dolph is with God. Would you start telling lies against one of God's saints?'

'It's the truth, Sister. Dolph wanted us to.'

'I believe you, sir,' she decided efficiently. 'You're fortunate you're not with God yourself—before your time, like Dolph.'

She turned to her desk, disapproved of the time she read from her large watch there, took a reading book from the bottom of a pile and gave it a spell on the top. There was a stick of green chalk on the desk which she moved six inches. Seventy eyes scoured her for the meaning of these ritual motions.

'And you wanted to save people's lives, isn't that so?'

'Yes!' By now I could scarcely force the cracked word up my throat. Grief poured from me like a malarial sweat, and I was alive again, *aware* of windows and sun and Stanislaus' brow and vast white sleeves, the blazers of the boys, the tight plaits of the girls, and the irreparable shame of bawling beyond control into a soaked handkerchief in front of so many people.

'Well, God may be satisfied with your reasons, sir. I am not. I will not have children from this school wandering in the darkness, traipsing into every kind of danger. Night-time adventures! None of you *dare*!'

The last word quivered above our heads like Damocles' sword in a breeze. Her jaw jutted abnormally wide, unchallengable, clear of her coif. She waited, considering the wisdom of her next ploy. But she knew that few children tell their parents of the more startling violences of the classroom. And it was worthy to trample on the graves of the dead for the sake of the living.

'If Dolph Conlon were here,' she told me, 'I would punish him as severely, Daniel Jordan, as I am now going to punish you. Helen Flanagan, bring me the feather duster.'

A ceremonious little girl rose and marched to the back of the room. From a bookcase full of Blinky Bill and Enid Blyton, she pulled a yellow feather duster with a long cane handle. Through space full of the roll of drums, she bore it to Stanislaus. It had never seen dust, and its yellow feathers came from only God knew what fantastic bird eyried on God knew what unconquered peak.

'Give me your hand, sir!'

The cane handle scorched my palm three times, singing as it came. I waited for the fourth stroke.

'Return to your class, sir!'

Eucheria was reading to them when I arrived back. I nursed my hand down between the desks and held up my head stoically. In the second last seat of row three, I sat and wondered at the superb cadences of Eucheria's voice. Sometimes, I would secretly touch the palm of the flogged hand with the index finger of the other, and the flesh would tingle excruciatingly. What a triumph it was in itself to shudder with that pain, to hear Eucheria, to have been judged and acquitted with three mere strokes of Stanislaus' ravaging cane. What a triumph it was to live on, and count on one's next breath.

But mostly, until dinnertime, I dreamt of revering Stanislaus who had raised me from the dead. If the school were on fire I would burst into it with a man's strength and haul her black and white serge sacredness into the open air. She would open her eyes in safety and see how much I loved her for her fierce physician's tongue.

After the bell sounded and we escaped to the playground by means of the *standing-like-a-statue* ritual, I sought out Hughie Green, who had a cast in his eye. We walked up towards the Church, to the verge of the out of bounds.

'We're going to go and live at the Cape,' I said.

'Where's the Cape?' he wanted to know.

So I told him all I remembered of it.

Two nights before the inquest, the Comrade came home to a completely locked house. He shook the windows and peered inside, but the blinds were down. *She's run through on me*, he told himself. She had pulled the blinds on their bedroom and their lounge-room and made him unwelcome to all the house. For half an hour he kicked at the door and worked at all the windows in the laneway. The sublime energies which had driven him to Hilda in the first place, which he believed had been smothered, began again to circle mutely in him. But all he could do for them now that she was gone was to batter at the windows of his and Hilda's dead house. When he got her back, heaven and hell, wouldn't he cherish her!

At half past five he started out for Hilda's parents' place, but the highway was cold and companionship gleamed from the doors of the Meatpackers. In the west, behind dim yellow clouds like snowfields, the sun left for other hemispheres where the summer might be. But it was winter there where the Comrade walked. He shivered, turned into the Meatpackers, asked for whisky, got beer, drank two of them, and decided to go back to Deakin Street and break in.

He smashed the glass in their bedroom window. The bed was made and all was tidy. In the mirror he noticed his own frantic image glancing across the room. The hall had the smell of stale gas, a failure smell of poor food and disenchanted marriage. It was something he detested, and made him furious at the best of times. By the lounge-room he had to push himself through it as though it were a wind which could be measured in miles per hour. He was blind as he opened the kitchen door, and a wall of cooking gas struck his face. Stumbling through the room, he flung open the outside door and lunged out suffocating. After some time he could see again. *Just like a bloody woman,* was all he thought, *going away on a bloke and leaving the gas on.* At length he rushed back into the kitchen to turn off the gas tap and a few feet from the stove fell swearing over Hilda's body.

When he had managed to get the gas out and the light on, he saw Joseph dead on the table with a pillow under his head. There was no pain on his face and a mild academic smile on his forehead. Hilda was on the floor with sticking plaster over her mouth. Why? he wondered. They were both equally dead. They had been dead since early morning.

'Dearest Leonard,' Hilda had written in an exercise book open on the table. 'It seems we weren't meant for each other. I will love you even in hell. I am in a terrible position and I will never get over Lennie getting killed. I made up my mind to send Joseph to God while he's still happy because this world is a rotten place. I love you Len and you are not to grieve. Us going gives you the chance to be the Len Mantle you used to be. We both love you better than our lives.

XXXXXXXX

Your adoring wife,

Hilda.

P.S.—Joseph will not have any pain. I gave him sleeping pills and he's asleep on the table already. I took some myself but I don't know if they will work.'

I was not told of any of these events until much later.

17

The Coroner's Court lay amidst pubs and warehouses close to some very deep anchorages. From fifty yards north along the street, you could have thrown stones against the funnels of ships loading for any beleaguered place you might care to name. From these ships, Scandinavians, Lascars, Americans, Scots passed without a glance at the one-storeyed drabness of the court, their eyes on the gaiety of the city a mile up the road. Perhaps across the harbour in Woolloomooloo or up the hill in the Rocks, one of them would be found knifed in the morning. That would be time enough for them to meet the Coroner.

The hearing on the deaths of Dolph (Adolphus Bernard Conlon, minor, to the Court) and Lennie (Leonard George Mantle, minor) began on a morning three weeks after the tragedy. This was the first of two inquests with which the Comrade was to be involved. Hilda's and Joseph's bodies had been released the day before from the morgue fifty yards to the east of the Court. Now their hearing was pending.

The witnesses who waited at five to ten for the Court's public door to open thought mainly of the Comrade, how it must be hell enough even for him to put one's flesh and blood beneath the ground, without having the Court's sterile hands rake the corpses over bone by bone. So beneath the plane trees, the milkman who had been first to the bodies, the red-headed sergeant, my mother, perhaps even the Conlons, were veering in quiet tones towards pity for the Comrade. Until at two minutes to, he came up George Street cleaner, thinner, soberer than we had ever seen him. Immediately faces hardened against him, against the basic indecency of a man who could scarcely manage to look better than a derelict when his family saw him with living eyes, yet came to their inquest as urbanely dressed as for a wedding. He wore a wide black tie, and that was indecently sham; he wore his best tweed coat and that was indecently gay. But above all, he had at his side a pin-striped young barrister, and a man who could care to avoid police prosecution when his follies had consumed his family whole, a man who in those circumstances could go to the trouble of seeking lawyers' names and, engaging one, stroll off a little chastened and quite upright to the Court with him, that man *was* indecent.

We had been standing in a circle, the Conlons and my mother and I, and Mr Conlon turning his head to look at a merchantman hooting its way out towards Middle Harbour, Mrs Conlon had whispered to my mother, 'I had to come with him. If I hadn't, he's just as liable to sit down in a gutter somewhere and cry.' On the far side of our group, the Comrade excused himself for a second from his barrister, and sidled into Mr Conlon's line of vision. Perhaps he was contrite or seeking pity or an exchange of pity. Perhaps he was about to make another clumsy attempt at lobbying for some sort of sympathetic support from us in the courtroom, since now, with his whole family vanished in a fortnight, to be arrested would be intolerable. When Mr Conlon saw him he shuddered and then chuckled, as if at some seemly afternoon tea banter on the part of the Comrade.

'Talk about swords being turned back into people's hearts,' he grunted, and moved his eyes back to us.

Stell and I were permitted by the Coroner to stay in the witnesses' waiting-room, four walls of aquamarine cheerlessness and a varnished fireplace which had forgotten its purpose. The rules governing witnesses were waived so that I could be guarded from the knowledge that I was now the one survivor of the grenade business. It was not until years later that I found out or wanted to find out how the inquest went for the Comrade. And then the first thing that impressed me was into how delicate a position the red-headed sergeant's family-man sensibilities had betrayed him.

He had not seen fit to bully Hilda and Joseph, he had been prompted to let things ripen for the inquest. Perhaps he had intended to call on them a few days before the inquest and really put the screws on them. In any case, it would have been easy to make Joseph crack amidst the solemnities of an inquest. But now the sergeant's humanity took on an aspect of negligence. Above all, as he sat in the witness box vaguely disturbed by the crown sergeant who acted as prosecutor but was quite brotherly towards him as a colleague, as uneasiness tingled beneath his armpits at the Coroner's beginning-of-the-day interest, he must have himself wondered at his own unprofessional kindliness. Without perjuring himself, he had for the sake of his record to ease the Court's attention away from the idea of the Comrade's guilt. For Hilda and Joseph were the only ultimate witnesses to the Comrade's criminality, my evidence being based on hearsay.

After wondering for years why the police had not sought information from the orange-crêpe lady, I found in the Coroner's reports the statement made by the police prosecutor, that incredibly she had died of virus pneumonia two weeks before. Death had had a spree in keeping the Comrade from harm.

After the police sergeant came the reading of the statements of Hilda and Joseph, shaky when given a few weeks before, but astoundingly strong on paper. Joseph had been in terrible shock when the statement was made, and Hilda had refused to leave the room. He had recited the story in which Hilda had schooled him, and the sergeant had had it taken down. Once more, why persecute a terrified eight-year-old semi-cripple? There would be time to let the truth sprout in him.

However, it appears that Joseph did oppose the sergeant's questions with astounding strength of will. He admitted to having told me lies about the origins of the grenade. In fact, he claimed, Lennie and he had found it in the swamps a few weeks before the tragedy. In the company of the sergeant and Hilda, he had pointed at the approximate area where he and his brother had come across it.

'Consider this carefully, sergeant!' the Coroner advised, having recalled the sergeant to the stand. 'Did the boy seem to you to be telling the truth? Did you believe him?'

'Yes!'

Hilda's statement was that she had never seen the grenade nor heard a hint of it.

Mr Conlon told the court of the Comrade's threat to blow up the Conlon family, but the Comrade's lawyer made Mr Conlon admit that the threat could have easily been a figure of speech, and did not in any definite way point to his client's illegally possessing a grenade.

My mother told the same story and was forced to the same admission. Any other evidence she attempted to give was branded as hearsay, which must have confused and angered her.

Now there was a ten-minute adjournment which grew to be a twenty-five-minute one. It was nearly twelve when the Hamitic-looking constable who was clerk-of-the-court came up to Stell and me as we waited on the steps. He winked at Stell and took me by the shoulder.

'Your turn now, cobber,' he grinned with his wide robber baron's mouth. 'Don't be frightened. They're all your friends in there, and the Coroner thinks you're a great little bloke.'

The Coroner did not look it. Above his grey suit, the face was craggy and wise; his mouth had the petulant upward curve of a mouth which is receiving a sour echo of breakfast. He sat side-on at the crest of a maze of cedar compartments which fanned out from the prosecutor and the shorthand typist to embrace eventually the Press, the witnesses, even the public. In the centre of the court was a large table inhabited by the Comrade's barrister.

The constable led me up to this grim old man on varnished battlements, burping behind his fist as if previous victims sat badly on his stomach. Yet his voice was amazingly soft. It questioned and taught me about oaths, and in the end directed the constable to administer to me an oath that the evidence I would give on behalf of our sovereign Lord the King would be, etc.

The police prosecutor rose as I sat and asked me if I admitted to my name, my address, and the fact that I was a schoolchild. I stared at him and at the shorthand typist, a middle-aged balding male glaring back at me, waiting to tap out my answer. The Coroner laughed dryly.

'I think we can take it sergeant, that the witness's answer is *yes*.'

One of the two men in the Pressbox lifted his bemused head and grinned painfully for a second.

The prosecutor read my statement as polished by the police stenographer. When he finished there was an unbelieving silence. At last he asked me, 'If what you told the police sergeant is the truth, if you believed Mr Mantle had brought home a grenade and was menacing—threatening, you know—his family with it, why didn't you tell anyone?'

'The Comrade would have . . .'

The typist frowned at me in panic. Over the top of the ramparts the Coroner's face appeared.

'Excuse me, Daniel,' he said. 'But who is this Comrade you mention?'

'Him,' I nodded. 'Mr Mantle.'

'All right. Go on!'

'He would have known it was me who told.'

'How would he have known that?' the Coroner asked before the prosecutor could.

Now, glimpsing the Comrade sagging in the corner of the witnesses' section, all his awesomeness neutralized, I found the Coroner's question hard to answer.

'He thought I was a blabbermouth,' I said. A savage joy pushed me forward on the chair. Up here, under the aegis of the Coroner and with my every word being cut into the Court's records, I could harm the Comrade. 'When the trucks were stolen, he said he'd kill me if I told anyone.'

'What trucks were those?' the prosecutor asked.

'He took Joseph and Lennie . . .'

'That's Joseph Mantle and Lennie Mantle, his sons?' asked the prosecutor lumberingly.

'Yes. He took Joseph and Lennie and me to the corner near the Glasgow Arms, and we saw three trucks of guns and . . . you know, bullets . . . pull up outside the hotel and the drivers went inside. Then six different men came out and stole the trucks.'

'Your worship!' The Comrade's barrister rose. 'I can't help but feel that this affects my client's interests, and I must ask for an adjournment to discuss it with him.'

'Yes!' said the Coroner and adjourned the Court until two o'clock.

'All rise!' commanded the Hamitic constable.

The after-lunch courtroom was emptier, for the Conlons and the milkman had been permitted to leave. To begin the afternoon, the police prosecutor put a question to me on the Comrade's threat at the time of the truck incident; and then the Coroner asked me if it was because of threats made at that time that I had kept silence over the grenade. At the table, the Comrade's young barrister wrung his hands on the verge of interrupting His Worship.

Now the prosecutor asked me when I had first seen the grenade. Though with a sense of outrage I found it impossible to remember Lennie's face and could evoke only the vaguest flavour even of Joseph's, I found that I knew perfectly the colours, odours, words of that morning when I had first seen the deadly thing in its shoe-box. Joseph had seen the Comrade pack it into the cabinet, I said. Here the barrister was allowed to rise and protest that this part of my evidence was hearsay. The coroner accepted the claim with a deep nod.

'You see,' he told me, 'we cannot believe everything that people have only heard about. Not everyone is as truthful as you are, you know. All we can take down is what people actually heard or saw themselves. You see, Joseph Mantle might have been lying to you. I mean to say, he did sometimes tell lies didn't he, as most boys actually do?'

'Sometimes,' I piped, though I couldn't remember when.

All day the Coroner had presented his bored, clinical gaze to the question of Dolph's and Lennie's death by blast. The voice had been fluent, concerned, alive, but the face dead. Yet now he continued to survey me for a long ten seconds, mild alarm crinkling the corners of his eyes. He was genuinely disturbed that a child should think the Coroner's Court to be armoured against the truth.

'When was the next time you saw the grenade?' the police prosecutor asked.

The fight night; Joseph drenched at the window; plucking the detonator out. They wanted to know, of course, how I'd learnt about the detonator, and I explained how Matt had been pumped.

It was the Comrade's barrister's turn, and he rose and took up once more the plaint of hearsay. There was no evidence, he said, for the truth of the tale which Joseph had given me, of the Comrade's sitting the family around his Mills bomb while he entered on a dialogue with it. Hilda Mantle's statement denied it.

However long in the forgetting, the rest of the affair was quickly, anti-climactically told. In the end, the Coroner thanked me, assured me that the truth would be found, regretted that I might have to be called back to the stand, and permitted me to wait out the rest of the hearing in the witnesses' waiting-room.

Stell and I spent the remainder of the inquest there. The sun must have slipped behind the warehouses across the street, and the little chamber was dim and as cold as a gully. Grey light, the colour of boredom, oozed through the opened tops of windows glazed with a large crown and the words *City Coroner* in gothic.

But we were in holiday mood. For us it sufficed that the inquest was all but finished, that by the weekend we would be at the Cape. I asked every now and then, with a kind of gaseous unease in my chest, if Joseph blamed me, and Stell persisted that of course he didn't. I would have to see him, I said, before I went.

'We'll have to see,' Stell murmured. 'He hasn't been well. He might be away. But he doesn't blame you. You were all trying to save people. It was the Comrade who killed Lennie and Dolph. Because the Comrade bought that grenade especially to kill. It was the Comrade who committed murder in his heart. You and Joseph and Lennie and Dolph were foolish. The thing is, not to mean harm.'

She talked on about the Cape; sharks in knee-deep water mad with hunger on Fourteen Mile Beach, a whale up on the sand and too big to cart away, the ghosts . . . since it is better to be frightened than bored . . . of dead convicts on Warialda. And at last, about five the courtroom door opened and the boots of the interested parties clumped in the corridor. I rushed to the door to see the Comrade and his lawyer hurry out. Then the red-haired sergeant came strolling along deflatedly.

'What's the verdict?' Stell asked him.

'Death by misadventure!' he said.

'What about the Comrade?'

He shrugged and screwed up his cheeks. 'There's no evidence against him. They might question him. But in the end there's no evidence.'

'Anyhow,' he continued, safe, fat, glibly pious, peering out into the dusk, 'he's been punished by a *greater One* than the Coroner.'

A glazed window glimmered as a light went by under the trees.

'It's going to be confounded cold tonight,' he remarked.

18

'Hell, if the old bream aren't nosing in again,' old Finnie whistled, reverent over the cycles of nature.

'Where?' asked Stell.

'They're like fruit in the jelly, girl!'

We leaned again against the footbridge railing, Stell and I. It tipped as it had always tipped after every full river for a lifetime past. Crystallized in the tide sucking around the pylons, the large complacent fish hardly swayed. At long intervals, the sun tickling their fins, they shuddered their flanks and jerked upstream a foot or two. Oblivious nations of those little fish which are leviathans in rock pools and faster than light, glanced through the upper levels of the water. Yet, through seven or eight feet of it, you could see to the scrubbed sand on the bottom.

This was the mother sea pushing up a tidal creek. Waiting with a vacant mind for Mass to start, I was hit again, after two years or so of forgetfulness, by the old saltwater longings. Had I been alone there, I might have begun by drinking mouthfuls of the stuff, and then, more than roll in it like a porpoise, let it drench each body cell and rinse the soul. But all this was an ancient, blunted mystery in the blood; this morning there was something younger to be served. Already the Cape people had gazed up to Warialda the mountain, which whined with Father Mullally's old Hudson. At the wheel, his whole face shaven except for his right underchin, a gob of dried oatmeal on his cassock, his lips beefing out the Magnificat in short-vowelled Irish Latin, and his water temperature gauge dancing close to the luminous 'H' for *hot*, the man himself had reached the crest, well on his way to consummate amongst a few Cape people the mystery of the Lord's body.

Stell, the baby on my left elbow, fondled my ear.

'I think Daniel would rather listen to the row of the trains along the embankment than the row of the surf at the Cape.'

'Oh, no!' I said, profoundly convinced.

Last night, after we'd come over Warialda in the Co-op truck, I had been clearly depressed by the blacked-out little town. Rolling down the mountain, I sensed and nearly saw the jet bulk of land, the satin bulk of sea. The village was something left by the tide; we came without warning amongst its dead glum bungalows hunched under the shape of the mountains, Warialda and Fourteen Mile. We ate steak and onions by the kerosene lamps in Finnie's kitchen. The range fire warmed us through, but medieval darkness thickened above our heads. After the meal, we found our way by torchlight through the bull-frogging night to Finnie's lavatory lying back in the arms of a pandanus. There, a classic story said, one of old Finnie's friends had been bitten in a private place by a frightened whip snake who had been resting in a fresh sanitary can. This had been a great joke in the district. Yet that night I stood half-naked in the darkness for thirty seconds before I could coerce myself down onto the rough wooden seat. Something, a half-pound of kidney, a frog, slopped onto my shoulder from above. It had fled under the door before its shock had begun to hum through my body, a sequence which I felt to be grossly unfair. Finished in there, I waited outside with the damp grass tickling my legs for Stell. Then we blundered back through the blackness to the kitchen and Finnie's two sinister kerosene lamps snidely sputtering, as if they were the only lights left in creation. This morning though, from the jagged big-sea horizon to the tree ferns at the crest of Fourteen Mile, the world was clean, honest, straight from the shoulder.

Father Mullally's Hudson slid down Warialda and was seen threading down pine-flanked Memorial Avenue. It advanced like a

9

young car on the surf shed where Mass was said at the Cape. But when the priest turned off the motor, it did not die without a seizure.

The priest ran into the pavilion with a lightness ill-fitted to his age and cloth. In his hand was a leather suitcase with sacred vessels and altar stone. An old lady from a hopeless dairy farm along the clay ridges towards Gilbert prepared the altar tenderly while Finnie fixed the cruets with his giant freckled hands. The room around us was sunny, and hung with surf pennants and photographs of surf belt-teams who had won at Pollyanna Rocks in 1927 or Wollongong in 1938. The straight-haired, half-naked young swimmers gazed down akimbo at the two old people pottering ritually, on the benches of silent people. In the adjoining kitchenette where supper was made at dances, Father Mullally sat with a sigh which could be heard above the surf.

'Whenever you're ready,' he called to the people, and his lips smacked as he kissed the stole. The old lady who had been arranging Father Mullally's alb on the altar was first to the kitchenette to be shriven. Then old Finnie. Usually during the confession of an adult, you would hear Father Mullally groan as deeply as Paul Robeson. 'That was a hellish stupid thing to do!' Every penitent in and within thirty miles of Gilbert was inured to this; it had become a part of the Sacrament and might mean anything—that you had tripped over the kneeler, driven off the road, procured an ulcer, told a lie, committed adultery.

At last, all penitents absolved, he marched out of the kitchenette, his gait crooked from sitting down. With his back to us, he put on the vestments. Occasionally you could hear him whispering a sibilant part of the vesting prayers as he tugged at the back of the alb which some holy wife of Gilbert had overstarched. Just beyond the wide back windows of the pavilion the surf broke over an arm of boulders and, having turned to count how many wanted Communion, he seemed for four or five seconds much taken with it all. Though year by year he had grown old in multiplying supernatural reality with his hands, perhaps he suffered from those same throwback languors that I had felt earlier that morning.

Father Mullally eventually put on his chasuble, dressed the chalice, came down to old Finnie. Together, they launched themselves into a thicket of Latin, both of them very familiar with what they were doing. *Not like some of those young priests*, Finnie constantly said in praise of his old friend. The priest hustled the rites along quite lovingly. A person was reminded of having seen some old man like him scurrying with his wife down an avenue where they had always lived, moving together into wider suburbs while there is still time.

In Gilbert, Father Mullally was said to be a deep man, which meant that no one understood his sermons. That morning he spoke of John Calvin and free will. A comatose generation slumped on the benches before him, one ear open for his cadences. They did not know John Calvin. There was no resentment against the man when the priest named him as the greatest enemy of the sovereign soul of man. Their eyes did not turn blazing with pity to inspect the millions of shackled souls lined up century by century—according to the preacher's gesture—between the tea urns at the back of the hall. The massive self-dialogue rolled on and over our heads, intimidated the terribly ordinary fibro walls. And the people seemed content, as did the priest himself.

Suddenly we could hear the Gilbert–Cape bus grinding over Warialda with the day's picnickers. The priest brought the sermon to a close by unleashing on it a sign of the Cross which was like three or four smart judo chops. He couldn't have our Protestant brethren hanging around the surf shed slaking their Protestant curiosity or getting good Catholic dogma without putting anything in the plate.

The rest of the rite was fitly performed while I daydreamed of Dolph and Lennie, of how if we had all survived that terrible night we would have all come at last to the Cape; and of how I would have hoisted them over Fourteen Mile Mountain to the splendid sickle of beach beyond. It was Communion time then, and I bore back to my bench the small wheaty flake on my tongue. Father Mullally very quickly had the chalice in its ornamental coverings. Turned to us for the blessing, he made an appeal for a man from Eden Bend who had been crushed by a cedar the Friday before and was close to death in Gilbert, in danger of leaving little else but a widow and four small children.

Sunday at Finnie's place meant, for the adults at least, staying in your best clothes till after dinner, when Father Mullally, having talked the morning away and eaten with his old friend, would turn the Hudson back to Warialda's scarp fifteen miles beyond which lay his cure of souls, Gilbert.

The morning went listlessly at first. After a desultory breakfast, Stell began work on the roast, Finnie peeled the vegetables, and Father Mullally sat shelling the peas. I lay on my stomach on the veranda, drawing up the Zulu, the Household Cavalry, etc., I had brought in a shoebox from Sydney. I could hear a bit of political talk from inside and then Father Mullally called for me. Out in the back seat of his car was a brown paper parcel. Would I bring it in? It gurgled as I carried it. The priest, in his shirtsleeves, unwrapped it with gusto, and on the table was . . .

'A bottle of Clonmel Irish Whiskey!' breathed Finnie. 'Father, where'd you get it?'

'You know Mrs Clohessy from the Pioneer's Hotel in town? She got it from a traveller and, being mindful of her spiritual heritage, gave it to me. Let's have a smahan or two!'

'Or five or six,' laughed Finnie.

They drank a nip of it with tank water while Stell went and fed the baby.

'You can smell the boggy westerlies in this. Dear heaven and hell, it makes a fellow remember!'

'It reminds me of wet streets in Waterford,' sighed Finnie. 'But I was happy there.'

'Why not? It's like honey in the hive, this stuff. There aren't many people sipping it in this sad old world this morning. Least of all poor Molly Clohessy who gave it to me.'

'How do you mean, Father?'

Father Mullally downed the last of his smahan, shook his head, both deliberately.

'You know,' he said softly, 'I was a late vocation to the priesthood. I'd spent five years training horses in Newbridge, County Kildare. And when God in his boundless wisdom called me, there was many a pallid little seminarian from sod huts in Cavan or some such barbarous place, traipsing to my door in that damned cold seminary in Carlow, trying to make me a total abstainer. But I always yelled in their faces, "Vinum quod laetificat cor hominis!"'

'*Vinum . . .?*'

'*Wine,*' declared the priest, '*which rejoices the heart of man.*

Wine in this case being a generic term covering Clonmel whiskey. Have another drop, Finnie Gavan?'

'Yes, thank you. But Father, what about Molly Clohessy?'

Being not much concerned for Molly Clohessy, I moved back to the veranda. Still, I could hear what was said, probably better than Stell who was unpacking in the front room. Occasionally, while Father Mullally was speaking, Finnie would rise to baste the roast, and the priest would follow him to the range fire and then back to their chairs again.

'You know,' the priest began, 'how everyone pities Molly because her son Jack's gone to the bad? And the poor woman's so scrupulous and all. It's prayer and hard work that've made the Pioneer's pub the pub it is.'

Finnie assented with a mighty grunt.

'Well, the lower Jack seeks in the gamut of female decency, the more blatant he's got, and someone told Molly that Jack was bringing lady-friends up to his room late at night.'

'I'd heard that myself,' Finnie sniffed.

'Everybody's heard about it. Only Molly was out of the secret.'

'It's often the way,' Finnie commented with peculiar melancholy. He told the priest how he fretted over Pat who'd stayed on in Sydney to work. You couldn't do anything with this equality of the sexes business. Father Mullally said that women could have their equality of the sexes as long as they didn't think they were as good as us. He gave a solitary short laugh, and proceeded again to the question of Molly and Jack Clohessy.

'Now, Molly has a large as life statue of the Blessed Virgin in the hall upstairs. It's on a little pedestal about as high as a boot box. And on Friday night she had the two cellarmen helping her get it down and away into one of the spare bedrooms. Then, about eleven, when the four paying guests were in bed, Molly got on her old Child of Mary gear and began her vigil on the pedestal. Nothing happened except that old Mr Forrest, who teaches science at the High School, got up to go to the toilet and didn't even look sideways at Molly as he passed.'

For a few moments there was a heightened sizzling, as if Finnie had done something to the roast. Perhaps the priest didn't speak up above it because he feared being overheard by Stell or myself.

Then there was the scraping of chairs as the two of them composed themselves again for the yarn.

'Well, towards one, Jack came in the back door and sneaked up the stairs whispering to some local judy of a woman he had in tow. Molly could hear them giggle and shush themselves every time they tottered against each other. They got to the top and began creeping along like a couple of Red Indians.'

'In his own home!' Finnie said incredulously.

'Yes!'

'God, what a filthy bastard!'

'Molly hasn't been lucky with her menfolk,' said the priest confirmatorily.

'Anyway,' he went on, 'Molly's heart was half-broken. That's the thing about this story, about all stories, by the way. They're usually only funny when seen from a distance. When Jack crept past her, Molly couldn't help herself reaching down and taking Jack by the elbow and saying in a voice quivering with reproach, "Oh, Jack!" And you know what Jack said? "Holy Mother of God!" Probably the first time the words have sweetened his lips since he was a little boy. "Holy Mother of God!" And he took off then, away down the hall. Molly thinks he tripped in a hole in the carpet. Anyhow, there he went, body and soul, through the end window, breaking clean through with only a little scratch on his corrupt head, and landing belly and balls on top of a crate and a half of lemonade bottles in the yard one floor down. But the Prince of Darkness looked after the lout even then. All he has is a cut in the neck, a broken collar-bone, and a fractured pelvis or something.'

Finnie laughed moderately, politely, with a parent's coolness. 'It's a funny, sad story,' he said. 'And I bet they're giving Molly a time over it in town.'

Soon after, the baby laid to sleep, Stell was back in the kitchen. Talk poured from the two old men. Talk of ancient, unreal times —evictions, migrations, a hundred different brands of defiance. Heroes and churchmen. The names of horses, and people of good stock who owned a pub in Casino or grew bananas at Murwillumbah. The Japanese and Pig-Iron Bob Menzies ('Thank God he's finished with politics for good,' said the priest. 'I'd prayed for that,' he said). The conduct of the war, rationing, the Labor Party.

'I can remember a time,' said Finnie suddenly, 'when if England were being bombed, I would have prayed my God to save me long enough to go across on the night boat to Liverpool and see all England in ruins and every bloody Englishman with her. But it's different now. Why, the new manager of the Co-op's a Pommie from Malaya. And I like the sod. Yes, it's different now, all right.'

'It's always been different. The reasons why revenge is forbidden is because it's impossible to obtain. If you *did* go to England, you'd find that all the bombs fell on the wrong people.' Even to me, it sounded that Father Mullally knew all this had to be true if he was to save his soul. 'The English are human, even if they didn't seem to think we ever were. We ourselves were a most perverse race. The heroes of Plassey and Waterloo and so on were all damned Pats. They could have ruined England just by laying by their arms.'

'We are indeed a perverse race,' Finnie repeated.

'Oh,' said the priest, and I imagined him waving his hand, trying to dispense with the rest of the subject, 'it's better to be here, away from all the old ardours. At the end of the Great War I was a fairly young man, and I can remember all sorts of strange, bloody names creeping into the Memento of my Mass. And I can remember a few cases I had in the confessional that still worry me. For I was a curate in a parish in Wexford where all the bright young fellers were. I say it's far better to be here. I always loved this place. The day I landed in Sydney in 1923, it was 115 degrees on the wharf and shipping clerks were running round with ties on. But I could feel a great relief. You know, it's a damned fine coastline.'

At least I could see the shingle beach below the Cape, the tussocky green of the Cape itself with the sea crisping into its caverned base and, miles beyond it, a long sliver of blue headland. The gulfs between were full of tropic-looking water. On the south of Finnie's house, beyond a small swampy tract, rose Fourteen Mile Mountain, olive with midday, its ghosts, for it had a few, asleep in the sun. I gazed at the lot of it as if it signified so many colourful tomorrows.

But first there was a roast for dinner.

19

When the roast had been eaten, Finnie asked me when I was going to see the Hogans. It was Stell he was talking to, I thought, and I went on staring at the congealed gravy and the twirls of gristle on my plate. I didn't even know he was asking me, let alone who the Hogans were, until his large bony knee reached out and jolted mine.

'Hey mate! Aren't you going to see the Hogans? They used to take you swimming when you could hardly walk, you know.'

'Aren't there any boys around here for Daniel to play with?' the priest asked languidly, from some merely automatic sense of fitness, for he was gazing at the tongue-and-groove ceiling with one ear to the floor, listening to his own digestion.

'Most of them are on the Estuary,' Finnie told him. 'Around the Cape, the only boy Danny's age is Colly Blakely and he's too shy, you know why.'

'Oh, he's the little . . . yes!' said the priest.

'And there's the Saunders. But those older ones are wild—they won't let them into the picture show here, not on your life, not a chance. And anyhow, old Saunders—though he's younger than me really—he hangs around the black gins.'

'Dad!' Stell protested.

'Don't you worry,' Finnie grunted, 'there're a few little boombra fellers in town have got Saunders' nose. And a few lubras that've got reason to wink at him while he's lording it up on the pub verandas. But no doubt you've noticed the same thing, Father.'

'Heavens, man!' said the priest. 'If we started looking for resemblances, where would it end?'

'I can tell you, Father, it'd end before you got to me.'

Finnie laughed, and as sign of his *bona fides*, ground a slab of tobacco ration between his palms.

I ruffled through my sparse memories of the Cape—a bald-headed little boy whom I'd known once on the sand, the big-faced cows cropping salt grass behind the beach—one of them waggling its horns at me; an old lady limping down Memorial Avenue in an equinoctial gale, and, quick as a flash, her umbrella blown inside out. A fisherman called Bumper hauling onto the landing a snapper with large blood-flecked gills, laughing and sucking the fag-end into his khaki lips, never a thought for the life-cells, kin to his, going out like the lights of a town, one by one, in the big fish. But there was no memory of anyone who might be called Hogan.

'Don't you go anywhere with that Fy Hogan unless you ask me first!' Stell warned me with the random wilfulness of the Queen of Hearts from *Alice*.

'Come on!' said Finnie, dumping his handful of weed on the lid of his raddled old Erinmore tin.

He led me out to the back veranda, his good shoes squealing on the boards.

'That's where they live, and they've been waiting to see you.'

His giant hand, speckled with years and labour, flourished along the back road to a little weatherboard house, so unadornedly square that it was the very house, down to the twirl of smoke from the square chimney, which every child drew sooner or later.

'What will I tell them?' I asked him.

'Tell them your name. And that you've come to play with Fiona. *Fiona*, you understand that? And watch out for mud on the track!'

Beyond the lavatory and pandanus was a sodden road, two slimy furrows encroached on by paspalum and blackberry bushes, with a central ridge of grass where a person could walk. I tramped down this central patch, angry at them for not having treated a child of my sad history with greater delicacy than to cast him out to face strangers the morning after he arrived.

The Hogans' place was girt by a slack wire fence. Only the corner posts were solid and solidly sunk. Along the front, the wire strands were twined around a few drunken sticks which made the whole thing definitely a member of the species *fence*. I ducked through the wire and tripped over a lawnmower laid head-on to the heavy grass. The house stood well above the ground on brick stilts. It had been built long before, in hard times; its wood had a weathered, iron-bark look. But, fairly recently, money had been found to paint it.

I went to the back. A little black spaniel rumbled threats at me and backed under the house. I wondered why dogs favoured these spidery places beneath the flooring. The Hogan place was much closer than Finnie's to the swamp, which you could see stretching away, clogged with dead gums and acacias, towards the river banks at Gilbert. Above it today a few big crows, or maybe ibises, wheeled, sabbatically lazy. But in flood time, it all became a tributary. Logs, dead cows, brown water swept down it, found the tidal creek, for a few days fouled the sea, which, like an old tomcat, then cleaned itself up in quick time.

There was a smell of Sunday meat as I knocked at the screen door. This was pulled back slowly by a man who was leaning back in his chair at what must have been a painful angle. He was a soldier in socked feet, whose army boots and gaiters stood by the door. Before him were the ruins of dinner; a plump dark-haired wife on his right; a square dark-haired little girl on his left. At the far end, his blond son sat, chin high to his plate, a razor slash of gravy from the corner of his mouth to his ear.

'Don't you remember me?' the man asked.

'Yes,' I said quickly, feeling suddenly intensely welcome.

The soldier was that fisherman called Bumper. I remembered a special brand of sunshine of five or six years ago, and being carried through the surf on this man's shoulders.

He and his wife now warmed me with questions—about Sydney and my father and the new baby and so forth. The little girl nuzzled her line of vision into her empty plate, and the small boy had been surprised in his chair by sleep.

'This is Fy,' Mr Hogan said, remembering that I'd never met his daughter before.

'Aren't you going to say goodday to Daniel, Fy?' Mrs Hogan asked.

The little girl gave a few strenuous shakes of her head.

'Chrysler bloody six!' Mr Hogan hissed to his wife. 'Game enough to hold a bull out to pee, and here she is pretending scared of a little boy.'

'Leave her alone for a while,' Mrs Hogan told her husband.

Fy mumbled something off her own bat, but it was too low to be heard.

'What did you say, Fy?' her father demanded, anxious for his daughter's social graces.

Fy mumbled the same thing, a trifle more loudly.

'She wants a bit of meat for Brownie,' Mrs Hogan explained.

'She's not still on that!' The soldier gazed at the small girl with the type of concern kept for outbreaks of ringworm and chicken-pox.

'Please!' Fy articulated.

Her father rose and cut two lengths of tepid meat from the Sunday mutton.

'Thin, please Dad,' Fy suggested. He handed the meat down the table to her and she smiled briefly. Then she returned once more to holding herself like someone who has been unjustly punished.

Mrs Hogan had me talking freely a few minutes later when the girl appeared at my elbow. I jumped at the glimpse of her old blue dress.

'Well, are you coming or aren't you?' she said with startling impatience.

The soldier laughed, tickled in some esoteric way. 'You're taking him to see Brownie?' he asked.

'Well, he'll have to get a move on if he's coming.'

'This is an honour, mate,' the soldier told me. 'Grab it!'

At the end of the table, young Jack Hogan opened his eyes momentarily, sucked in his glum cheeks and went to sleep again. To him, Brownie was old hat.

'Who's Brownie?' I asked apologetically.

'*Who's Brownie?*' Mr Hogan lifted his stockinged feet off the lino to laugh the better. 'That's something the fifth column'd like to know. Brownie might be one of those elves or pixies or I don't know what. Brownie's just about Fy's best friend. But none of us've ever been allowed to meet him, her or whatever it is.'

He pulled the humourless little girl to him, his big arm under her armpit and then raised vertically to stroke her hair. Her eyes followed a wild circle of the upper room to avoid mine.

'But the thing is that Brownie's Fy's mate. We never saw Brownie, but he's all right by us.'

The three conscious members of the Hogan family beamed on each other so complacently that the earlier sense of my being quietly, intensely welcome was largely destroyed.

'Come on,' the girl mumbled suddenly, a snap decision, take-it-or-go-to-hell offer. She was gone so quickly through that ajar gauze door, that although I waited only to have Mr Hogan say, 'After the little witch!' the little witch was already a good thirty yards ahead of me.

We were off at a pace I knew I couldn't keep up. Fy knew the terrain and deliberately led me the long way round the Hogan shed where an ancestral 'T' model decayed without wheels on stilts of bricks and timber. For someone younger than I was, for someone with a full stomach, Fy ran alarmingly well. Her path was over the fallen strands of wire which were the bounds of the Hogans' place, and up another dirt road. When we took to this, we had our backs to the brown-grey luxuriance of the swamp and were on rising ground. We had already come a hell of a long run from Fy's back door.

It was a necessity of pride to catch her, but having done it, I was gagging for breath as we stumbled over the thigh of Fourteen Mile, where the road became a foot-track through fuzzy grass.

Up there cows grazed, we ran, the land slanted, at forty-five degrees to the surf, up whose translucent gullet, just before it broke, you could see the shapes of fishes swaying. It would come spoiling into a little cove where, ages ago, much of the side of Fourteen Mile had fallen into the sea. Today a man and woman with lines on beer bottles fished from the little beach. A few whitings' tails showed over the level of a man-made pool half-way up the beach, and four gulls circled them on the axes of four pairs of greedy eyes. Biting breath out of the air, I saw a little boy running with a dog through the shallows, thudding over onto the wet sand, rising to brush himself with his hands, as the woman rolled the line and bent at knees and waist for hilarity.

The little girl Fy was still running like an animal. The sand-shoed feet, the plump olive legs moved as decisively after a quarter of a mile as after a yard. I kept to her left rear, partly because she was hostess, largely because my mouth yawned for breath, my shoes were full of sweat, and the calves of my legs were as if hung with sandbags. Then she reined herself in with such perverse abruptness that I stumbled past her and fell in the grass.

We had arrived at the mountain end of the small beach. A bald lump of sandstone and conglomerate formed its headland and sheered down to a blue, rock-bottomed bream hole. A small wax-leaved tree survived there, one of its tap-roots exposed between two layers of rock. Its dark arms cringed. It had the look of being bullied by the wind and cheated by the salt air. Yet it was also inordinately beautiful. Without it, the green heights behind us and the steppes of sea would have been oppressively splendid, an elegantly vast and musclebound landscape. Its shade fell on a shaggy old sand-coloured log which must have seen life far up the river, been felled and rotted hollow by fire (its edges were charcoal), then washed down to the sea in a flood to be soaked and salted and swept up onto this ledge by some preposterous tide.

'Have a rest!' insisted Fy, and had one for about ten seconds. Then she pounced forward to the log, knelt down and knocked politely—there is no other word for it—on its rim. I leaned back on the slope which was the side of Fourteen Mile. The tough grass yielded enough to make a good bed, enough to buoy me off the damp black ground beneath. I idly watched as the girl pulled a few shreds of meat from her store and extended them into the black hollow. For a quarter of an hour we did very little. A few times she peered into the log, her cheek laid along the rock. But it was blackness in there, and she couldn't tell whether her friend was eating up.

'I used to give him too much,' she explained softly. 'I remember I gave him a big lump of sausage once and he just stayed there—oh, a long time—with it sort of stuck down his throat. He couldn't move. I thought he'd died.'

I sat up. 'Is there really someone in there?'

'Yes. Besides Colly Blakeley, he's my best friend. And *Me*, of course.'

I must have frowned.

'*Me*'s my brother. Everybody calls him *Me*. He hasn't even learnt *I* yet.'

Again she squinted into the log. 'I think he's eaten the lot,' she said.

'What's in there?' I whispered, for whatever it was, I didn't want it put off by my surge of interest.

'Come over here!' she bade me, pointing to a spot on the rock where I was to kneel.

'Now watch,' she said when I was beside her and conscious of pebbles cutting into my knees. 'And don't you say anything, because it's easy to scare him. I didn't knock hard. Don't you talk hard!'

She had another piece of meat in her hand and, putting it down near the lip of the log, knocked softly again on the outer rim.

'I used to have to wait way up the track after I'd knocked,' she articulated in a stage whisper. 'I'd put the meat down and go way up there.' She pointed up the track. 'You'd have to wait a long time for him to come out because he'd be frightened. Now he's got used to me. You know Finnie Gavan?'

'He's my grandfather!' I hissed.

'He said they don't come out much in the daytime because they're knocked something. Knocked-earn-all. That's right.'

I was relaxed, sitting back on my heels in the way Eucheria wouldn't let you kneel in the church. It was easy enough to understand Fy's anxiety. To the little possumish creature whom I expected to come blinking out of that log, I would be a largish, lordly, tolerably fast and unpredictable animal.

'Now don't move!' Fy concluded with a quaint compelling intonation which convinced me that tolerance demanded I should be absolutely still. She had me diffident even of looking directly at the rim of the log, and it was out of the corner of my eye that I got my first glimpse of Brownie, turned my head to him incredulously, and was paralysed in that position with terror.

Brownie had just nosed crookedly from his home, and his savage right eye—I was watching him from the side—was fixed, blood-red and big with hate, on Fy's meat. The maniac iris blazed for a second before the daylight quenched it. Now I saw his tan scales, had a glimpse of his yellow ventrals and the livid flesh beneath. His tail also appeared from the hole and was tucked back under his neck. The terrible head with its superb pattern of scales wavered towards the meat, and his tongue worked with a frenzy that belied the sinuous nonchalance of the rest of the serpent.

He drew back his neck and was motionless for seconds. Seeing this, I believed that Fy's snake must be the only creature who could stay for so long on the brink of movement. Then, showing the yellow tray of its lower jaw, it struck like a piston for the meat.

I found that I was galloping away down the top of the beach, scrutinizing the tops of the grass for broods of vipers. It was best, I decided, to clear away from anything which could hide the abominable length, the dishonest colour, of a snake. Where the grass ceased, I fell down a sand embankment to the beach, rolled onto my feet, ran fifty yards and pitched forward onto the warm sand. Not more than fifteen yards away, the couple fishing in the surf ruminatively faced the sea and had not seen me arrive.

Finnie having once told me (falsely) that snakes kept away from sand since they got their belly scales clogged with it, I would have been willing to go to sleep there, drugged with the regularity of the surf. But in a startlingly short time, Fy had arrived beside me.

'You frightened him,' she accused me. 'You frightened him and I won't be able to get him to come out for a week.'

I tried to seem contrite.

'I told you not to move.' She regarded me closely through narrowed eyes, searching for the cleft in my soul from which had issued my boorish conduct towards her second-best friend, the brown snake.

'Where does he get his water from?' I asked, trying to introduce into what was a merely academic question a note of the politest concern. The girl's face smoothed. She settled herself down placidly in the sand and began to instruct me.

'There's a hole in the rock and it's sort of Brownie's tank. But don't think he's too scared to go down there near the swamp if he wanted a drink.'

I shook my head with vigour to show that I knew Brownie's attitude to the swamp to be nothing but the most valorous.

'Sometimes I sneak up there with a bottle of water and empty it into the hole,' she went on. 'Always I taste it when I go up there. To see if it's too salty. It's always all right. Except it's a bit slimy.' She frowned. 'Only I didn't have time to taste it today. Never mind!'

Fy sat up quickly then, for the lady fisher had hauled briskly on her line. She hauled again, jerking her head around towards us. The mouth was wide open with hope. The fish was on. Calmly the woman backed up the sand, like a person used to taking fish. Fy and I closed in on her to see what she had. She wound and wound the line until a shovel-nosed flathead came flapping out of the shallows, biting on the long-shanked hook. Damp sand caked on its brown, soapy, five- or six- or seven-pound flesh. Its wide spiked gills fanned the air savagely. It threatened me with its dark half-dead eyes. They were teddy-bear's beady eyes which had been suffused with instant hate and ferocity. They hinted how it would go with us when the fish in their deeps and the ants in theirs got overnight the mastery, when giant swamp beetles came nosing up like monstrous cattle to Finnie's back wire door.

Then the lady's husband came up, cracked a bottle down on the flathead's skull, drove his knife down either side of its neck. It twisted about madly for a few seconds, as if it would really rather suffocate. Without warning, the gentlest of shivers ran through it, killing it. For a little while, death seemed sapped of half its dread.

The husband didn't let the fish lie, but flipped it over and aimed his knife at its soft white gut. Fy sprinted away and sat down at last on the embankment above the beach. I followed her without thinking. The two of us stayed there while the woman baited up again from a tin of blood-worm.

As we watched, Fy began to argue me into climbing up past that snake's place to the top of the Cape. Up there, apparently, was a monument for someone who'd crashed down into a gulf of mad water you couldn't see from where we were.

In the end, Fy had her way. Behind her, I eyed my way past Brownie's rock. Beyond it, the climb began. Ten yards from the track, the black cliffs went down smoothly like the nigger brow of a chieftain engulfed to the eye-sockets by sea. Soon we could no longer see the village, and found ourselves huffing in a place of giant and simple beauty.

It was such a place as had bred totemism in an honest race of

Stone Age men and, crawling over its scalp, I too felt a totemist reverence. Here you were aware of a sad, alien spirit, hidden somewhere in the eucalyptus clumps like a prince amongst commoners. It was amongst the scrawny paperbarks, standing on one leg and ochred white. It stood close to the darkling trunks of she-oaks, and hid its blazing eyes behind their draperies. You could feel the glaring of the dark old trees which Finnie called the mess-mates. Rounding on some red-gum, you found its maniac limbs frozen in the act of hurling something. You had the intuition, even Fy had the intuition, that up here it was best to be reverent.

From the top, dizzy on the little black-soil path, we could take in a thousand square miles of sea swell—Pollyanna Rocks twenty miles to the north, Frewin Needles spiking up through the swell at the far end of Fourteen Mile. Over the top of the Needles, we could see Hat Head, which some people said Cook had named because it looked like a hat, and others that it was the great cartographer Flinders, having lost his hat there over the bulwarks of *H.M.S. Investigator* in the old, old days.

A little way down in a fold of the Cape the monument faced the sea, dark-blue under those black cliffs. We slouched downhill to the small fenced-off obelisk. It was hard to read, and we had to trace the letters with our fingers. The gold leaf had been scoured out of the grooves. The marble surface was pocked and blasted by wind. Fy, who seemed to know the whole text by heart, insisted that I read it, largely as a test of my previous schooling. Over words I couldn't master, she would shake her head over and over, and eventually make good my weaknesses.

Facing the sea which took his body, (the monument said)
Honouring the God who has taken him home,
This monument is erected to the Memory of
Maurice Archibald Stewart,
who perished descending this cliff-face,
July 18, 1910,
Aged eighteen years.
He had all the valour of story,
As he faced the dark, terrible night,
But he found himself called in his glory,
An heir to God's kingdom of light.

The monument was in fact in an angle of the Cape. The boom of the surf was channelled up to the little memorial. A vertical wind seemed to rise with the sound, wreathing Fy's hair up above her ears, making her clutch for it. Occupied thus, she advanced towards the edge of the cliff. Twanging with vertigo, I was unwilling to go forward myself and find just how she stood to that black drop which had taken Maurice Stewart away in his glory. Her dress ballooned backwards from her and her hair splayed in a thousand wisps in all directions.

'My name is Fiona Hogan,' she yelled in the direction of New Zealand, while far below the surf once more homed in roaring. 'I am seven and a half years old. I am the most beautiful girl in the whole world. I've got a new friend who's very stupid, but it doesn't matter.'

Delivered of her bulletin, she moved back to me and told me we were going home. She pointed to the sun, hazy and low over the swamps behind Fourteen Mile beach; and I wished she hadn't, for from that moment on, the wind was far colder, and the dusk seemed to fall behind us like a grey powder as I followed her home.

The sight of Cape township came to us at the top of the last sudden rise. It was like a revelation, it was like the justification of a person's faith. We ran down the slope laughing, until the only solution to our speed was to roll over in the springy grass. Yet it would be hard, especially after dark, not to go on savouring, if *savouring*'s the word, the images of the dark spirit, the warrior-looking trees, and the vanished rock-climber.

20

I can remember shivering that night when Stell opened the bathroom and let in the wind blowing the course of that vast billabong which was the swamp. She was mad with me for going off climbing the Cape that afternoon. She showed no delicacy for my feelings about having a person's back dried by his mother lest he get asthma. She dragged me up goosefleshed out of the tepid water, and abraded my back with a very coarse towel. On the chair near the door, she had dumped some fresh clothes for me.

'And get changed quickly because Mr Oakley's already here.'

Since I had arrived home from our excursion, Fy's and mine, Mr Oakley's arrival had been portended. Our wandering off like that had developed an extra edge of malice, for I should have been washed and sitting up at the table long before the man arrived. He was the staff of the Cape school, coming to tea to meet me. All I knew about him was that Finnie said he was a hell of a difference from the nuns, that he had two big faults and God help him if it wasn't for the shortage of teachers; but that he was a good honourable bloke despite all that, and he had a great tenderness for his pupils.

When I arrived in the kitchen, there were only Finnie and Stell working over the range fire, and across in a dim corner, the bassinette with the little fellow. Finnie gestured towards the door in a way which gave me to understand Mr Oakley was down the back; and I considered for a while how different it would be to have a teacher who had natural functions to perform, for I refused to believe that the nuns had such.

'Sit down there,' said Stell, with one eye on the knuckle soup and one on me. Finnie's primus stove was roaring under the soup with a noise like rain on the roof, and I took to my seat before the set table, closed my eyes, and imagined a great storm outside.

The clinking of glass made me open up again. Finnie was pouring beer but only into his own glass. Before Mr Oakley's place at table, he was putting something which he considered indicative of his own blazing Irish wit. It was a tall glass of cold tea, topped up with a collar of candle grease. Finnie had in the past offered it to many a thirsty man; it had looked authentic enough to fool the lot of them, so authentic, said Finnie, that it was a dangerous trick to play unless you had a bottle of iced Toohey's to bring forward straightaway afterwards.

There were footsteps on the boards of the back veranda. The door opened with us all staring at it. This seemed to embarrass the stooping man who came in and stared at me down his long nose. I noticed his hair running lank and russet-grey on his long intelligent head, and his faded, soft-boiled eyes. His was the head of an elder. I was to find out later that at this stage he was no more than thirty-two or so.

'Who've we here?' he asked.

'This is the little pirate himself,' said Finnie. 'This is Daniel.'

Mr Oakley extended his hand.

'He looks like a good sort of fellow,' he boomed. I felt that to amuse himself, he was putting on a caricature of a schoolmaster, and that he wanted me to be somehow in on the joke.

'What position do you play, Daniel?' he asked in an entirely different voice.

'Position?'

'Mr Oakley's a great centre-three-quarter,' Finnie explained.

'*Was* and *mediocre*,' Mr Oakley corrected.

'Sit down, John!' Finnie told him. 'I've poured you a glass there.'

Mr Oakley glared down avidly at the glass and, since Finnie sat down, sat down also. The two men raised their drinks. It was not in the circumstances funny to see your teacher, so plainly desirous of downing his ale, about to be made a fool of. He held his glass in the air, half-turned to me and to the bassinette in the corner, and said sombrely: 'To the boys!'

'To the boys!' Finnie did no more than mutter the response, as if he were beginning to see how outlandish his little trick might prove to be.

Mr Oakley sucked at the candle-grease, and for a split second, when it did not yield as beer froth should, bit down into it.

'Oh!' he said then, and put it down, smiling a thin, dutiful smile. He took out his handkerchief and, glancing towards Stell, spat into it with as much gentle dignity as a man could in the situation. Stell and I looked on grimly. Finnie laughed, an attempt to glide over the uneasy incident.

Stell moved from the range to the table, to collect our soup plates.

'I'm terribly sorry, Mr Oakley,' she muttered. 'You'll have to excuse an old Irishman.'

'And what in the hell's wrong with old Irishmen?' Finnie asked petulantly. I suppose he was only just then beginning to see that Mr Oakley was the last one to try gross bush tricks on. 'No, no, look John, I am a bloody old fool.'

'I won't have that!' the schoolmaster insisted, winking at Stell. 'No, I won't have that!'

He plucked up and held sideways the glass which could have ruined the evening.

'This is marvellous. Tell me, Finnie, how did you make it?'

Finnie told him precisely. Stirring the pot of soup, Stell shrugged. It was far too late now to teach the old fellow his manners.

Finnie had a fine store of folk yarns, both Irish and Australian. Not that there was necessarily a specific difference between these two types; there was a little more of the supernatural in the Irish. Both would usually end in a strange anticlimax which left you faced with a boggling series of monstrosities. One of his stories that night—he had so many, and most of them were put beneath the earth with him—was of giants, *giant* being a term relative to the audacity of the story-teller.

'There was a fellow I knew in the old days, up in Dorrigo,' said Finnie, 'a big Clare man, a timber worker. He took a liking to me for some reason. When he'd come into town for weekends, he used to sleep on the floor in my room. Only at my invitation, of course.

'That's when you could see how big he was—when he was stretched out on the floor on a blanket, fully dressed in his best suit, his tie loosened, his boots off, and his big flat head of copper hair shining in the moonlight, I'd say he would have been close to seven feet tall. Everyone called him Big Red, and of course, no one had ever seen such a man for a fight. Other men would come in from the timber camps with the firm intention of getting drunk or doing some other thing. But Big Red was a religious man, and when he came into town, it wasn't to get drunk or do evil. It was to better a man in a fight—and there were a lot of big blokes round Dorrigo in those days to oblige him.

'By half past nine every Saturday night, Big Red would have found himself someone drunk or angry or proud enough to take him on. The lights would be blazing, and a hundred or more drinkers yelling in the long bar of Riordan's Relief of Mafeking hotel. Perhaps Red would take on a series of blokes and, two hours after closing, the mob would still be yelling—illegally. But that didn't matter. The sergeant of police would be down at the end of the bar, organizing the betting.

'Stripped to the waist, and his Sunday pants hanging round his thighs, Big Red took no more than ninety seconds to wallop pulp out of men as big as cedars, men who'd been felling and chopping and living in tents amongst monstrous trees up on the plateau from the time they were ten. He was the fiercest damned man—bar one—that I ever saw.

'On Sunday mornings it'd be on again at the Relief of Mafeking, if Big Red could find anyone. Riordan was of the faith, and he wasn't scrupulous about ridiculous liquor laws, but would open up for the sake of good Catholics who had done their Sunday duty. And there were plenty of them up Dorrigo way, making their peace with God at Mass, and then going off to break it again perhaps at Riordan's.

'Then Big Red would simply walk up to a likely fellow in the bar, tap his shoulder, and say, "I'm Big Red. I'm the toughest coot in Dorrigo, and I'm going to *do* you!" And *do* them he would.

'Of course, the week end came when there wasn't a big bloke around Dorrigo who hadn't fought with Red. When Red'd come up to a man in the bar and challenge him, it was no disgrace for that man to say, "No thanks, mate! Not just now." In fact, Red became a pitiful figure of a man, wandering Dorrigo in search of a triumph. Everyone *knew* he was the toughest man in Dorrigo, and no one thought it necessary to underline the fact by swallowing his own blood at Big Red's hands.

'At length, one Saturday night while he tossed about on my floor, he said, "Finnie, how about coming to Sydney with me? I could get the two of us a job on the wharves."

' "I'm quite happy with Dorrigo, thank you," I said. "And those Sydney wharfies are the toughest men in the world."

' "I know," he said. Then we both dozed, but after three or four minutes he woke the two of us by calling out, "Well, I'm going to Sydney in any case. I'm not staying here to die of shame and boredom."

'In Sydney, Big Red got daily employment on the wharves, and as he'd pass the clocker, he'd look at the poor fellow out of those furnaces of eyes in a way that would singe the poor man's hair, and say, "I can't work without my mate," thumbing over his shoulder towards me. So I never lacked a job either.

'Big Red opened his Sydney season at the Hero of Waterloo in the Rocks, and he began on a big Russian off a whaler. The old crones, down from their hovels to spend their rent on a nightly pint, were crazy with joy at the way those two giants fought, as if Big Red had brought back into their poor old lives something that had been lost long before.

'Red had his troubles with the police, of course. There was a time when he threw a slaughterman through the roof of the bar of a North Sydney pub, and landed the poor fellow in the bridal suite above—fortunately unoccupied at the time. But, Red always paid his fines. There was no better citizen than Red.

'After a year, he had used up Sydney's biggest bucks as if they were tissue paper. He then took on teams of two and three, and smashed them all over the place with plenty of vigour. But the joy was gone. Sydney was just a bigger Dorrigo; it just took longer to work through, and where in the hell did you go after Sydney?

' "Pine Creek," a publican told him. "Pine Creek. It's in the Northern Territory, and I used to own a pub there. That's where you'll find the biggest, toughest men in the whole of Australia."

'It took us a year to get to Pine Creek. We worked our way, cutting slab timber, stevedoring, digging gravel, labouring in railway yards, driving bullock teams. We went by schooner from Cooktown to Darwin, and followed the overland telegraph towards Pine Creek. When I'd faint from heat and tiredness, Big Red would sling me over his shoulder like a rolled-up blanket and carry me for miles. We met up with an Afghan with a camel team. He had wandered away from the overland and found it again only when his beasts were in a shocking state. He himself was half-mad, for an Afghan, which is nine-tenths mad for any other race. In the end we had to leave the camels, and for the last five days Big Red carried the Afghan delirious over one shoulder, and me delirious over the other. And all night nearly, he would go digging with his hands for a mouthful or two of muddy water—for our parched mouths, not for his own. Fifty miles from Pine Creek, the Afghan died.

'Pine Creek was a desert row of iron and slab timber and wattle-and-daub dwellings, but it looked like a garden of delight. Big Red laid me in the shade of a big baobab tree and got me water. After a rest, we went scouring the place for big Pine Creekers.

'The first one we saw was a vast blond-headed yokel of a storekeeper who might have been, if anything, bigger than Red. He was hammering shutters over the windows of his store. We could see through the half-open door that the counters were cleaned and the fixtures empty. You would have thought that he expected the town to be bombed, which, in those days anyway, was an impossibility.

'At the moment, Big Red needed food and water and just about anything else that could help him get over his trek. But maybe he was afraid that the storekeeper might be about to lock himself away.

' "Hey!" said Big Red quietly. "I'm Big Red. I'm the toughest coot in Australia and I've never been beat in a fight. And—I'm—going—to—*do*—you!"

'The big Pine Creek man hardly turned away from his shutters.

' "Not today, mate!" he muttered. You could tell he wasn't scared of Big Red. "Any other time, but not today. Today Big Louie's coming to town."

'He couldn't be got to say anything else. He was too wrapped up in the business of getting his property, his earnings, his wife and his children under cover.

'It was a busy midday in Pine Creek that day, with a lot of fine big blokes doing what the storekeeper was doing. Not one of them seemed afraid of Big Red, which was a scalding insult in itself. Their muscles were as big and taut as his were, yet all they could talk about was this Big Louie person. The town faced the coming of something terrible. Perhaps Big Louie was a giant camel of the type who sit on a fence and down comes the fence, who lean on a shed and down comes the shed. Or perhaps he was a big mad buffalo. But none of them would say. They just rolled their eyes and went on hammering.

'Of course, we came at last to the pub, both of us dry again, dry down to the pits of our stomachs. Big Red put me down on a row of chairs in the bar, and though half-dead, I could see the place was empty. Yet there was the fine icy noise of bottles clicking together. Beneath the bar, a little publican was packing his spirits away for a happier day.

'Big Red leant over the bar and ordered us beer, a quart for himself and a pint for me.

' "Not today, mate!" the publican said without even looking up. "Big Louie's coming to town today."

'That name! It was like spittle in Red's face, and it put him in a fury. He dragged the little fellow off the pub floor and flung him against the mirror behind the bar. The glazed mermaids on the mirror broke and fell in pieces, and the poor little publican bounced back within Red's reach.

' "Now, how about that beer?" Red screamed. I could tell that he was not himself. He was not by nature a cruel man.

'We drank, and our host gave us some cold cuts of beef. Mid-afternoon came to the pub and the busy little publican, but nothing and no one else. We went out on to the veranda to sit in the shade, and that dustbed of a street was dead. The shops were closed. There was not even a dog wandering around the corners. The heat, even on the veranda, was as thick as treacle.

'In the north were great dreary hills of red stone. About three o'clock, we saw a column of dust over them. It moved down on to the plain, and raced towards us like a storm. And then, about four o'clock, we could see what it was.

'And from now on, it's only the fact that you know I'm an honest man that will make you believe the rest. There was a giant camel, twenty-five feet from hump to hoof, galloping. A man I would say no less than eleven feet tall, with a chest like a water tank, rode the mighty beast, walloping its flanks with a crowbar. He rode that camel with crocodile-skin reins, and draped over its neck like a sort of mane was a string of sleepy taipans, hardly twitching in the afternoon sun. Both of us, Red and I, stared and didn't move, believing we had some sort of desert madness.

'The giant reined in his mount, and tied it to the hitching rail. He could see us there on the veranda, and he probably wanted to show off. For example, he lightly flicked the crowbar into the ground, and it speared in so that only a few inches of the haft were left showing. Then he ranged past us, and the veranda shook. It was for all the world as if one of those giant sandstone pillars you see in the desert had grown legs and come into town on a spree. Poor fellow had probably had some gland trouble when he was young.

'We followed him into the bar, and sat down goggling at him.

' "Get me a gallon of rum, mate!" he called to the publican. "I've had nothing to drink but taipan juice for the last two weeks."

'While the publican obliged, the big fellow sat on a table. The piano was in his road, so he flicked it and off it rolled, like a bit of rolling-stock, into the far corner. The publican hardly looked up, but with both elbows high, poured bottles of spirit into a kerosene can for his guest. At last the giant's cup overflowed, and the publican lugged it across the room. The big man lifted it with one hand around its rim, and drained it like a dipper of punch.

' "I don't like that man," Big Red whispered. "I could *do* the big fool."

' "He'll kill you," I hissed. "It's all right fighting mere men, but this fellow's probably the angel Gabriel or something."

' "If I do him," Red muttered, "I'll be the best man in Australia. If I don't, he probably *will* kill me. But I don't want to live unless I'm the best."

'As the last of the spirits went into the giant's rowdy gut, Red therefore walked up behind him. For the first time, Red seemed to me sadly small. He had to stand on his toes to tap the big fellow on the shoulder.

' "Hey, mate!" he roared. "I'm Big Red."

'That was courage—calling himself *big* to that man. "I'm the toughest coot in Australia, and I've never been beaten in a fight. And I'm going to *do* you."

'The giant belched, wiped his lips and looked down into Red's eyes.

' "But I've got to go home," he said. "Haven't you heard, mate? Big Louie's coming to town." '

21

In the little weatherboard school beneath Warialda, seventeen children received their moulding from Mr Oakley. There was about him an air of being steeped in the routine of teaching on many grades at once. Clutters of frayed and fat dusty manila folders on his desk bespoke the security of Mr Oakley's system; and every child could feel secure beneath that iron roof grunting in the wind.

My class was Fy and a wizened little boy, completely bald from dengue fever, which people get in the tropics. He wore always, even in school, even when the inspector came, a little flannel cap; and when Fy ushered me into our long desk, I was disturbed by the wide brown resentment in his eyes. Fy, I found, was strength, pride, normality to Colly Blakeley. He had no wish to share any of this.

On the afternoon of that first Monday at the Cape school, he wanted the three of us to go down to Gunulla's beach. 'To race,' he said. Fy approved the idea; there was a queer avidity about her as she did.

We were off to the tidal creek therefore, where beyond the landings of the fishing boats, on the lee shore, a crescent of sandstone and slate guarded a narrow beach which hardly existed at high tide. Some explorer or other had once met a chieftain called

Gunulla here, who at the time did something quaint or kind enough to be remembered in the name of the place. For some reason, I was never tempted to ask Finnie for the story of the small beach. *Gunulla* was a name which meant contentment, the contentment of an old chief. The giant monolith we called the Cape was a nest of mighty ancestors for Gunulla. The Cape's black lip was sacred; and when its shadow fell on him, it was the shadow of heaven.

The beach itself was littered with rocks, no more than calf-high, but studded with jagged oyster and mollusc shells. When Fy, Colly and I climbed down to it that afternoon, it was the first time I could remember having been there. It seemed an utterly unreasonable place to have a race.

'There are rocks all over the place,' I told Fy.

'Of course there are rocks all over the place,' she said. Her eyes flashed to Colly. The initiates were closing ranks against me.

We lined ourselves up for the race. The sand was still wet from the tide, and Gunulla's creek seemed abnormally close and wide. An oblique afternoon sun had turned it the colour of mercury.

'Ready, steady, go!' said Fy quickly.

It was a terrible race for me. One foot out of place, and it would have been diced to a bloody mash on the shell-pocked crust of those rocks. Colly and Fy sped away from me as I chose a lumbering course amongst the gibbers. Their size and Sheffield sharpness curdled my blood. The second time I looked up, the other two were fifty yards ahead. When I got to the end of the beach, they had been resting there, puffing victory through open mouths, for a long time.

'Beat you!' grunted Colly without necessity, and, though I wanted to start a fight, with a sort of drowsy kindliness.

I said nothing, and sat on the smooth dome of a rock. It chilled me through my trousers. My eyes screwed up with shame, which the others probably thought was mere exhaustion. Fy's well-fed litheness, Colly's terrier legs flaunted before me. Most of the other people I had ever raced against were content with a thirty-yard dash. These two raced over the length of beaches, the length of their *own* beach anyhow, beside their *own* sea. They exuded a sense of possession, as the Mantle boys had on the day of my first meeting them. And in many ways, the way they stood for example, they looked as old as the beach itself.

Colly turned his capped head to me. 'Want another one?'

Between two gulps of air, 'Yes!' I said evenly.

'Wait a while!' Fy told him, and began to steady her own breathing.

For some time, all I could hear was a snuffling in my nose, and the tide taking little sips at the beach. And of course, there was the noise of the surf three hundred yards away but, at the Cape, this was merely an element of silence. My rock was getting very cold. I stood up.

'Ready?' asked Fy. She showed a certain bureaucratic fairness, wanted to give me every advantage and still see me fail.

'Yes!'

We arranged ourselves again for the start. I stood close to Fy. Her head thrust forward to the far end, the sea end of Gunulla's beach. Only time separated her from another triumph down there by the heap of washed-smooth slate where the sand finished. If my feet should be ripped off, if I had to finish on the bloody stumps of ankles, I would not allow myself to be beaten this time by either of them.

This time, to show that all the rules were of her making, and if she wished, of her breaking also, she separated the *Ready*, the *Steady*, and *Go* by three unpredictable intervals.

From the start, I was conscious for a short distance of being in front; then I could see a blurred Fy and Colly coming up on my right, and hear the sound of their feet thwacking on the wet sand. We ran together for perhaps a hundred yards, until out of the blue canopy of air above the Cape, I couldn't drag down one sufficient breath. Then for some reason more akin to cowardice rather than to the question of how closely the rocks were placed, my feet scraped up the agonizing surface of one of them. I felt shells scoring down the ball of my foot, and tripping up the instep of the other. Hand-first I came down on the rock in front, and its edges sliced up my palms. It was terrible lying breathless in wet sand, stinging hand and foot. I wailed once, even more piercingly than the agony warranted, loud enough to make Fy and Colly turn back. You're going to look really impressive, I told myself, done up in all that iodine and lint. The blood was making in runny gouts for my wrists, so I licked it away, and swallowed it and tears at the same time. Far along the beach, Fy and Colly finished in a sprint where the tide had begun to splash companionably at their ankles. Fy turned back to me then, her dress heaving as if it and not the small animal beneath it needed to get its breath. I turned my head away, wanting to worry her, and lay indulging my agony. The south wind sliding down that tidal creek turned all skin goose-fleshed.

At last Fy had arrived above me.

'Whatever happened to you?' she said with an intake of breath.

'What in the hell do you think happened?'

I jumped up and stretched my slashed foot towards her. Sand had half caulked up the bloody trough which had been the ball of my foot.

'Good heavens!' she said primly. Like a hospital matron really. 'Come on!'

Her quite plump, quite strong little arm went around my shoulder. Limping over the amphitheatre of smooth stones with the low sun making our backs anonymous, we must have been like two symbolic extras from *Gone with the Wind*. But Colly did not find us awesome at all.

'Hey, come on, Fy!' he called, like a curlew. He stood out black and forlorn against that anodized creek. 'Hey, come on, Fy! Who in the hell said we'd finished?'

For an indiscriminate second or two she turned to him, keeping a hold on my left hand as the rocks wobbled beneath our feet and little crabs ran out between them. Just a second or two for Colly, and then straight back to me.

'You're dripping blood all over the rocks!' She sounded impressed. 'I've never seen anyone bleed so much. What will your mother say?'

'I'll tell her I tripped,' I said, and squinted. I was full of manly pain.

'Hey, Fy!' yelled Colly masterfully. 'Hey, Fy! We aren't finished. Hey, come on, Fy!'

But with Edith Cavell tenderness, Fy had me over the stone embankment, having had no ear for Colly, having stared at each ball of sandstone expertly, all she cared about being whether it would rock beneath my one good foot. Occasionally I remembered to lick the gobs of blood from my hands. On the cuffs of the blue jumper I was wearing, blood would show up in an unseemly fashion. The way poor old Dolph's cuffs looked unseemly with mucus. Poor old Dolph.

We made good time across the reserve, because I tired of hopping and used the heel of my bad foot. Colly went on yelling behind us, but by the time he lost his temper with Fy, we were too far away to hear clearly the few blunt frightened words he'd learnt in fishing launches, pubs and kitchens when people had forgotten his presence. I looked back to see him lift a large, too-heavy gibber of slate and hurl it a miserable yard or so from where he stood.

Along Memorial Avenue, the pines were clogged with dusk. A sad lamp, like a light of remembrance, fought darkness in the general store where yesterday morning's Sydney paper was at last on sale. The sun dropped as it had the day before, homing down behind Warialda at an unreal rate. In the sudden dark, a few slivers of gravel got into the trench in my foot. I yelled and tried to shake them out, which all seemed to make Fy angry against Colly.

'That Colly Blakeley!' she said; and after a few more yards, turned my left hand so that she could see the cuts on the palm before the light gave out entirely.

'That Colly!'

And though poor Colly's pride was understandable to me, and hers was not, I became instantly warm with a useless, thoughtless hate for the small capped boy going home in shame, somewhere behind us in the dusk.

That was the way it went with Fy, Colly and myself. We were no co-equal trinity, and Colly and I were the only ones who could lose. Face, dignity, independence we lost and won many times a week; and no one coming into Mr Oakley's school and seeing a plump little girl flanked in a long desk by two scrawny boys, would have guessed what august supremacy she held over both our wills. She believed we were inferior by reason of our very boyhood, boys being undeserving of etiquette or the truth or any knowledge of the special mysteries she pretended to carry about with her, locked in behind her wide, Mediterranean-blue eyes. In those days, I saw her in my ignorance as a special phenomenon; as a misplaced boy who had in some way wandered into the wrong bodily format, rather than as a cameo world, a cameo history of the world and history of women.

One day, I hauled off a long hard fist at Fy's complacency. Mr Oakley saw the incident and chastised me on the stingy part of the leg. I had to read a social studies book standing up in moral leprosy for the better part of the afternoon. Towards three o'clock Mr Oakley called me up to his desk and told me confidentially that girls were weaker than us and no gentleman would hurt them. Below us, Fy worked on a pattern of wool and cardboard, and a brand of modesty made her face look strangely thin.

In the circumstances, there was no reason why I should not become Colly's friend, even though it was his stubborn dependence on Fy which began our trouble. Take away a certain lassitude and the shock of the grenade disaster, and I could have been his mentor. But I too, like Colly, had a reason to fall back upon and, trust in, her dominance.

A number of times a day, Mr Oakley would hint at his own ill-health. 'A poor sick old man like myself!' he would say. 'If it wasn't for my ruinous health,' he would roar, usually at one of the Saunders who were his sole disciplinary problem, 'I'd come down there and *really* lay into you.' A number of times a day, he would produce a metal flask (with dents in it that Colly claimed were bullet scars) and sip at it in a convincingly febrile manner.

One day, the eldest Saunders heard Colly and me talking about this flask. It was lunch-time, and Mr Oakley supervised us from his kitchen window. But the eldest Saunders had little reverence for him, about as much as we had for the eldest Saunders, who was lumpy, fourteen, and still only in his sixth class. Mr Oakley was nonetheless a branch of knowledge in which he was expert.

'Cold tea!' he said and laughed, for cold tea was what Colly had suggested was in the flask. 'Well, wouldn't that give you the gripes? Cold tea! It's brandy or some other booze in that flask. I'm telling you. It's just plain booze, and Mr Oakley's just a plain booze-artist. I seen him in town. I seen him when I was about as big as you. He was lying flat out on one of them tables they've got in front of the Imperial. There's a lady chemist in Gilbert won't marry him because he's a booze-artist. He's been trying for years. You ask any grown-up. I hear all these things.'

The biggest Saunders spat in the dust in the sunlight. I wished he hadn't, as there was no reasonable place, situated as we were, to look any more without seeing either his thick, knowing face, older in some ways than Mr Oakley's, or the foul spittle on the ground like an ill-formed slug. But he didn't stay long. Into the thicket of poor scrub behind the school he made his normal lunch-time way. What he was at, vanishing away towards the swamp like that, we didn't know. But the fact that he did wander off each dinner-time, without Mr Oakley's knowing or perhaps without his caring, gave this boy a peculiar authority. He was a challenge that Mr Oakley chose not to take up. And that is why we were especially boggled by the giant, enthralling scandal he had given us, and settled down to digest it at leisure.

'And anyhow,' the biggest Saunders murmured, darting back on us from the edge of the bush, 'if he's such a great bloke, why isn't he in the army?'

'Your father isn't in the army,' Colly said coldly, an unexpected glimpse of steel. I had the same thrill of horror you get when you wipe your nose with your hand and, looking up, find a stranger staring levelly at you.

But the big fellow had the grace or stupidity or languor to laugh.

'But my old man doesn't pretend to be anything. At least he doesn't pretend to be a God-almighty schoolteacher. He pretends to be the best booze-artist around Gilbert. But Mr Oakley's the second-best.'

Then he went defiantly away into shaggy, olive scrub. Colly's face, which followed him, was very small, peaked and white.

22

In early September of that year, Colly displayed chicken-pox. This happened in the second week of the holidays. When we called at his window, Colly seemed to be fretting over his own inefficiency in developing such a favoured disease in out-of-school-time, as if it finally proved that the odds were stacked against him, and he didn't want us to see the fact in his bald, pocked, calamined face.

What would we be doing that day? Colly asked. *Oh, we were going to climb right over the Cape to Fourteen Mile beach*, said Fy. *Were we let?* Colly wanted to know. He would not suffer as much if we were not let. His eyes were wide and liquid with desire while he waited for the answer. *Oh, she thought so*, said Fy (lying, but why not? since we'd be back by lunch-time if we hurried).

'Shake hands, Colly,' Fy demanded in the end, 'and Daniel and me'll get it just when school's starting.' His mouth set in lines of self-sacrifice. Colly obliged with the pensive nobility of the poor. His hand was sweaty. 'We'd better get cracking,' said Fy.

The morning lay quivering beneath the long pines in Memorial Avenue. The last of the winter was treed in their matted limbs. Shushed by a big September sea, the after-breakfast town was absolutely silent, and all the boats were gone, out towards Pollyanna since before the two of us had even been awake. I was very happy with Fy beneath the row of Norfolks, striding by the little slabs of marble, each one of them with the name, rank, number, regiment and place of death of a Cape man dead in World War One. There were thirteen slabs, which implied that the Cape had in those days been a bigger town. But not as big as one might think, for seven of the names were of the same regiment, and died on the same day in June 1918. There was a great mystery there and you couldn't read the slabs, as we often did, without becoming thoughtful and thinking of Lennie and Dolph, and praying to Dolph, who rightly or wrongly, according to the words of comfort bandied after his death, was Saint Dolph, home and housed, and a jewel in paradise to me.

'Sit down!' Fy hissed, out of the blue, and *did* seat herself beside *248309 Hickman, Gerald Pte. 57th (New England) Volunteer Btn. France June 22nd 1918*. 'Come on, sit down if you're game!'

'Who said I'm not?' I asked and flopped beside her.

About two hundred and fifty yards along the road, limping in our direction, was an old aborigine with a sugar-bag over his shoulder. His face was an ebony splotch beneath a wideawake hat which even at that distance looked flaccid with sweat.

'I know something that makes the blacks mad,' Fy whispered, though if twice as close, the old fellow couldn't have heard her. 'It makes them so mad that they put a curse on you, and one day you just step up the street and turn into a tree. Unless you show them you aren't scared. So if you're not scared, take off your shoe!'

'Why?' Meaning why take one's sandshoe off, why make the blacks mad, why provoke a curse?

'All right then!' Fy herself was savage with fear. She had already hitched her right foot up to her mouth, bitten the shoelace loose with her teeth. Now she pulled the shoe off. 'If you're going to play the dingo, go back home!'

'Like hell!' So I pulled my right shoe strenuously off, and had begun to undo the left, when Fy whispered with a ferocious, sibilant shrewishness: 'Did I tell you to take the other one off?'

I left it, and sat very still, sensing, all but hearing, the petulance of fear beating in the plump little body next to mine. The very dark old man was much closer now, his face still utterly black and eyes squinted up from walking towards too many afternoon suns.

An old blue shirt held in his chest and belly, and a charity pair of brown trousers just managed to encase his thighs. His feet were bare and scabby. Gazing at them and at his ulcerated left hand, the hand not engaged on the gunny-sack, I very nearly found it beyond me to be predominantly afraid. When he was only yards away, however, my eyes were impelled up to the wide and convoluted features of his awful, somehow kindly, old face.

'Gunulla?' I asked half-thralled.

'Don't be mad!' Fy whispered. 'Listen, do what I do!'

All she did was to begin to scratch the sole of her right foot. Of course, I did the same. The old man halted on the side of the road and stared at us. His eyes were impossible to find in the folds of black flesh and the shade of his hat. Like those ancient trees up on the Cape, he was the soul of resentment and tolerance, and he all but frightened the insides out of us.

Fy kept on scratching sturdily. The old fellow, in alliance with time which could make us vulnerable in the end, in alliance with the shadows which made his eyes a mystery, stood and glared at us for the best part of a minute.

Then: 'White bastard!' he muttered at me, which was unjust. He kept a further long silence, took a war-like step towards us, and yelled, 'White bastard!'

We sprinted away, one foot bare and a sandshoe in our right hands. Behind us, the old fellow laughed and laughed; but we didn't stop till the post-office store.

'There!' Fy grunted. She held her waist and walked back and forward in a small arc, gulping air. It was the way women athletes at the German Olympics had behaved after their exertions, and Fy had seen the film of it all only the Saturday night before.

'There! Doesn't it make them mad?'

'Why?' I asked her.

But she couldn't tell me why.

Too much water from the reserve tank swayed in our stomachs as we mounted the slopes beneath the Cape. We were very tired suddenly, and feared that next time we yawned, our soft, companionable flesh might turn to the shard-harsh likeness of a eucalypt. But yawn we had to, the higher we went, and I doubted that we'd ever make the far side.

She couldn't seem to rouse Brownie that morning, so left a dead mouse from the Hogans' woodshed for him. As she attended to the surrounds of the log and wondered if her serpent was inside, I stood forty yards further up the track, yelling with the prevailing wind for her to hurry up.

It was spring-time, you could tell; and spring-time and the slope made me take my jumper off. The damp of the seaside winter had gone. There had been no dew on the grass that morning. On top of the Cape, the old brown trees aimed not to be seduced by the flow of the seasons. But you could smell the eucalyptus; the seed-pods were straining; look closely, and there were a thousand underhand blossoms. Even that temperate earth throbbed with some sort of resurrection.

We sidled past the old trees, and a line of young wattles which had fallen frankly in love with September and dolled themselves up in yellow. The monument we passed, and in a black-faced gulf above a mess of fearful rock and spume and liquorice-coloured water, headed for the last crest. If we were to be turned to timber, I thought, this would be the place. It seemed clearly to be the old black man's mother earth, to have extruded his soul.

At last we sat, with some breath left, on top of the last rise. I could not remember having seen before the fourteen scimitar miles of that wild beach all at once. The surf moved like cavalry, and the flank of one unit tangled itself with the flank of another. We could see the deep blue trough which bore the cross-current and ran for miles within easy casting distance of the shore. This was supposed to make Fourteen Mile a good place for fish. But no one lived here except the lighthousemen at the far end, above the Frewin Needles, and two old meths drinkers who sold bait in front of pubs in Gilbert and even Pollyanna Rocks. The Cape not having a pub, Fy and I had never seen either of them.

The story was that one of them, a Gilbert man gassed in World War One, had turned to beachcombing on Fourteen Mile. Everyone thought it would have been better for him to be a slab in Memorial Avenue but, with the perversity of all futile things, he had outlived most of the sober ones. After twenty years of drunken squalor in a tin and hessian hut in a glade behind the beach he had, without warning, gone social and gathered into his life another half-crazed tramp whom he'd found in a pub in Gilbert. Somewhere down in the scrub, the two of them were now gathering their tins and stinking bags of berley, were slumping on their hessian cots or limping off to their fly-blown latrine in the sand-hills. Like the lives of sand-flies, funnel-webs, and black snakes from the swamp, their lives were hidden under the matt-green purity of the terrain.

It was easy going down the side of the Cape to the shallows four hundred feet below, to the rubble of sea-honed quartzite which fringed the Cape on this side. From half-way down, I became aware of schools of mullet mouthing through the perfectly diaphanous waters, and began running straight-away to get knee-deep amongst them and send them panicking off towards the caverns under the Cape.

As we came down, we saw that there was a man on the beach who had been hidden from above—perhaps by the salt haze of the heavy surf. This man was fishing or catching bait, and his short midday shadow splotched the wet sand behind him. But he must have been the better part of a mile along the beach, so we took no notice and crashed into the shallows, stampeding mullet.

We found it pleasant to put our socks on again afterwards, for a strong sou'-westerly slewed around the beach raising goose-flesh on our ankles. By now, the man had worked considerably closer to us, and was hunting blood-worms with a sugar-bag full of berley. He would draw the bag of rotting fish-flesh across the wet sand, and as the worms came up to savour it, grab them in his fingers and drop them in a billy-can. This man, poorly dressed in a ragged jacket and rolled-up trousers, we quite naturally made the turning point. When we reached that man, we would turn back home to dinner. The fishing boats would eventually be in, and all afternoon there would be good sport at the landing.

The distance to the bait-catcher we used up with a long walking race, degenerating, because Fy cheated, into a sprint. The winning-post was that man showing black against the dull brown of wet sand. I concentrated on the thin shabby back. An oblivious back. It failed to hear me until the last few yards, when its left shoulder cringed alarmingly. Then the horny feet and rolled-up pants, grey jacket and turnip head turned on me.

'Oh!' I said, and refused to believe in the face I saw. For it was, under the tan and beard and lip-blister, the face of the Comrade. It was shockingly afraid, and he had me by the elbow. I accepted him as authentic when I could feel his thumb and fingers much too firmly on my shoulder. Forest, dune, beach, water, the scared face of the Comrade, the distant sweaty face of Fy, all swung in crazy orbit as he shook me to the edge of nausea. When the shaking stopped though, after an unconscionable time for shaking to continue, I was looking him full in the face. His eyes behaved like the eyes of a drunken Negro I'd seen in Sydney once, rolling his eyes up like a prophet on the look-out for tongues of fire or the elective hands of angels.

'I'm sorry,' he mumbled. 'You gave me a bugger of a scare sneaking up like that.'

He let go, eyeing his berley bag, its malodorous flap swaying open on the very edge of the sea.

'Wait till I get it please, Daniel,' he said temperately, retrieving the bag and a billy-can part-full of worms.

'I didn't hurt you, did I?' he asked. 'I wouldn't want to hurt *you*. You're the last of the tribe.'

It wasn't until he made this unintelligible statement that in some strange way I knew him to be the same Comrade and myself the same Daniel.

'No! I'm all right.'

By now, Fy had come a few yards towards us, wandering in a lackadaisical arc. She was breathing more heavily than she needed to, for this was her way of hiding interest, but above all, of advancing arguments why she should not be shaken or beaten or killed.

'I've wanted to see you a long time,' the wistful Comrade said. 'I don't remember much. But I remember you. And I remember your mother, I've often wanted to sit down and have a yarn with the two of you.'

He made up the beach towards a sheltered place between the two spurs of a sand-dune. The southerly cuffed grit and shell-dust stinging against our legs, so that there was a taste of ill-considered irritability about the words when I asked, 'Have a yarn, Mr Mantle? What about?'

He stared at me confusedly, but I mistrusted the confusion drooping from his eyes, making his cheeks so narrow.

'About the old times,' he explained. 'About the old times. I can scarcely remember them. Come and have a yarn about it all, Daniel. Over there!'

It was useless to think of running away. Running away would provoke him. And he was only a yard from me, with his scabby right index finger, gory from the insides of broken sea-worm, pointing to a hidden little groin in the sand-bank behind the beach.

'Hey, Fy!' I yelled. All I wanted was that if the Comrade pierced me with his clam-knife, or scraped my hide off with his scaler, Fy should be with me at the time.

'Hey, Fy!' I repeated, fully treacherous. 'This is a friend of mine called Mr Mantle.'

Fy nodded to the Comrade's right shoulder-blade. He was set on a yarn and his long right arm shepherded me along.

'How is Joseph, Mr Mantle? How's his legs?'

The Comrade issued a jagged little laugh which was no surety on the state of his soul. And as the yarning place closed in, and spines of grass from scrub behind the beach ran out and bound the naked hips of sand, I felt a more than vested interest in the Comrade's state of soul.

'His legs don't give him no trouble any more,' said the Comrade. 'He's dead!'

'Dead?'

'He died in his sleep.' The Comrade spoke with envy. He spoke as you would speak about someone who had found a haven in a cool place amongst trees. A different sort of tree from those front-line ones along the sand-banks, standing racked with purpose and straining every sinew to hold the earth together and stop it dipping down into the sea. In the shade of one, the Comrade sat down.

'That wasn't so bad,' he said. 'Dying in his sleep. I always thought it wouldn't be as easy as that for Joseph.'

Across from him, Fy and I slumped rigidly, and despite the danger, our backsides sank into the sand. The Comrade talked on with his eyes all but closed and a speculative look on his face. That much was true. He did seem very much to want to yarn.

'On a day like this, I know that Lennie and Joseph and Hilda are dead,' he stated.

Though I wanted to raise a point of order about Hilda, of whose death I knew nothing, it was only questionably safe to interrupt him. 'And I don't blame *anyone*. I don't even blame myself. Certainly I don't blame you, Captain Bradley—not Captain in the army but in the Sallies—you know, the Salvation Army. He said I'd be damned if I blamed you. Anyhow I can't even remember if I ought to or not any more. My memory's gone right to buggery since all that trouble.'

From the afternoon tea talk of adults, I chose something soothing to tell him.

'You ought to take better care of yourself.'

'Yeah! I ought to, all right! But I keep on forgetting. I've just about forgotten the works. What Hilda looked like, the colour of our eiderdown, the front windows. They had some glass in them that was coloured. But I can't remember what colour.'

'There were blue diamonds,' I supplied him. 'And there was sort of—slices of green.'

He shook his head slowly and said in a monotone, 'I don't want to know anyhow.'

Fy now shifted and sat up straight, ready to get up and run. But the Comrade had a lot of yarning left in him yet.

'The late afternoons are bad. The darker it gets the more I think it was all my fault. I can remember the police yelling at me it was all my fault. Saying "Are you satisfied with what you've done, Mantle?" And all that smart-arse stuff. Now look, Daniel! You were there. Whose fault was it? You tell me! Was it mine?'

'No!' I called out with sublime conviction. 'No, it wasn't yours.'

'Then whose fault was it?' His voice was very quiet beside the steam-hammer industry of the surf.

'It was . . .' I would have blamed Dolph but that would be virtually sacrilegious. 'It was no one's fault! It was an accident!'

'Yes,' the Comrade intoned. 'It was an accident. I know that much. And anyway, Captain Bradley—you know, of the Sallies—said, "Leonard Mantle, murderer, drunkard, whatever you are, you are only a challenge to the Mercy of God!" God, I wish I was dead, Daniel. With Hilda and the boys. I wish to God a ten-foot black snake would come down out of the scrub. Or a funnel-web spider bite me on the seat. Or I wish they'd shoot a bloke in front of the firing squad. They're the luckiest blokes of all. But we're such a great bloody democracy, they don't shoot blokes. They just put them in jail.'

Fy and I glanced round on guard against that snake the Comrade had all but conjured up. Through the seat of my pants I imagined the unspeakable hole of a funnel-web fat with venom. But I was too afraid to move an inch.

'The Cape!' he went on simply. 'Everyone knew you'd come to the Cape. The house was as quiet as a dead horse and full of the smell of gas, and I can't stand that. I tell you, that bloody house clammed up on me. It never changed any more. Even the tiles on the roof wouldn't rattle no more.'

He cupped up a handful of sand to pour it out between his legs. 'But, just the same, I didn't have to ask anyone where you'd gone to. I heard it first of all in the grocer's. Someone was talking to that old lady who has her glasses on a chain. You know . . .'

'Mrs Smart.'

'Yeah, Mrs Smart. I went in one day to get sardines. They're horrible all right, sardines. I hate sardines. But they fill you up and keep you regular, and with them under your belt, you can't get a whiff of gas and death, because *they* keep on repeating.'

In verification, he belched, as if sardines were beneath his belt, functioning as sardines should.

'I beg your pardon,' he said. 'While I was in Smarts' just as I came in, I heard the old lady say, "They're gone to the Cape!" to another old duck. Mrs Smart saw me. But the other old Judy said, "Where's the Cape?" and Mrs Smart shushed her like hell. Where-ever I went people shushed other people like hell.'

The Comrade closed his eyes so tightly that if there was so much as a tear inside him, it would have to come out now. No tear came. But all at once, I saw an image of the pit and dome of whisperings in which this man had lived. The musical comedy tramp dances and dances over the darkness, and cannot shake off his relentless cone of spotlight. And the Comrade writhed likewise in his cone of whispered imputations. Whispers had brought him here, where nothing whispered. The sea, the greedy gulls, the whip-cracking snake who panics off through dried-out reeds—none of these could be said to whisper. Nor the bott-flies roaring in the glade round his unseemly home.

'I've seen you,' he said, and his eyes popped open. 'I've seen you often. Maybe not face to face. But sometimes I go up to the mountains in the daytime. I like to look down at the town, and think about the things you might be doing. The last of the tribe. I'd never go right down in the daytime. That'd spoil things. I'm a bloke who can't help spoiling bloody things. Really, Captain Bradley said, "Never go near the Jordans!" and got me to swear. But I go down in the night. I wander round. It's a lovely little place. I stand under the trees, and look at a place and wonder if it's yours or not. I like to think about you sleeping safe inside there. I don't know why I like to. I suppose I haven't got many friends. Not since the Party told me I couldn't be of use to them any more. After all I'd bled for them. Anyhow, I stay down there till I'm shivering like a cat with the cold. Then up over the top, home. There's usually a hell of a wind on top. But I like big winds.'

On the beach, the wind boomed in appreciation of the Comrade's sentiment. It sounded as if it were filling giant sails. The Comrade was quiet for a while and let it have its roar, which it did so loudly that a natural pause fell on our conversation, or rather on the Comrade's dialogue with himself. If I was brave enough, Fy and myself might now be able politely to withdraw. The wind fell. I swallowed; and the Comrade spoke before me.

'I go up Fourteen Mile a lot,' he stated. My back itched with impatience, but we had to sit and listen. 'I go up there a lot, and if I told you why, you'd laugh.'

'No!' Fy muttered. 'No we wouldn't.'

'Then, I go up there to pray. I go up there to pray to that convict bloke. You know.'

'Martin McQuaid,' Fy suggested, looking momentarily over her shoulder towards the mountain.

'McQuaid's his name!' the Comrade nodded.

A dumper of a wave slammed down a confirmatory fist on the beach. McQuaid was a ghost of Fourteen Mile Mountain, known to the tortuous magnificence of the Cape as the red-gums are known to the heart of the black earth. Escaping in chains from Port Macquarie convict station one evening some hundred and twenty years before, McQuaid had fled up the mountain. Below him, on the beach, dragged along by bloodhounds, were the pursuing redcoats. As if this obscure, antipodean hunt for one scared man were to rank on the regimental colours beside Culloden and Talavera, Bayonne and Waterloo, they pushed him on and on. Until, at dusk, he died an Absalom death. Stumbling over a crest, he found his chains grabbed by a tree limb, and his feet left dangling in free air. Then standing up as straight as justice, that sad old tree strangled him slowly, by his own iron collar round his neck.

'He killed his people too,' the Comrade said, confidently aware of what McQuaid had been transported for, a question of which no one at the Cape had any clear information. 'Like me, by accident. By accident, poor bugger. I know how glad he was when he started choking to death.'

'Well,' Fy breathed, 'have you seen him?'

'I reckon I have. I can't help seeing the poor coot. He's a shy sort of bloke though, and he only half trusts me. He stands back in the mulga. He doesn't really know I'm in the same sort of mess as he is.'

The Comrade sat and thought about McQuaid. A cloud of flies seethed round the berley bag. It and the Comrade and McQuaid were a good trio, all variously dead. My desire to get away from them strained my chest and belly drum-tight.

'I think we'll have to go now,' I said quietly. 'We've got to get home for dinner. Be seeing you, Mr Mantle.'

'*Home for dinner*.' The Comrade mouthed the words luxuriously. 'That sounds good. It'd be great to be able to say you were going home for dinner. Well, I suppose you can't stay here for good.'

'No. We can't. There'd be terrible trouble if we didn't get back.'

'Hey, d'you know you won't be able to say a word about this?' He was matter-of-fact. Perhaps with his many trips up the side of Fourteen Mile, he lacked the energy for violence. 'Look, Daniel, you won't be able to. It'd be the end of me if you do. See, I'm a deserter.'

We stared at him evenly, blankly.

'Look!' he persisted. 'I joined the army. I mean, I wanted to get killed. But it's more complicated than that. So I left after two weeks. Now, you can't do that. It's called deserting. That's what I said. In a full-blooded country they shoot deserters. Here they just put them in jail for years. And I couldn't take that.'

He pulled himself groaning into a standing position, brushing the sand from the back of his coat.

'I couldn't take that bloody army neither. Bloody Liverpool Camp. Up in the morning with the frost. Ordered round like something that's got no dignity. And making fun of a bloke out on the firing range, laughing their bloody heads off when I got a red-hot Bren cartridge down my shirt. See, there's some bloody

Federal law that they can't just send you out to get shot, they've got to humiliate you first . . . I suppose you reckon I should have just shot myself if I wanted to die.'

I rushed to assure him that I'd never reckon anything of the sort.

'I thought of it all right,' he went on. 'But the funny thing was I could never do it, straight off like that. I used to be able to cut myself with a cleaver when I was at the abattoirs, and I bet that hurt more than shooting yourself. But that was two things I couldn't do—shoot myself, and squeeze my own boils. Ever. Hilda used to have to do the boils for me.'

He shut his eyes tight again. When he opened them, he asked, 'You wouldn't want me to go to jail?'

'No, I never would!'

'What about your girl-friend though?'

The *girl-friend* spoke for herself. 'No, *I* never would,' she said.

'I'm not always soft and easy like this,' the Comrade told us apologetically. 'I can't trust myself. Neither can you. Trust me, I mean. If I ever thought you'd tell the others about me here, I couldn't trust myself not to bust into your place one night. Or yours, girlie. And then I'd do you a violence.'

Our eyes must have begun to widen with fear.

'I'm not threatening you,' he assured us. 'I couldn't be bothered. I'm just saying, I can't trust myself any more. So I've got to be able to trust you. I told you, I'm often down there in the dark, circling round the place.'

He stood as a self-aware Moloch clothed in a skin of geniality. We had no doubt, neither did he, that appeasement was his due. With heads strangely bent down, Fy and I appeased and assured him for all we were worth. At last, we managed once more to gaze up at his face. His head seemed empty, and his face the colour of old and leprous Sicilian marble. I believed that if we had the courage to poke at his dead eyes, we would find them paper-thin, and an empty skull beyond.

'You'd better get home,' he said. 'But I'll be watching you to the top of the Cape. It'll be a sort of token if I do that. I'm your friend now, Daniel.' It was a sort of threat, for the first time that day. 'I'm your guardian angel.'

While we made a slow path up the beach, a fury of a surf came running in, siffling round our ankles. We didn't run, and a full three-quarters of an hour would have seen us up the side of Fourteen Mile. But when we turned back to look at the beach for a last time, we could see the mile-off, tiny man still gazing up at us to find if he could trust us. At last he turned away with his old berley bag, and the scrub reached down the dunes, consuming him.

23

Fy may now be insulated, as I shall point out later, by the talents of Press agents and so on, against that plump, scabby-legged fisherman's child in too capacious, hand-me-down dresses: yet she no doubt remembers, with an intense remembrance, the Cape days.

Sometimes, perhaps in February or around the equinoxes, you had to huddle under iron roofs roaring with cyclonic rain, and watch the sea go fully as mad as if this were the coast of Iceland. But most of the Cape days were, like melons, split open with ripeness and the sun.

At the end of the front beach at the Cape were a series of low hills tipped forward into the sea to make a number of small, steep beaches. These we used, on the right sort of day, for a game invented by Fy, and called *dodgings*. As presiding spirit, Fy sat on a lump of sandstone under one of the palms that managed to live, the tips of their fronds dead with salt, along the coast. In the pauses between breakers, she ordered us to run across the wet stones. One of the rules was, of course, that we had to abide by Fy's word; and Colly and I watched each other, waiting for a disobedience which would have meant cowardice. Fy could judge the waves perfectly. As we neared the end of our run of fifteen yards or so, we were often aware of the green palate of water arching up beside us, and would have to fling ourselves to safe ground. The sea came in with a constant fury in those little gulfs, and would have ground us down a strand of gibbers before drinking us whole, if ever Fy had made a mistake in timing.

In such sport, whole mornings were passed.

In the clear and utterly contented mornings, you could hear or be woken by the Amberleys waking each other. Mr Amberley was a wealthy draper patently consumed by a boyish love for Mrs Amberley. Towards the end of 1942, when it became clear that the coast would not be invaded, they came to live at the Cape, in a long bungalow on the side of Fourteen Mile Mountain.

Mr Amberley would usually be the first of the two to wake in the morning; and raising himself on his pillow, he would begin to sing *The Indian Love Call* to his doughty love, trolling lightly at first, but pealing the song out in the end, and filling the village with his fine baritone. Waking, Mrs Amberley would join her less self-sure soprano to the song, and together, the deeply attached couple would battle up and down the hills of sound. It was a thing worth waking to. Both had good voices which rang well in the amphitheatre formed by the sides of Fourteen Mile and Warialda, the mountains.

Then, after breakfast, they would stroll down the hill to ask at the Post Office if there was a letter from their son, believed to be a prisoner-of-war in Malaya.

About fifteen miles north of the Cape was a headland called Blazing Head. Beyond it was a three-mile sliver of beach, and a town on a low hill which flung an arm of rocks wide out towards the sea lanes. These rocks were called Pollyanna Rocks, after a ship which had been wrecked on them. The town bore the same name.

Blazing Head carried on its hump the still substantial ruins of a nineteenth-century granite jail. During World War One, this had been restored to hold German prisoners and internees from Papua and the whole Pacific, even from the Gilbert valley itself. In late 1942, it appeared to be still in good condition, standing up as grand as Tintagel on its granite outcrop above the sea.

As summer began, a company or so of Army engineers arrived in truck convoy on Blazing Head. The Pollyanna Rocks people were disquieted to see an entanglement being set up around the jail. Suddenly, the editor of the Gilbert *Argus* brought out a special newssheet claiming that the Army meant to put Japanese prisoners-of-war on Blazing Head. The government prosecuted him under some special war-time security act (which has probably never been repealed). On the day he was escorted aboard the Sydney Mail at Gilbert, the whole valley was along the station and all the way along the railway line down to the river, cheering him. The government had told them that the Japanese were anti-European fanatics with their eyes on Europe in Asia, and Europe in Asia was Australia. The people did not want the Japanese in their valley, on their coast, watching the fishing boats from Pollyanna and the Cape, watching the evening smoke waft up from dairy farms along the river, plotting fantastic escape.

'Down on the Lachlan or Murrumbidgee,' Finnie kept saying, 'where they can't see a damned thing. That's the place for Japs!'

Mrs Hogan, being not given to political agitation, minded young Brian and me while Stell and Finnie went into Gilbert to attend protest meetings. At one of these, a spokesman for the Department of the Army told how the Commonwealth government had acquired the use of the Crown Land on Blazing Head, stated that the old jail had been found unsuitable for human habitation, but that the government would not be swayed from its decision to place a P.O.W. camp on the Head. A great part of the materials and personnel required for setting up such a camp were already allocated, and could not be re-allocated without great expense. He assured his audience that the Japs would be adequately guarded by two companies of infantry.

As the Gilbert *Argus* said, Argive tongue in cheek, 'The meeting burst out into pandemonium. Curses were yelled from the body of the hall, despite the presence of women. The representative of the Department was asked why didn't he put up the Japs in his own home suburb, and was called on to do a number of unnecessary and unnatural things with his two companies of infantry. The crowd began to invade the platform, and Mr Malone was hustled out of the back door of the hall by the police. Many people in the audience who have sons, brothers and husbands fighting overseas, feel that their home soil has been betrayed, and that in a way, a part of their valley has been delivered into the hands of the enemy.'

In December 1942, my father's anti-aircraft regiment was shipped from Libya to Ceylon, and Stell made novenas against his being sent to New Guinea. Matt had already gone off to that theatre of war as if to the Riviera and, on New Year's Day 1943, was wounded, suffering shocking damage to that mighty left arm he had thrown around so prodigally on the night of the fight in Sydney.

Fy's father, stationed at the Army Training Camp near Gilbert, found himself assigned to one of the two far from full-strength companies which were to guard the Japanese at Blazing Head.

Mr Oakley came often to call on Finnie and, for a time, Finnie and Stell seemed to consider him the soul of wit. Towards the end of the year, sitting and yarning with Finnie became Mr Oakley's main recreation, and Stell warned me against doing anything silly in the classroom on the basis of the teacher's familiarity with us, and on the basis of my knowing that his name was Jack, that the taste of fish (which children often brought him—*a luvly snapper, sir*) nauseated him, that he voted Labor, and looked forward to the coming of conscription as a slave looks forward to his emancipation.

It must have been nearly the end of the school year when our relationship with the school-teacher had reached its zenith and began, sourly, disconcertingly, to decline. Finnie would be found grumbling around the kitchen on the nights when Mr Oakley was due. Stell would, on some unreal pretext, take Brian and me to pass the evening in Hogan's kitchen. I can remember waking on a rug and pillow in front of Hogan's hearth, and gazing about, mind out of joint with sleep, to find Finnie half-kneeling beside me, saying, 'Come on, mate! The men have all gone mustering, and it is nearly day.' Which was a line from an old shearing song.

And then, he'd lump me home, past the edge of the droning swamp and his aboriginal lavatory, picking a way through the grass, Stell following with Brian in her arms. To be taken back into Finnie's house at those times was like returning after temporary dispossession.

In school, I found myself examining Mr Oakley when he wasn't looking, which wasn't often. For a new element had come into his teaching, a symptom, as it turned out, of new hope and new youthfulness. He would launch himself from some simple historic or geographic fact and commence to glide away, doctrinizing, moralizing, his eyes flicking around the room, seeking mine, pushing his ideas into me with neophyte fervour. It was as if an insoluble connection lay between me and these truths which he had only now begun to believe in again. I would lower my head and look at some feature of the desk, or at Fy's proud double rubber with F on the pencil section and Y on the ink. But Mr Oakley would keep up his homily in such a way that when I couldn't see him, it seemed even more indisputable that what he said was meant for me.

The school year ended without my knowing whether Mr Oakley was priest or prophet, wizard, torturer or nuisance.

Although he declined to eat snapper, the school-teacher had at one stage asked Finnie if the old man would consider taking him out in the boat for a day's fishing. At the time, Finnie had agreed with some enthusiasm, but by December he was talking about getting the damned picnic over by Christmas, as if he didn't have to go out fishing for a living in any case.

Having fixed on a particular Saturday for Mr Oakley's fishing trip, he asked if Fy and I would like to go. 'So that at least those two will enjoy it.' Finnie gave his off-sider, a vagrant sort of bloke, part-aboriginal, called Hindu, the day off; and Hindu headed away towards Gilbert as if he would enjoy it too.

The six o'clock on which we left the landing at Gunulla's beach was very like the midday of many another day, and beyond the green tidal entrance the sea was cobalt, the horizon held itself as firmly as blue steel. Shouldering its way up the wide swell, Finnie's little petrol-driven boat sounded like the voice of insolence. The engine cowling, painted green and stuck amidships, jumped with the effort of those crucial organs it shrouded.

Finnie headed the boat into the swell and rounded the Cape. The black cliffs rose glossy with sunlight as we swung irreverently close to the cliff base. We could see the fizzing green water slopping into black caves, booming against their furthest walls. There were three such caves in the gulf beneath the Cape's marble monument. Fy and I sat quietly in the stern, thinking of the rock-climber washing into one or all three of those places, sliding down past the wide eyes, the amazed lips of bream and jewfish, to rest perhaps not so far from the obelisk to his memory.

Finnie decided to anchor on the shady bottom of the lee of Frewin Needles. The engine grunted and seized and died. The quiet filled up with lazy water noises; the boat lolled up and down, nestling into the luxury of slack tide. Then lines were got ready for Fy and me. There were little bollards along the gunwales round which Finnie wound the lines once they'd been dropped, and told us to call him if we hooked anything. It was clear that he was annoyed for not having got away from the Cape earlier, at the time we'd used up waiting for Mr Oakley to arrive at the landing.

The slack tide served us well though, and for a while Finnie had no time to fish for himself, being so busy hauling in whatever we found on our lines, gaffing sizable jewfish, knocking flathead on the skull with a hammer.

After nine o'clock, the sport became irregular. I regretted the absence of Hindu, who had been known to swim to the beach at times like this and scale a tree and sight new shoals of fish for Finnie to go after. But today was a picnic outing, so Hindu would be gulping down port in the lavatories behind Clohessy's. I wished for another fish, and spat into the sea. Fy subsided asleep in the shade of the bulwarks. Further forward, under the cabin awning, Mr Oakley and Finnie communed over a Thermos of tea, but I would not be distracted from living from second to second for that brisk, electric strain a fish hooked through its living jaws sends up the line. Dull, tea-bibbing conversation from the two men rattled on, not worth the heeding. Fy rolled in her sleep and her soft cheek went down plush on the decking. Eternal mid-morning set in then, and a straggle of gulls, rounding the Needles, groaning with boredom. We can skim the water at six inches, they said, hardly flapping a wing, playing with the updraught from the backs of waves, using the wind and water as no fighter-pilot ever did. But we've been doing it for aeons.

Towards half past nine, the sound of Finnie welting home the cork of the Thermos came like a starting pistol for a race. Until then, the two men had waited, undemonstratively, with their tea in their hands, but now it was as if tea-break was over in the wings, and two actors stepped into mid-stage to give of their lines and their assumed emotions as loudly as they could.

'Well, if a man your age can't tell when a woman's embarrassed . . .' Finnie began.

I turned my head to see if Finnie was smiling, and reverted to my fishing when it was clear that he wasn't. I found myself looking through screwed-up eyes at a hazy blue sea and, with a peculiar anguish, tried to yearn a fish on to my hook. The line trailed fairly limply in the opaque blue. There would be no fish to distract Finnie.

'Listen, don't you think it'd be better to talk it out later,' Mr Oakley suggested. I hunched my shoulders as I felt his eyes flick across them. Yes, I concurred, this is one bit of gossip I don't want to hear, for the man who teaches and corrects you for most of your day, teaches and corrects in such a way that only God is above him, can't be told off by Finnie as if he were the baker or Hindu. 'But let me say,' he went on, just as loudly, 'that people have minds like Guernsey cows. All I've done, Finnie Gavan, is to go back to school again, and learn what beauty and decency are. *You* know how I'd stopped believing in them, Finnie. You've seen me, I suppose, in Gilbert. So've others. Because some . . . somebody wrote to the Department about me. I'm the sort of bloke who's either on the mountain-top or in the swamp. And there's been more swamp than mountain-top these last few years. So when I say things like decency and beauty, Finnie, I bloody-well mean them. And I've learnt to believe in them through the influence of one person only. If I knew whether I had a soul or not, I'd say she's saved it. There, I'd say that much!'

Finnie groaned. 'I know she's a fine girl and all. But you think she's some kind of bloody missionary!'

'Listen, Finnie, there's a word I always thought was garbage. But it applies to . . . this lady we're talking about, and me. And that is *platonic*.'

'*Platonic!*' Finnie echoed. I, of course, had no idea of the meaning of the word; Finnie gave it a tainted emphasis.

'I've heard the word used by wantons and tarts in the picture shows,' he said. 'Like that strumpet Bette Davis.'

'Use any word you like,' conceded the schoolmaster. 'I haven't done anything that anyone could put an indecent interpretation on.'

'Couldn't they?' Finnie whistled, and looked out to sea, invoking the cosmos. 'And the man's just said they've all got minds like cattle!'

Mr Oakley made his hissing sound, the same he made in the classroom whenever a child put him beyond words. Neither of them said anything. They had become aware of me again. They were eyeing my laboured silence, reproaching themselves.

'It's no use arguing about it,' Finnie said, quietly enough to justify him in his tacit assumption that if I overheard him now it would be purely as a result of my own malice.

'All I can say, Finnie, is that unfaithfulness is in a person's mind long before it becomes a fact,' Mr Oakley mumbled, trying to get the last word said and the argument packed away. Then all the way home, beneath the hawking of the engine, he could be quiet and melancholy on a magnificent day, and in a fit locale for that sort of thing. 'And we both know it's not in her mind, and I can tell you, it's not in mine.'

'I know it's not in hers!' the old man agreed. 'She goes out of the house of a night just to avoid you. See, this platonic business isn't much use to her.'

'Stop using that bloody word! It was a slip of the tongue.'

Far out, a cloud-burst loomed, nudging along the rim of the ocean. It was immense and galleon-like, multi-masted with cumulonimbus the colour of pain. Unaffected, the sun went on mounting and stinging my arms. A little southerly scuttled through the Needles and gradually it would mount, putting an end to the day's fishing. I began to doze now, subsiding beside Fy. The planks were clammy from heat and wind and moisture. But I laid my sunburn down on the sticky deck, and, though it began to itch like a rash, I did not move.

'Look,' Finnie began again. 'You can't trust this platonic business. It's an excuse for other things. It's a wolf in sheep's clothing.'

'Thank you!' Mr Oakley said savagely. 'Either I'm a liar, or I don't know my own mind. If you were a bit younger I'd ram that choice right back down your bloody throat.'

'*Every man is a liar*, one of the psalms says,' Finnie told him, far too calmly. 'And if a man of your intelligence still thinks people know their own minds, well . . . Dammitall, people go after what they want in a pretty roundabout way. There was a bloke off a dairy farm out near Pollyanna. I don't suppose you know him.'

Mr Oakley spat overboard in anger and, unfortunately, into the wind. 'Don't you think we could get started for home?'

'In my own time, thank you, in my own bloody boat.'

'All right, tell us about your dairy-farmer, and let's get going.'

'He wasn't a dairy-farmer,' Finnie said deliberately. 'He did share-cropping with the Truscotts, and his younger brother married one of the Truscott girls. Vera. I think it was Vera.' And then, savagely, 'It might have been Fay.'

'All right!' said the subjugated teacher.

'Well, this share-cropper used to hire the Oddfellows' Hall in Gilbert for every Sunday night. This was over twenty years ago. He could preach, that man. He could preach rings round any monsignor I ever heard. He was so good we were warned from the pulpit not to go near him. They told us that he was some sort of heretic, that he taught salvation by faith alone or some other thing. But partly it was because even if he came off a dairy farm and learnt his Bible in the cowshed, that man could preach better than they could.'

'I'm not interested in church matters,' Mr Oakley grunted.

'This isn't a church matter. If you want me to, I'll get you so tangled in twenty-year-old gossip, you won't get away before bloody midnight.' Finnie laughed shortly then, and there came no answering noise from Mr Oakley. 'This bloke was like you and me. He started off to do something good. He started off to preach faith. And there'd be a few hymns. After a while, the preacher's sister began dancing to the hymns. So did all the women of that bent, and there were some wild ones up there swaying in those days, I can tell you. Then she began to have fits, and she'd pick up a sabre and hack herself with it. There were people who reckoned she had the gift of tongues. A lot of people got a bit frightened and stopped coming to listen to the brother. All sorts of people got mixed up in the dancing, and the fits, and flogging themselves until they collapsed, and slicing into themselves. People would be wriggling on the floor like blood-worms. Some were bleeding, and a lot bubbling at the mouth, and women lying around screaming. And in no time of course, Babylon was builded there, beneath the roof of the Oddfellows' Hall in Gilbert. You can understand what I mean?'

'I can understand you!' Mr Oakley said jaggedly. 'I can see you think I've got rotten intentions.'

'Oh, you're not that sort of person.' Finnie was diplomatic in view of a little fishing boat's deck being so unsatisfactory for brawling. 'I think I'd be the first at anyone's throat who said you were. But that bloke off the dairy farm wasn't a complete freak. We're all a bit like him. Especially when we start using fanciful words. Platonic's a word like that. It's a sort of slogan, and it's bloody suspicious.'

The brunt of the southerly now arrived, inevitable destroyer of a solstice heatwave. It was one of the rules that fishermen seem to make and the fish tolerantly keep, that a brisk southerly is the finish of fishing. But we had a few baskets full, so that, even from the business side, the day was not utter failure.

'Here's the big wind,' Finnie said, an old man expressing an old heart's relief. 'At least a man'll be able to sleep tonight. Hey, just look at those two Dogger Bank fishermen there. Laid out like marines.'

His voice gave over to the wind. It filled my shut-eyed universe, occupied the silence which grew to become primeval and terrifying. Through half-closed eyes I had a glimpse of sunlight, and that at least was a reassurance.

'The simple fact is,' Finnie stated at last, 'you'll never get a decent woman to believe in this platonic business. They can smell a rat in all that sort of thing. A hell of a rat. I used to go in for it myself, thinking of a girl as if she was the Madonna or Joan of Arc or Saint Bernadette, expecting her to talk as if she was Sappho the poetess. And, you know, the beggars never will. They go on talking about the price of pumpkin. That's how they protect themselves against blokes like us.'

Then he paused. 'You've got nothing to say?' he asked.

'No, I haven't,' Mr Oakley said, laying down the words like final cards.

'We may as well get going then. That's a day's petrol ration gone.'

'I'm sorry.'

'No need to get all offended. We got a few baskets. And it was well worth coming out here, for other reasons than fish.'

Finnie stepped over me to pull in Fy's line and mine. This was a judicious time to stretch and stir and sit up wide-eyed and cranky at myself for slipping off to sleep.

'Hullo, Dannyboy. Had a good rest? How's that anchor, John?'

From the bows, Mr Oakley gave a bland Winston Churchill sign. Finnie got the engine turning with the second pull of his greasy old trip rope, and its raucous grunting woke Fy who sat up puffy-eyed, looking displeased.

I ran forward for the pure excitement of moving. The wind boomed in my ears, and Finnie smiled at me. He was happy to have the day over so soon. No doubt, he would wash and dress, and get into town on the quarter to one bus to spend the afternoon and an illegal portion of the night at Clohessy's pub, seeing friends.

Fy came up, gobbed with the loft of the wind, challenged me with her eyes to gob further than she could.

'Well,' Finnie growled, 'if you two aren't the elegant ones!'

One leg up on the gunwales and one arm laid along the top of the cabin, Mr Oakley spent his time gazing beachward to the piratic-looking sands and the olive forests behind. He kept his lean shoulders away from us as if the coast were a novelty to him, and as if he had to face far more than the three of us if he turned around. As the Cape came wallowing up to us, he swung towards us and yelled, 'Let's get this clear, Mr Gavan. These people we've been talking about. They don't want me to go near them any more?'

'I'd be a liar,' Finnie told him cheerfully, 'if I said they did.'

'All right!' said the schoolmaster.

Soon Finnie turned into the tidal creek and cut the engine, gliding in towards the whole fishing fleet, such as it was, lying at sabbatical anchor along the landing.

'I can see I did make you waste a day's fuel,' Mr Oakley commented, nodding at the other boats.

'It's all right, Jack. Those others are just too bloody foot-loose to work of a week-end.'

But helping to moor the boat was the last thing the schoolteacher ever had to do with Finnie Gavan.

24

One thing that you'll no doubt say of this random coverage of ten months of childhood is that it's shambling. But not as shambling as you had begun to fear. For those ten months *were* an era. The Mantle era, you would have to call it; and it extends beyond the inquest on Dolph and Lennie to a time in early 1943 when a more sizable disaster than the grenade put an end to it. These being the only two disasters of which I can personally speak.

And so Fy and Colly have been introduced, a shallow introduction, but I can't help that. While, more shallowly still, you have had the great Cape represented, the spirits native to it, the wild inestimable forests that dwindle down to its edge, and the azure coasts that can be seen from its crest.

There will be no time later to tell you about Fy whose very face you know as well as feature articles and films can make a face known. It began with a season at Stratford, where she played Desdemona and other parts. Lately I saw her myself from a three-guinea seat in Melbourne when she toured in a series of Sean O'Casey. I mention the three guineas to show that a tour by Fy Hogan is a foregone triumph, costing the public more than a Test match or a Victorian Football League Grand Final. Even from the gods though, I would have recognized her by the way she flounced, which has not changed since the Cape days. And then her films.

Having won a Cannes award, she earned an inverse notoriety in the tabloids for her wholesomeness. Her Italian ski-champion of a husband is said to keep a censoring eye on all her film parts.

Every two or three years, Colly and I blunder into each other for a few minutes. As on a fierce January day last summer, when I was fishing alone knee-deep in the surf on Fourteen Mile. About mid-afternoon a Land-rover catapulted over the edge of the sand-bank behind me. Colly was at the wheel, and his small son in the back. We talked of Fy of course, and he asked me what I did for a crust, and clearly disapproved. He himself sells bait to tourists and molluscs to a fish-paste factory. In winter he cuts timber. The blue distances of the cedar forests, the golden farm which was Fourteen Mile Beach, he seemed, by the colour of his eye, to have firmly in control.

He looked like an utterly happy man.

On a Sunday in early February 1943, Mr Hogan took his monthly twenty-four-hour leave pass. He liked to let leave accumulate, but the orderly room sergeant had bullied him into taking his leave for the sake of keeping the books straight. Later, when Mr Hogan knew that, but for that leave, he would never again have seen Mrs Hogan, Fy, and Me, he felt a surge of respect for the orderliness of the orderly sergeant. But that Sunday evening, leaving the blacked-out village unowned and unprotected in the wide, luminous night, he knew only an unmanning pathos for his wife and children, alone below Warialda with kerosene lamps for company.

His way of getting back to Pollyanna prisoner-of-war camp before the pass expired was always much involved with fish. Into Gilbert in the Cape Fishermen's Co-op truck, loads of fish in the back to be sent south on the Sydney Mail. Then he'd hang around the Pollyanna Rocks truck, going back empty, until Alby Rood, the ikiest of men, would tell him he might as well ride back in it as catch a taxi. Alby, of course, like his breed, made you beg for a ride, then dumped you at Rood's place in Pollyanna with hardly a grunt of good-bye.

That was the way things went on the humid Sunday evening in February. Hogan was set down on the edge of Pollyanna. Before him was a three and a half mile walk to the camp below Blazing

Head. Hogan did not resent walking. He resented nothing, and resents nothing today. But he was quite frankly scared of what you could call *the dark*.

This behind-the-beach dark, which his second-sighted forebears from Mayo or some place had summoned up and peopled with phantoms, this was what frightened him. *Darkness* you could call it, yet it was dark only in its lower reaches. Higher up, it was a purple dome painted with burlesque stars. A little off the road, the night was a show of wizened shapes and pallid, epileptic trees. Where one second you saw a tortured gum, the next might show you a likewise stunted soul.

It was not the Japanese he feared. His first few times on his way back from leave, he had looked for them and forgotten the ancient ghosts. There was so much propaganda about Japan, about what suicidal buggers they were. For a while there, at the start, you would have expected them to charge the wire in their underwear, in daylight. But, separated from most of their officers they showed, with an alacrity that would have done credit to any European, that they could tell which side their bread was buttered. The fish and fruit and rice which went in quantity into the Japanese other-ranks compound at Blazing Head had made the prisoners into a genial race. Captain Saito, who could speak English and acted as liaison officer, most of the time anyhow, in the other-ranks compound, had complained apologetically that the rice was short-grained. 'Perhaps he wants us to import some from Malaya,' the C.O. told his officers later. Altogether, the Japanese were nothing but amenable, and amongst themselves very peaceful. They had their basketball and baseball, wrestling, boxing, judo, and so on. They had classes in obscure Oriental subjects; and every likely day, a party of them would be taken fishing on the camp end of Pollyanna beach. Whatever these men caught went to the two half-strength companies guarding the camp, for the army did not supply its own with anything very edible or fresh in the way of fish.

In the evenings you would hear the prisoners sing, sometimes in disorganized bunches, sometimes joining in, hut-full by hut-full, until the night was full of the twisted poignancy of their songs. At times such as that, Hogan knew with a shock that the race beyond the wire was human. It was a knowledge which disturbed him, forced him to mistrust the War Cabinet, the films, the newspapers, who, in the interests of total war, had convinced him of the sub-humanity of Japs.

So he reverted to the old homely terrors he had known as a boy. For there were apter ghosts than skulking Japanese to fill the scrub around him. Ghosts like the ghosts of blacks who had stolen a red-headed infant (later Hogan's grandmother) and fêted her as a princess on their walkabout along the beaches. When caught by police and armed settlers, they had given her up as quietly as they gave up a continent, and disappeared amongst the she-oaks. They were what Hogan hoped not to see that night. Or more intensively still, he hoped not to see the spectres of the twenty chained felons who went down cursing amongst the bream in H.M. George IV's sloop *Pollyanna* the night it ground itself to bits on the Rocks that bore its name.

The prison camp itself, hidden to seaward by the low bulk of Blazing Head (there had been bushfires there the day Captain Cook sailed by, bushfires in the southern autumn of 1770), was circular in shape, and straddled the road. Compound M, on the west, was for N.C.O.s and privates, and was nearly half-full with Japanese captured at Lae and Salamaua, Milne Bay and Buna. These being battles in which few prisoners were taken by either side, there were fewer than five hundred men in Compound M.

The semi-circular area across the road was divided into a large compound for Japanese and Indonesian internees, and two smaller areas, one at either end, the first being the hospital at the south end, the other occupied by thirty Japanese officers.

One thing Hogan was attuned to was silence; and a lot of people think they hate the dark when it is only silence they fear. As part of his silence, he had always had the row of the sea, which was to him no more of a noise than the pounding of his own heart. Living his whole life at the Cape, he could hear trucks which changed gear on the far side of Warialda or the moo of one of the Cape's big-hipped, stupid cows that had wandered off into the swamp. Tonight, it being now almost ten, he could hear the Japanese sing-songing when he was still a mile and a half from camp.

That was something the C.O. seemed a little wary of—noise in the compound at night, especially after half past nine, his own bed-time. He wanted to be able to forget a camp that had been fed and pacified for that day, wanted to bed himself in quiet with a whisky bottle and a novel. But some nights, he had to let the noise go on until theatre-closing time. These were special nights for the Japs—the Emperor's birthday for example, or the day of the Divine Wind.

To Hogan, the noise that night seemed not at all menacing, but companionable. It helped him hold his breath less for fear of what might be beyond a corner whenever he came to one. So he swore all the more plentifully when, out of the shadows beside the road, someone stepped with a rifle and yelled, 'Halt!'

It was apparently a young fellow from the infantry training school in the hills beyond Gilbert. He and his mate—the mate was in darkness and Hogan could hear only the voice—were part of a training company which was at this moment securing the camp end of Pollyanna Rocks beach from invasion. That particular stretch of sand was secured from invasion on at least one night a month by young recruits who would be formed up at one in the morning and marched all the way back to their camp. These two men—and Hogan believed the term to be purely nominal—had been detailed to secure the road against use by fifth columnists, who might try to guide the enemy invasion barges into the beach by means of lights. All they wanted for now, they told Hogan, was some identification. His pay-book would do.

Hogan told them to go to hell. What was the use of a stripe if you had to show your pay-book to every snot-nosed recruit who asked for it. A very young, slight officer came up, listened to his men, and likewise demanded Hogan's pay-book. Hogan refused. The officer asked him his name and number, and Hogan, with all the heavy insolence of his breed, not only told him to go to hell, but asked him for his own pass-book, as he, Hogan, was in no way certain of the officer's authenticity. The officer had enough character not to lose his temper, nor to pursue a lost war. He told Hogan to get on his way and to expect to be reported to the C.O. at the prison camp. Striding off, master of the dark now, Hogan called back that the C.O. was already undermanned to buggery, sir, and that he'd be likely to take a lot of notice, like hell, sir!

It was well after ten now, and the first watch-tower on the left of the road was looming. Hogan called to the man up there from quite a distance away so as not to alarm him. The singing in the main compound continued, more lurchingly now, less concertedly. You could hear the genial spirits the Japanese made from rice and potato peelings flooding into the voices, separating one from another, making them lurch round the curves of the song. Soon the sing-song would be finished. It had gone drowsy as the whole night had, from the sheltered waters of Pollyanna Bay flapping the beach below him, to Hogan himself, drowsy with triumph, having stood up for the common soldier against some Great Public School pansy of a grazier's son.

In the orderly room, the corporal had been dozing.

'Bit of a noise among our Nippon brethren,' Hogan mumbled, signing the book the corporal heaved towards him. 'What's the big occasion?'

'Don't know, mate. Might be their wedding anniversary.'

'Well, why's the C.O. letting 'em make all that racket.'

'C.O.'s gone to Sydney. Wife's sick. Adjutant's in charge. Anyway, no need to shut 'em up. Not doing any bloody harm.'

'Yes, but a bloke's got to get his sleep, mate.'

'Amen to that, dig! Go to bloody hell or someplace, will you?'

Hogan brewed himself a spot of tea in the cookhouse, went off to wet on the edge of the scrub and, self-indulgently omitting to wash, fell into bed 'like an abo'. There were five men from Hut D who'd just gone on watch an hour ago. If he'd refused to be bullied into taking leave, he also would have been on watch tonight with the leave accumulating in a sunny limbo somewhere between heaven and the orderly room.

By arching his back on the bunk, and pulling away his blackout curtains, he checked on the position of the Southern Cross—the Pot stars his wife called them, for their profile was that of a saucepan. She'd told him when he'd first joined to look at the Southern Cross each night as she would, so that they'd know they were both under the same heaven. Fat bloody consolation! They were queer cattle, the ladies. Yet, he'd found himself seeking out so often the Southern Cross in the night sky that it had become a nocturnal habit. Well, so was cleaning your teeth, but he'd managed to skip that tonight. So that looking for the Pot stars had become a worse habit than cleaning your teeth. But this was surely only a manly failing in a bloke who'd used strong language to an officer and probably got away with it.

On the penumbra of sleep, he was aware that the singing in Compound M had sputtered out. The adjutant also lifted his head and heard the customary silence of the camp, *his* camp tonight. How demoralized, he thought, in the strict sense of the word, the Jap 'other ranks' were. And yet how contented.

Down the middle of the camp ran George Street, simply a wired-off section of the road up which generations of picnickers had come to eat cake and drink beer in the shade of the old granite jail on Blazing Head. The main gate of the camp was at the hospital end of George Street and, a hundred yards inside it, the gate of Compound M debouched on the road. Two soldiers patrolled George Street, and it was a weird place to be alone in at night, with the Japs sawing away at their homesick ballads, and your mate anything up to six hundred yards away. Each of these two guards carried only three clips of ammunition in their flabby basic pouches, as it was believed, rightly or wrongly, that the chances of escape via George Street were clearly slim, and that guards would tend to be more prudent if their means of self-protection were limited.

At half past eleven, the nineteen-year-old guarding the south end of George Street saw the door of a hut in Compound M fall open. This produced an effect very much like an instantaneous combustion of part of the blank barrack walls. Within an instant, the blazing gap in the darkness spilt out five blunt-headed figures. Their loping indistinctness terrified him as they moved in a pack to the Compound gate and began shaking it, as if to shake it down. All the while they babbled drunkenly, no longer the patient, contented rabble the camp commandant had begun to believe them to be, but now the traditional incomprehensible Asian, indulging an insane gesture.

But the boy could see their faces in the moonlight now, and was no longer afraid of them. He kicked at the wire.

'Get back or I'll blow your bloody noggins off,' he yelled.

They were like men in a debased sort of ecstasy. You could smell them. They were all sweat and frenzy and gibberish.

'All right, then,' he said, like a schoolmaster. He cocked the rifle and flipped the safety catch. Taking aim on a star, he shot it down. The Japanese backed from the gate reproachfully, then bolted back to their hut.

The main gate, all wood and wire, shrilled like an orchestra tuning as it opened. Through it crunched the officer of the watch wanting to know what and why the hell.

'*They were shaking the gate?*' he roared. 'Look, private, it's a bloody solid gate and you know it. Isn't there a standing order about discharging firearms?'

He didn't give the soldier time to reply.

'You fire only when ordered, except in an emergency. Now I don't call drunken Japs shaking a gate an emergency.'

'You'd be more likely to if you were here alone, sir.'

The boy could hear the officer swallow.

'All right, private! What if you report to me for special duty at midday, tomorrow? And perhaps we'll get you to shake away at the main gate all afternoon, and see who's still standing in the end. You or it.'

There was no sound any more from any of the compounds. The awakened garrison was told it had all been a mistake. Men swore and creaked back to sleep. In the four Vickers gun emplacements, guards untautened their back muscles, rubbed and relaxed their eyes. The men on the Bren guns slipped off the magazines. On the watch-towers, the safety catches of hair-trigger Owen guns slid down into place. The watchers around the perimeter became dazed once more with the opalescence of sub-tropic moonlight on iron roofs. Next thing, they thought, it would be morning.

The kerosene lamps were still burning, however, beneath the placidity of the hut-tops; and only the most drunken slept. In one of the huts, two soldiers who had volunteered for the wire moved down the avenue of cots, gathering all the clothing they would be needing when the time came for them to lay themselves like mats against the barbed fence. Half the hut sat on their bunks talking in low voices. The other half were gathered around Private Aggai Haduchi and his school atlas. Although they were arguing, it was somehow easy for them, tonight, to argue as quietly as any men in any argument could.

Aggai had his atlas open at the page where, in a few strong, basic colours, the Pacific area lay explained. It was a greasy-looking page. Tonight many an emphatic finger had stabbed at it. Aggai's thesis was that, however much this was to be regretted, it was impossible for a Japanese army to have landed in Australia. He did not claim that Captain Saito lied, but that he must have been mistaken. Through their illicit shortwave radio, they had all heard the war news. They had heard cautious Japanese bulletins, rhapsodic American Japanese-language broadcasts. They knew, by taking a middle road between the two, that Japan had for a time lost sea power in the South Pacific. I also, Aggai said, wait for a Japanese army to land in Australia. But this army which you claim to have arrived, where has it come from? From New Guinea? (This must have been a rhetorical question, for all the men about him had fought in New Guinea, and knew that the Japanese were somewhat more than contained there.) From Java? A Japanese convoy moving from Java towards the east coast of Australia would be open to flank attack, and eventually to frontal attack, in a great number of places along its route, whichever route it took.

From Aggai's diary, we can tell that his profession of a desire to see a Japanese army invade Australia was a lie, a pious lie, a lie to help save lives. Aggai did not feel the want of anything any more in the emotional, frenzied way all those others did. He was a Methodist in whom the loneliness of prison life and a lack of spiritual kinship with his fellow soldiers had provoked a latent mysticism. His life had become strangely sterile, improbably detached and easy. So much so that he expected this detachment to become obvious to the guards, as obvious as contempt would be on the face of another man. One morning, he couldn't help believing, the prison authorities would call him to the gate, and let him go off seeking botanical curiosities in the strange green hills behind the beach.

Since half past nine that night, Aggai had been stating and restating his few clear arguments, tracing the course of a possible convoy, running his finger through the blue straits, indicating Lae as a possible trap on one side of New Guinea, and Port Moresby on the other; reminding them of the obvious strength of Allied airpower in the Pacific from the increasing numbers of planes they themselves had seen flying over Blazing Head, escorting troopships or engaged in less easily ascertainable operations.

His difficulty was not the geographical naïveté of his comrades. Nor was it the ease with which their fingers slid down the incline of the East Indies, and came to the immense natural terminus of the Australian continent. It was not that they refused to be quiet long enough to allow him to present his argument as a whole, that they attacked examples as if they were principles, and enmeshed his logic in a net of peasant inanities: his true difficulty lay in that they were content with this new-found exultation and didn't care at all if a lie was at the base of it. It was all they lived for now, to fling themselves at the fifteen-foot wire, which was, no matter what they were fed, or how they were diverted, the wall of Limbo.

In the lamplight, one of them belched and smiled ponderously. Another then accused Aggai of having a Japanese body but a European spirit. At this, Aggai pulled his fatigue trousers down from his side to show the scored blue-white formlessness where a Bren gun bullet had borne away half his hip at Salamaua. I am a cripple for Japan, he said, and I will die for Japan if that is needed.

This gesture initiated a series of wound showing, and those with a scar to bring forward were so vocal that the sergeant moved along the aisle and ordered them all to their bunks. Aggai, watching them grope away, was all but panicked into a state of despair. They were content to be silent, and loll on their bunks, and prepare their belongings, when in an hour or two, half of them would be slaughtered at the wire. If he betrayed their intentions, it was treachery; if he did not betray them, they were carrion, and their souls would curse him in hell.

The prisoners were unnaturally quiet now, reclining with every appearance of thoughtfulness, each on his bunk. After a time, Aggai became aware of the sergeant and four other men making their way down the aisle, their eyes fixed on a point at the far end of the hut. Without warning, they wheeled and surrounded Aggai's bed. 'We need your clothes,' the sergeant explained, and Aggai smiled irrationally, pleased at being asked to have a small part in their insane scheme. Of course they could have his clothes. There had been no need to send a squad to get them.

He had time to undo a shirt button. Then two held his legs, and two his arms, while the sergeant smothered him to death with some thing typically Western, a pillow. He probably did not suffer as much as other men would, dying that death. He had his faith; and he knew that beyond the syncline of agony lay release from his terrible moral burden.

The men he had reasoned with watched the murder quietly. When the flutterings of his lame little body had ceased, the sergeant and the four stripped the corpse and covered it with a blanket.

There were other huts where dissidents from the escape plot were variously assassinated. The five men who had earlier tried to appeal to the sentry in George Street were all cajoled back to their hut and knifed. In another hut, a man was hanged; and elsewhere, some were garrotted.

The two liaison officers in Compound M remained in their shut-off quarters at the end of a hut near George Street until early morning. Yet one of them, at least, must have condoned or even ordered the slaughter of such men as Aggai. Captain Saito, being in command of the escape attempt, would appear to be the one.

He was a neo-Samurai career officer, the Intelligence officer to a brigade of infantry at the time he had been captured at Buna. The temporary badges of rank of staff major he had been wearing at the time he had stripped off for the purpose of confusing the enemy on a matter that was of potential importance, the matter of his rank. He had then succeeded in passing himself off to his captors as a mere company commander.

Saito was squarely built, with a wide, bland face, and a constant twinkle of thought and judgement in his eyes. His mouth was small, taut, but not necessarily cruel.

As a result of his father's having spent four years during the 'twenties as Secretary in the Japanese Embassy in London, he spoke excellent English. He seems to have been quite fearless, with a Hannibalic disregard for loss of life, his own or those of the men in his compound. In his code of values, they were all freakish, as he himself was freakish, in being prisoners at all.

The other liaison officer had been attached to the same brigade headquarters as Saito on the afternoon it had been overrun. He had been shot in the chest, and by the time of the escape attempt was still convalescent. He had a long, pale face, and a trace of adolescent pimples round his chin. His English was university-learnt. There was a quality about his pale eyes and long, delicate lips that let you know he had not learnt it for military purposes.

It may have been his state of health, and not at all his state of mind, that made him seem to disapprove of the escape plan. But Fomaguchi knew, as Aggai knew, that there would be carnage at the fence, and those who reached the outside would all, or nearly all, be recaptured as they blundered northwards to find Saito's mythical invasion force.

Since the escape had been ordered by the senior Japanese officer, however, Fomaguchi was bound to go. Over the next four days, he would show himself to be a man of considerable endurance, bravery, and mercy.

No 1 Vickers gun was on the south-west of the fence, nearly two hundred yards back from it. So that, in fact, the gun could traverse east and west to cover nearly a third of the perimeter. At two o'clock in the morning, the three men slumped around it sat up straight when most of the occupied huts near George Street burst into what seemed spontaneous flame. Banners of orange fire fluttered straight up on this soft, humid, none-too-windy night. Almost immediately, black shapes blotted out the wire in a number of places. At first, the Vickers gunner, his offsider, and the third man in the emplacement, all thought that the wire had merely disintegrated in these places. But then it came to them that the Japanese were assaulting the fence. In the same instant that the blaze filled out the open parts of Compound M with yellow light and definite shadow, the mass of Japanese milling up to the fence sent up a sustained, barbarous yell. A number of prisoners seemed to materialize in open ground, with only the little two-strand secondary fence before them.

The Vickers gunner flicked his safety lever to automatic. His off-sider fumbled at the belt of ammunition and with the lock on top of the gun. A hundred and fifty yards to their left, a Bren gun, placed to cover one of the blind spots of the Vickers, began its cross-fire. Half a dozen escapees were clipped sideways off their feet.

'Come on, Cec,' the gunner roared to his mate. 'Talk about a gin at a bloody christening!'

He was an old digger, nearly fifty, veteran of a World War One machine-gun regiment. Though he had a complete and self-important inside-out knowledge of the Vickers, he found himself firing in bursts, traversing very little, creating a shambles just this side of the secondary fence, without having been aware of starting. Up the main fence, over the bodies of the wire volunteers, a horde of Japanese were coming whom he had to ignore.

The whole affair appeared to him not as a developing and fluid chain of actions, but rather as a series of manifestations, and, out of the blue, a doomed line of Japanese were manifested fifty yards from him. They came forward screaming, and in their hands were baseball bats and knives and staffs with honed blades in the end. The old fellow shot them neatly, and they fell with a gymnastic regularity. When he saw a wall of others racing up to fill his sights, the old gunner knew that No 1 gun position would be overrun, that in the fire-lit madness the Japs were probably already on both sides of him. He poured out the last of his ammunition while it was still of some use.

There was a queer silence when the Vickers shuddered to a stop, and the three of them knew there was no time to re-load. The third man, the one with the ·303, finished a clip while the other two watched him. Then even he had no time to re-load, but sank down into the pit, mumbling something irreverent.

'The lock,' said the old gunner, and plucked the lock out of the Vickers and hurled it far into the long grass. He was off-balance from the throw when a baseball bat cracked the side of his skull.

The Bren gun crew to the left were also beaten and hacked to death.

Lieutenant Fomaguchi walked out to the wire behind Saito. Their leisureliness was impressive, but not really brave, since all the slaughter seemed to be on the far side of the fence. This barrier was ordinarily fifteen feet high but was considerably less now, sagging outwards under the weight of the fifteen wire volunteers spaced in tiers of three along its length, and of the men who mounted over them to a dubious freedom. Fomaguchi, short of breath and climbing slowly, found that at least one of the men in the human ladder was severely wounded but held in place by the barbs, whimpering when Fomaguchi's weight was placed on his back.

The jump to the ground beyond brought the young officer close to fainting. He sought a safe part of the wire with his hands and leant against it, swearing, willing for a bullet, aware of himself, as he had often been since his wound but never before that, as a blister of blood and muscle and viscera. He was able to stumble forward beside Saito though, and able even to forget the authentic delicateness of his body when they found themselves under fire from No 2 gun position, and from the tower facing down George Street. In a few hundred square yards around No 1 gun site, there must have been nearly a hundred men dead.

In Compound M, the blaze had sunken to less sinister heights, but still the camp's strong carbon lights had not been turned on. Captain Saito reasoned that once the command were aware of the escape attempt, the searchlight would flare up, so that there might as well be a series of fires in the compound itself, lit simultaneously in a number of huts, by cracking kerosene lamps on piles of bedding. This would be an awesome thing for the guards to see. It might even provide enough light to cause the enemy to forget about his carbon lamps. And this, Fomaguchi assented in the midst of the dead, was what had happened.

Mr Hogan woke to the blabbering of a Bren gun, asked the darkness what silly coot had gone mad this time, and noticed the radiance of the fire crinkling the window pane above his bed. Ripping the black-out curtain back full length, he saw a crowd of black figures, spilling over the fence from Compound M, while behind them, dominating and pin-pointing, the fire sent waves of flame and luminosity up to blot out the Pot stars.

All he could think of was, 'History repeating its damned self', and 'Dark Satanic mills'.

'Here they come!' someone announced.

'After rifles,' said someone who was still lolling in bed with his eye over the window sill. 'As if they expected every joker in this bloody army to have his own personal rifle!'

Hogan watched them, and the rest of the hut watched them, in silence now. They padded forward with a terrible loosenses of limbs, in weird fluidity of body which suggested that they could cover ground endlessly in that coolie jog. Hogan fumbled for his webbing belt, and found it draped over the back of his bunk. He fingered its heavy buckles.

Unnecessarily; because the fat little corporal who worked in the armoury staggered out of it now in pyjama coat and underpants, carrying a Lewis gun. It was an antique armament which they sometimes trained with, and it was ineradicably a jammer. The corporal fell on his stomach on level ground, and emptied a pannier of ammunition into the hypnotic Japanese advance, scattering it to the corners of the night.

Saito circled to the back of the tower and, leaving Fomaguchi waiting at the bottom of the ladder, took an N.C.O. with him and overpowered the guard who stood firing into the scene before him in a cordite haze.

Dismounting the tower, Saito thrust the newly captured machine carbine at Fomaguchi, to the lieutenant's surprise. Together with the N.C.O., the two officers re-crossed the line of fire of No 2 gun and plunged into the scrub. Above them was a forested hill which bore a peculiar knob of granite at its eastern end. This was the pre-arranged site, where by four o'clock they were to meet three chosen N.C.O.s before descending the far side of the hill to the edge of the swamp. For although three hundred other escapees had been ordered to move north, *they* would be following the network of swamps southwards until inevitably it would bring them to a tidal creek, and fishing boats.

25

I made transitory contact with the Comrade on two occasions, both some time before the escape.

One morning a week before Christmas, I woke at four o'clock, woke without lingering and with the strange certainty that some renaissance was going on beyond the window. Pink light hung from the iron roofs of Cape village and I had a glimpse of a pink sea.

Finnie had set aside for my use a broken-down rod and a reel given to seizures. It lay in the corner of the back veranda with too many of its eyelets sprung. I fetched it around the side of the house. One rod, one sinker, one bream hook. Finding pippies for bait, I would get a wet seat, and then lose my lead after one or two casts off the rocks. But that was better than using up this superb mock-daylight in looking for one of Finnie's rusty tinfuls of all-species hooks and all-weather sinkers.

Across Finnie's front yard stood a pair of pudding-shaped lantanas with minute purple flowers. They had an unobtrusive fragrance which worked its way into the very grain of life at the Cape. Rounding one of them that morning I came on the Comrade, flat on his back, scabby face agape in sleep. He had the look of something washed up there; but in a second or two he stirred and sat up as straight as Lazarus.

'Oh!' he said thickly. His finger wagged soddenly. 'Don't say a word, Danny! Don't say a word!'

He clutched a lemonade bottle on which he must have been lying during the night.

'Another day, another dollar. Never grow up, Danny.'

The bottle he used to push himself crookedly upright, groaning all the way.

'Here,' he said, when he was finished with it, 'throw that away for me, will you?'

He headed across-country for the back lane, tripping over Finnie's two-strand fence at the side of the house. No one stirred inside.

I ran down to the beach, fishing line over one shoulder, and the bottle held lengthwise under my left arm, as if its origins were printed around it in scarlet. The easy sand came like the blessing of secrecy. But before hurling the bottle into the sea, I stared at it for a long time, and then, blushing on an empty beach, closed my eyes, put it to my mouth, drained its last few drops.

It was not simply a matter of chemistry, but a strange repugnance also that knocked me backwards and blinded me. No longer could it suffice to roll the thing into the surf. I found my pippies by digging with my feet, furiously impatient. Jogging across to the rocks at the head of the creek, I smashed it on oysters well below the high-tide mark.

The next time I saw the Comrade was on a sizzling day in the dead of January, when the only sound in the world was of locusts raving with heat. It was early afternoon, and for some forgotten reason we took to the side of Fourteen Mile. This was, by Fy's obscure astrology, the day we were to climb to the highest point of the mountain.

The sea was flat, no leaf moved. Birds had left or blended into the hard, brown forest. Heat quivered in the streets of Cape town and came in crinkled waves off the roofs. As we climbed, Fourteen Mile became all grey sandstone and spiky scrub. Grey clods of rock got in our way. Dried-out briars scratched at our ankles. Fy and I would have given up before half-way but Colly kept us going, his skinny legs taking great strides, and his face turning back to us, glistening beneath the cloth cap with uniform sweat.

We got to a place from which we could see only part of the village. Of that, the Co-op alone seemed alive, pumping a lot of smoke up its stack. Beneath its red roof, some poor beggar was curing fish. We sat for a spell, to get control of our breathing again, to let the sweat cool. Then Fy pointed along the contour of Fourteen Mile, and we saw the Comrade.

'Do you know him?' Colly asked

'He's an old drunk from across at the beach,' Fy told him.

A little below us and to our left was an exposed platform of rock. On it, the Comrade was talking to someone. Despite the stillness of the day, we could not hear what was being said. Keeping his back in view, we shuffled closer, ready to run, making amongst the leaves and thorn bushes and wilting acacias a noise I thought any sane man could have heard. Yet the Comrade never looked around at us. The time came when we were only yards from him.

As well, we saw another man who had been hidden from us till then. This one was unshaven. His face was grey from the heat. He wore a long smock-like grey shirt and grey baggy trousers. Fy's face expanded with terror as she stared at me. 'McQuaid!' she whispered. 'Martin McQuaid!'

We panicked away down the side of Fourteen Mile, looking for footholds in the confused terrain, and slamming our feet down in them an instant later. Though he didn't know why, Colly came with us, and at the bottom of the mountain we had an indecisive brawl, since I would not tell him the reason. Fy wanted to take him into our council, but I could remember the grenade business, and dissuaded her for all I was worth, using tears in the end.

Colly believed that this was simply another temporary coalition between Fy and myself, and against him. It would in that case be his turn tomorrow or next week. He went home sulking.

For two days after the Pollyanna Rocks escape, a guard was kept on the road beneath Warialda. When it became clear that those escapees who moved with any measure of decisiveness at all were striking northwards, when spiritless Japanese were brought in under shot-gun guard by dairy farmers, and recruits from the training camp marched them back to Pollyanna in dozens, the three-man guard was withdrawn. Some N.C.O.s having been found hung from trees by belts and bits of cords, it was presumed that the two officers involved in the escape had killed themselves on some uncombed mountainside. By Tuesday night, there were scarcely twenty Japanese who had not been recaptured, or at least accounted for.

The Wednesday was Finnie's birthday. His compatriot, Father Mullally, was due to a birthday tea at Finnie's place, petrol rationing notwithstanding.

It was a day of terrible heat and in Mr Oakley's small school children dozed and were unresponsive. Half a dozen blowflies sizzled discontentedly round the ceiling. Colly was away in Sydney at the specialist's, so that Second Class was now a matter of two parties, Fy and myself and, like parliaments similarly blessed, was all the more stable for it. In those torrid February days, Mr Oakley had read us a children's abridgment of Faber's works on insects, and it was Fy and I especially who kindled to the subterranean orderliness of the insect world. This surge of interest did not however imply any benefit to the insects.

The classroom was hung with projects, mainly ours, of captioned mites and moths and spiders, all stuck on to sheets of cardboard. In little bottles around the shelves, tarantulas, beetles, and white grubs gyrated in kerosene. The results of the field work of other children quickly became unbearable in the February heat, but Fy had paid attention to the problems of decay and preservation. She would first impale the creatures on a needle, then dip them into a pot of lacquer belonging to her father, and lay them out in the sun to dry. Under this process, the round red eyes of cicadas took on a baked gloss which drew Mr Oakley's praise.

Fy had become especially interested in those black scorpions which you find under rocks. She liked the way they stood up to people and doubled their poisoned tails above their heads. On that Wednesday, we planned to spend an hour after school hunting them on the side of Fourteen Mile, where there were many leverable slabs of sandstone. We had a bottle and a pair of tweezers for our work and, by the next Monday, we hoped to present to Mr Oakley a project featuring two ranks of dead and varnished scorpions.

A good southerly began to blow that afternoon and, far away down the coast, a bank of rain clouds stirred. There was shade on the mountainside, and the cool sound of leaves. We moved quickly. My work was the brute one of grabbing the rims of the stones and flipping them over. In the moist clay, a variety of creatures would lie exposed, some of them half-way down their holes. Fy's tweezers would flash down at the enamelled midriff of the scorpion who usually stood there, blinking and full of fury.

Five o'clock came. The sun was on a slant to the trees, and fell on us filtered red, rouging up the excitement in Fy's cheeks. She held the jar above her head and towards the light. It was a third full of the lean black fury of scorpions. They tried to fight, seeing each other as blameworthy for the circumstances which had come on them. But there was scarcely room or a proper surface for that. Any small wood beetle or centipede we dropped in would be dispatched with a great show of spleen, in a flurry of black pincers.

We were standing fingering the jar when Father Mullally's Hudson, stuttering like a sick aeroplane, shunted through the town and towards the reserve. The dirt road brought it in the direction of the spur where we stood in natural ambush amongst the trees.

We charged down yelling on the slow old vehicle, and patterns of sunlight and handfuls of shadow like dust flew at our eyes. Fy ran well on this sort of ground. I have seen films of her ski-ing classically in the Tyrol, within twelve thousand miles of which I have never been. Still, she learnt the principles of balance in the sandstone confusion of Fourteen Mile.

She was a little way ahead of me, to my left, when I had a furry glimpse of an arm held out in my path. Amongst a welter of ill-exposed visions of tree limbs, grey, red, tettered brown, I ducked my head to it, but it grabbed me around the underjaw, and spun me to the ground. A second later, I was hauled upright, but had seen nothing as yet. As I waited for the concussive humming to stretch each band of gristle in my head and then die out, I knew, by a faith in the logic of human relationships, that it was the Comrade. When I did look, there was that immemorial face, both tanned and unearthly pallid.

'Look!' he urged me. The car had by now arrived below us. In the front seat, the priest could be seen. In the back, a khaki jumble of men knelt on the floor. The moment Fy emerged whooping from the trees, one of them lifted his face to the glass and saw her.

'Let her go, Danny!' the Comrade hissed in my ear. 'No use sending good money after bad.'

For the man had a Japanese face, and one of those little caps which Tojo wore in the *Sydney Morning Herald* cartoons. The Comrade's advice was the wisest, whether the two of us were cowards or not. Yet I was not yet afraid of that frightened man at the window. Fy could so easily be retrieved. Apart from that, the Cape was ours, our home ground. We knew its ancient surface, and had heard the vital poundings beneath its skin. The blunt face of Father Mullally's car had not suffered this quasi-mystical experience. It seemed therefore that the crisis which had rolled down Warialda, and stricken us out of the blue, found Fy and me as devout and primitive pantheists, leaning back on our spiritual kinship with the Cape as reliantly as any of the vanished black race ever did. Throughout that curious afternoon, we were therefore not half as scared as we should have been.

I took off after Fy, and the Comrade after me. We were all in the open when the Hudson braked. Stepping out of its far front door, Mr Oakley called to us. I had not known until then that he was inside the car, and this sudden piling of known faces (the Comrade's and Mr Oakley's in particular) on my senses, dizzied me far more than fear of whoever it was keeping their heads down in the back.

'Fiona, Danny!' the teacher called, and saw the Comrade as he spoke. 'And you too, mate. You're all to run across to the surf shed.'

He lifted his eyes to the Comrade's while a muffled voice came from inside the car. He nodded.

'Now, listen to this, digger! We've got some of the Japanese from Pollyanna Rocks in here.'

His eyes flickered when he saw we didn't believe him.

'They might be wallowing round on the floor, all right. But they've got a gun, one of those little machine-guns, so you've got to do what they say, and then you'll be safe. Look, cobber or Jack or whatever your friends call you, take these two straight over! Whatever you were doing chasing them around the mulga, I don't know, but if you want them to live, take them straight over there to the shed.'

Fy, on her own between the car and us, gazed around straight into my eyes, and seemed to reproach me for the extravagance of this nightmare. Mr Oakley misread her turn of the head.

'No!' he barked. 'No, Fy! Listen, you'll live for another eighty years, and we'll get you home in time for tea, and do anything. But don't run away just now! They'll shoot you, girlie!'

Throughout his appeal, a voice from the back slowly grumbled him back into his seat.

'Go on now!' Father Mullally called in a tone kept for acolytes who spilt the altar wine, 'you three get over there!'

The salt grass reserve lay ahead of us with a few knobby cattle grazing on its edges. Not far away but empty, right on the edge of the rocks so that king tides came slopping round its tables, was the long wooden shed where gusseted matrons spread tablecloths on Sundays, while their husbands fished from the rocks, and Shirl or May or Beryl swam with the boyfriend. *Many a poor beggar's destiny was settled over ham and lettuce in there*, Finnie said once. But Sunday was the day for settling destinies in the picnic shed at the Cape. The rest of the week, it stood empty with people's names scrawled all over its boards. In another direction, towards Gunulla's beach, a few tentfuls of holiday-makers fried their evening fish. Too far away. Between the purpling sea and us lay only the surf shed, and the car herded us along and shot ahead only when we were all but arrived. It waited for us in front of the wooden steps of the shed.

The Comrade shambled beside us, mumbling reassurances, promising to save me. Of Fy he had nothing to say.

'I'll just scout the ground,' he grunted. 'I'll be looking out for the main chance, don't you worry. When I tell you to run, you run like buggery!'

Fy wept querulously all the way, and swallowed her tears as we came up to the car. Mr Oakley had already emerged from the front, and smiled broadly at us. He smiled more broadly still, crinkling the corners of his eyes, crooking his long mouth, when he thought his normality had solaced us. I became strangely peevish over this false notion. Fy had ceased crying for the same reasons that I had not yet begun. In the first place, we did not believe that the few glimpses we had had of the Japanese could ever materialize into true, commanding shapes. We even felt that our absurd advance in stumbling line across the reserve was part of some droll experiment, testing a point of metaphysical argument between the priest and the teacher. But if there *were* Japanese squatting in Father Mullally's Hudson, tears were an ultimate device which, once used, left you no further recourse but hysteria. And we had learnt the lesson in the dark of picture shows and from the radio, that the Japanese would not tolerate hysteria.

Father Mullally had already left the car and turned his key in the surf shed door. He made genial eyes at us, saying quietly, 'This won't be for long. They want us all to go inside now. That gentleman there'—he nodded to the Comrade—'had better go first.'

The Comrade moved in sideways, bobbing a head and shoulder to the priest. Fy and I followed him, both fitting through the doorway at once. Inside, we stood blinking in the mats of light thrown down by the windows facing west. We would have liked to stop at the door, and ask the priest would we be shot. A reassurance would have reduced us to mere misery, but we would not have believed him in any case.

Now we were enclosed in the meaningless, be-pennanted fibro walls, and squinted at the sleek possibility of death. Still I must have been only half-afraid for, above all, I did not want to die amongst the dusty streamers, the echoes of Saturday night intrigue and sweat and talcum. When a child can afford to be preferential about the decor of his death, it can be hazarded that he is not yet fully afraid.

So we surveyed the room like prospective buyers, and the Comrade came up behind us, mumbling, 'I won't do a thing till the right moment. But you'd better be waiting for it. You know what they say about thieves in the night. You've been taught your Bible, Danny!'

He grinned for a moment, thoroughly pleased, full of alcoholic complacency.

I could hear people milling behind me. The priest and Mr Oakley, and then, startlingly passive, the Japanese. The second last one in walked with a gait meant for blucher boots, strode to the middle of the hall, and established his sovereignty over us. This, some of us learnt much later, was Captain Saito, a man with the gift of command, which hunger, fatigue, and a barbarous stubble of beard could not take away from him.

The one who came in last was quite tall, and held a light machine-gun. His body bent back and forth across it. A minstrel who has caught a long slow beat quakes so over his ukelele. His muddy index finger curled around the trigger guard, and he gestured his four subordinates back against the wall. His grey face, half-consumed with sickness, was intent enough to terrify us.

The door was bolted.

For a long while, we eleven waited gazing at each other with different degrees of tactfulness. Now that we were conclusively imprisoned, fear pressed more closely, and I told myself that soon I would start crying quite deliberately, as befitted an eight-year-old locked up, and guarded by aliens, and threatened with death. Still my proximate emotion was a humanist interest in the men facing us—the peasants and fishermen and businessmen of Japan.

There were no criteria for a child to judge such people by in the summer of 1943. For they were a people possessed of bad faith throughout, and of unpredictable cruelties. Through their hooded eyes deadly thought patterns glinted, fixed and maliciously so, as evil and deliberate as the scale arrangements of serpents. Besides this, their further vast crime consisted in having contumaciously refused to be reasonable in an Anglo-Saxon way; in that they did not have white souls. Metro-Goldwyn-Mayer and government propaganda had prepared us ill, for Fy and I expected any fate at any moment. As far as we knew, they all stood there near the wall, not for any rational purpose, but simply to consummate a wanton cruelty on the two of us.

The man closest to us, in the position of command, wore a loose tunic still elegant. His khaki trousers seemed to be ankle-length, but it was hard to tell since below the knees the legs were thickening in layers of mud that could be smelt throughout the room.

'There!' he ordered, pointing the Comrade to the far corner of the hall. Here the surf reel stood, blue and gallant, reminiscent of the week-end heroism of men whose photographed chins had jutted towards the empty room for years on end. Like a parody of this brave mechanism, the Comrade slid down beside it.

'There!' the Japanese told Father Mullally, sending him to the centre of the far wall. 'There!' and Mr Oakley went to the other corner.

Now, with the adults safely disposed, the officer made a spacious gesture with his hand, granting us the freedom of the back wall.

For some reason, we went straight to Mr Oakley, and hunched down beside him. Glancing along the wall, I could see the priest with his eyes closed, seeming very old, and, past him, the Comrade's doleful stew of a face turned on us, with the eyes in it like two lumps of random gristle. He glared at us, and I understood that he wished to be sole saviour and sole champion, and that he saw disloyalty in my approach to the schoolmaster. But we stayed with Mr. Oakley, Fy reclining, snuffling like a person with a terrible head cold inhaling vapours. On occasion, I would find myself crying softly, though I believe this to have been intermittent.

'Will they shoot us, Mr Oakley?' I asked.

'Oh, I don't think so. They'd want to escape in one of the fishing boats, I'd imagine. Now, in case there was a sea chase, and one of our boats or one of our planes caught them, they'd want to have us with them so they could say, 'If you don't go away we'll shoot these people'. So, of course, our ship would go away for the time being. No, the Japanese would never shoot us, because then they would be unprotected. We're only hostages, and sooner or later we'll come back home again.'

The teacher grinned, seeming overjoyed with our hostage status. Yet the very concept, as explained by him, involved an infinite progression—rescuers drawing near, the gun being placed to our heads, rescuers withdrawing. Only callousness on the side of the right, and spilt blood, our blood, on the side of evil could break the unholy circle of which a hostage was part. But I said nothing, and Mr Oakley laughed and hissed at us that we weren't scared, were we? because we'd be home by tea time. And Fy played with the lid of the jar of scorpions, who writhed as she did in their own subliminal captivity.

At a nod from their officer, the Japanese sat down themselves. One of them flopped a sugar sack on the floor and drew from it a blend of food, fruit cake first, then a bag of plain flour. 'Huh!' said one of the Japanese in impatience, and the four of them crowded in on the sack. Next came what looked like a bundle of sliced meat, and there was a groan of approval from those waiting to be fed.

'Ham!' Mr Oakley laughed to the priest. 'My tea for tonight.'

The meat was unwrapped, and offered first to Captain Saito, a man accustomed to plumpness, who took a good third of the sliced ham with a princely, indiscriminate sweep of the hand.

Next, the man with the machine-gun, who also remained upright but leaning against the wall, took a small slice. Lieutenant

Fomaguchi, we found out later, was his name. He was tall, with a sensitive mouth, large ill-fed eyes, and boyish pimple scars under the three-day furze of beard. The collar of his thin, sweaty tunic hung open, and around his throat were the cavities you find round the scrawny necks and collar-bones of old men. At that time, he was sick but would not succumb; he let the wall prop him and, above all, he clung to that Owen gun with its skinny magazine of blunt little bullets.

The remnants of Mr Oakley's Sunday roast were offered then in order of rank. Saito ate well of it. Fomaguchi looked at the roof and waved it away. When it was brought back to the other ranks, they laughed and passed it around, for they had suffered three bad days. Since Captain Saito believed in his escape plan, they had therefore needed to move southwards, but could not forage or steal, nor go near any roads or settlements. They had moved along the swamp edges by night, for the swamps were an infallible highway. They had rested on the forested hillsides by day, and all they had had to eat as they rested was what they had taken with them from the camp—a few pocketfuls of cold rice and boiled fish. By day and night the insects of the swamp had come after their living blood, and their sleep had been a few hours' half-conscious twitching on slabs of sandstone. At last, they had come out of the swamp system between Warialda and Fourteen Mile, and ambushed the Hudson as it slid down the last curve before the swamp-bound corduroy road into the Cape.

After school that afternoon, Mr Oakley had gone into Gilbert to see the bank manager. The interview was brief, for the bank had neither time nor finance for the Cape schoolmaster, whom his lady-friend the pharmacist had slandered up and down the dinner tables of Gilbert. He slouched back across the East Gilbert bridge, drank a few lonely whiskies at the General Kitchener, and waited on the veranda for transport back to the Cape. When Father Mullally's old car came racketing up East Gilbert hill, noisy as a travelling saw-mill, he trotted beside it for ten yards, his head in through the left window which had no glass. When the priest nodded, he flung the door wide and vaulted into the front seat.

Not that the two of them were friends. They had wrestled over the dogmas together both in private and otherwise, and I am sure that each of them harboured a private image of himself whenever they clashed. Mr Oakley being the humanist teacher guarding the minds of children from the gothic blackness of clericalism, Father Mullally being the simple curé whose sword of faith lops off the forked tongues of secularist pedagogues.

But even secularist pedagogues want to be home before dark. Thus, they had come together along the poor clay ridges, and were in sight of their evening meal when the six men descended on them, Fomaguchi stumbling right into their path, and hitching the gun to shoulder height. In this way, Captain Saito's party had acquired the Hudson and disposed themselves throughout it, one on the floor at Mr Oakley's feet, one even in the boot. They wanted food, Captain Saito told the priest, and they wanted hostages and a quiet place to hide for perhaps an hour, perhaps a day. It would have to be an excellent hiding-place. Because if any of the townspeople stumbled on it, they would be shot.

So there was a short stop at Mr Oakley's place, where he filled a gunny sack with all the food there was. Father Mullally's contribution was the surf shed, usually empty the whole week, and of which he had one of the two keys. But for Saturday dances, a rare surf club meeting, and the Sacrifice of the Mass, it was not used at all.

Twenty minutes of captivity made me used to the tall sick young man with the gun, and I crawled along the wall to Father Mullally.

'We're going to be home for Finnie's birthday,' he assured me. 'Don't turn those big doleful globes of eyes on me, son! I have said the *Memorare* of St Bernard. Do you know the *Memorare*, Danny?'

'No, Father!' I was relaxed enough at the time even to feel that I should.

'Well, I have said the *Memorare*. I don't do this often, because you could change the world out of all recognition. It never fails, you see. It is a magnificent prayer for getting what you want.'

I remembered Eucheria who had insisted that there was no such prayer ever composed and, now that the question was more than theoretical, I wanted to argue it out.

'But what if it isn't the will of God?'

'Huh!' said Father Mullally. 'That's the damned Jesuits for you, with their will of God line of talk. I can circumvent those Pharisees! I prayed that God's eternal will would be that you'd be home for Finnie's little do. God saw my *Memorare* going up to the Virgin Mary, from all eternity, and His will was fixed accordingly. So, I tell you, you'll be home for tea.'

The old man beamed with the sense of his own subtlety. He closed his eyes again.

I crawled then to the Comrade's side. His face cracked, like some dubious egg, into a crooked grin. There was a harmony of smell between the Comrade at one end of the hall and the Japanese at the other. They all gave off the peculiar methane smell of a swamp, the heavy, rotten smell of swamp-mud. Yet the Comrade had taken time to reach this stage. Mud had dried in the sun and been blown on to him, and not washed off. The odours and sweats from the reedy marshes behind Fourteen Mile had risen with the wind and been swept to him. Beside him, the Japanese were still dirty, but honestly so. Yet, between the Comrade and me there was a kinship which I would not deny even in front of Father Mullally and Mr Oakley, who watched me whenever I talked with him.

'Well,' he chattered, 'I'm definitely running for it. I've never felt better, Danny. I'm ready, son! When we leave here, I'll choose my ground, and take off in one direction, and while they're fixing me up'—he waited a second, to give me the chance to spot his brave euphemism—'you head off in the other. It's going to be so damned easy.'

But I doubted my own willingness to run at the Comrade's word. I doubted the Comrade's judgement and sense of purpose.

'But I don't want you to do that,' I said, and the words came out like a repudiation of the value of any sacrifice he could make, like a doubt on the possibility of his spilt blood being of strength to any person or any cause. All of a sudden, he knew that he would shun death and woo life with as much ardour as any child.

'They'll steal one of the boats,' he growled, 'and take us on it with them. We'll have to try to get away before then. We ought to try, anyway.'

I looked the length of the wall to Fy who had fallen into exhausted sleep beside Mr Oakley. The closed pits of her eyes were nearly blue with crying. She had rubbed away the tears with hands dirtied on the side of Fourteen Mile, so that her face seemed bruised. Against her stomach, she clutched her jar of monstrosities.

At the Japanese end of the hall, Saito had allowed his N.C.O.s only the most moderate of feasting. Now a few of them dozed, but Saito kept by the long windows, gazing at the Co-op which had closed for the day. You could hear a pump throbbing water out of the ice-box hold of one of the larger boats and, when that was done, even those few fishermen would swear and go home to tea. Saito had his eye on the boats.

It was not on behalf of a dozen and a half 'fishermen in a small way' that the Co-operative fishery operated. It increased their earnings, arranged their marketing, and halved their transport costs. But it would not have existed at all if a Gilbert combine of retailers, undertakers, and graziers had not created a fleet of long-range fishing boats, registered for New South Wales *and* Queensland waters. When the Gilbert rose, for instance, which was often, and the swamps were flushed out and fouled the sea with brown water stained by the ti-tree, these larger boats could go prawning off Stradbroke Island or trolling off Tweed Heads.

While he waited for the last of the fishermen to go home, Saito selected the boat he meant to use. *It* was the secret of his patience, his moderation, his solid control of played-out men, his keeping of the gun in Fomaguchi's hands. He could be vengeful to the back teeth if the town became aware of us, or heard the gun go off. But, in that case, he would die on the beach or, at very best, a few miles up a long, long foreign shore.

As it turned out, he decided against the clumsily named, yet forecastled and refrigerated mother ship, *Gilberta*. Its fifty feet and diesel engines were full of confusion for a simple soldier. It had the vice of being easily recognizable. Yet none of the others had any crew accommodation of the type which would have satisfied the Seamen's Union. If the boats were out for a number of days, tarpaulins were rigged on stanchions fixed around the bulwarks. Not that the boats had often been out for long lately. The week before, thirty-five men had been lost when a freighter was torpedoed a little way up the coast. The June before, a store-ship within sight of the Lighthouse at Frewin Needles, cleft by a torpedo, rolled sixty men into the snapper fisheries a few miles out. Sharks were always found there. From the Lighthouse you could see them through binoculars, and they moved in packs. Five men were saved, and all that week savaged corpses and boxes of butter had lolled up on the beaches. A trawler from Pollyanna Rocks had been shelled and, north and south, a dozen cargo ships had been sunk with almost total casualties. The burghers of Gilbert, cherishing their investment, kept their fleet close to home and in sight of the coast.

Outside, it was twilight, a little after six. Saito beckoned Father Mullally, and the two talked for a while, the priest's face crinkling into leathery folds of earnestness. He was asking Saito to leave Fy and me locked in the hall when they all left, but Saito feigned incomprehension to begin with, and ended in pointing out that often old men do not mind being punished or even killed themselves, yet will do anything to avoid having children punished or killed in their stead. He told the priest that the two of them were going out to fuel a boat and fill its water tanks. The same was told in Japanese to his own men. No sign of understanding showed on their flat, drained faces; but he got a nod from Fomaguchi, who writhed with fever but shook his head at the N.C.O. who, Saito suggested, might rest him with the gun.

Mr Oakley was called then, and his tweed coat appropriated. On Saito, it reached to the beginnings of solid mud on his trouser legs. There was a flavour of pantomime about him as he spoke to us.

'This gentleman and myself are now going to leave, to go to one of the boats and fill it with its fuel and fill the water tanks. If my man who will be at the window does not see a signal coming from me after a half an hour, you will all have to be shot.'

In the dark at matinées, I had seen men shot, Indian scouts felled without warning, stoolies tracked through dripping alleyways, ivory-hunters shot in the back as they gloated at Tarzan over open sights. A little surprise regularly showed on the faces of the newly shot, the good seemed disappointed, the evil offended, and there was no more pain than from a broken boil. Now that the word had been used with some immediacy, it anaesthetized me. My head roared. I found myself on my feet.

'Sit down, Danny!' Father Mullally muttered. 'We'll be easily finished in half an hour.'

His voice, however soft, woke Fy. She blinked, and her face went grey from despair as she verified the circumstances of her capture. She glared from the priest to Saito to her jar of scorpions, curled her mouth in immense distaste for the insects, and put them, the jar on its side, away from her sight against the skirting board.

'You are all to come with us,' Saito told us with a terrifying lack of emphasis. 'If you obey me, you will survive this journey, and our government will repatriate you when the war is finished.'

Repatriate disturbed Fy, for it sounded involved enough to be a torment. Mr Oakley smothered her face against his white shirt and clucked his tongue.

The door was opened, and Saito and the priest strode away across the reserve. Though he must have known how distinctive were Father Mullally's clothes, the captain chose to *walk* to the Co-operative. From the town came no shout or roar or sound of understanding. Southerly thunder tried to slip some warning into the chore-drugged wives and wearied men of the Cape. But no one seemed to hear.

I sat in the place left by Father Mullally. I rubbed my eyes, itchy from many half-secret tears. But Fy shook, and grief bubbled out of her lips; and it was better to be alone than caught up in her jeremiad aura.

'What's re . . .? You know, repasture . . . ?' I hissed at Mr Oakley.

'*Repatriate?* It means they'll send us home,' he said, and forebore to tell a lie about *when*. Perhaps through lack of time. Fomaguchi had placed a man at the window to look for Saito's sign. The lieutenant himself shouldered away from the wall, and came down the hall. His crooked gait made him seem to caress the Owen gun with extreme military tenderness. Small scabs of mud fell from his flimsy shoes and clotted leggings as he walked, and the quietness of his tread hinted at some malice in him, but was only extreme weakness. Against dark opposition from our eyes, he moved just as Saito spoke, each unit of movement or speech having so much labour inherent, that you doubted whether the next would be forthcoming, and were strangely delighted when it was.

He stood above Mr Oakley and Fy. The teacher blinked. Fy put her hand half into her mouth.

'There!' he told Fy, indicating me. Fy joined me. We were lonely against the middle of the back wall, far more lonely than we would have been if separate. At the other end, three of the Japanese

N.C.O.s faced us, sitting up quite stark and tense, and it struck me that they were as incapable as we of predicting their officer's next act.

As it turned out, he spoke very quietly to the teacher, even smiled once, wagged his head often. And when he and the teacher were involved in fluent negotiations, he jammed the butt of the gun down on Mr Oakley's shoulder. It should have fired then, that Owen gun, unless Fomaguchi held on to the safety slide with his thumb. But this is a small mechanical mystery, as there is no way of finding out from the man himself, and what would it matter now? Mr Oakley slid down the wall without any grimacing. He gave out only the smallest moan, and his face had the sweaty paleness of the faces of injured footballers. Fomaguchi waited for him to faint or recover, and when he recovered, ordered him upright again. The officer went on speaking intently, with no apparent fury. In the end, he nodded, and managed to make his way back to the front wall in stages. His shoulders trembled.

Mr Oakley beckoned us over. He had seated himself crookedly in regard for his injury, but he smiled as we crowded solemnly against him. I glanced at the Comrade who opened his eyes just at that moment. He winked at me momentarily, as if he had regained a sodden sense of mastery which nothing in his past justified.

'He had to give me the thick end of that gun,' said Mr Oakley. 'Now I'm going to tell you something you must not mention to anyone else. They're going to take us away with them in one of the boats.'

We knew this, but to hear it now in the same voice as quavered over the Saunders' shambling homework, and reproved us over the state of the playground, made it foredoomed. The N.C.O. at the window stirred at the sound of our combined anguish, Fy's and mine, a cough like a thunderous hiccup. For Mr Oakley cut it short with a crisp wave of his good hand.

'Listen!' he spat at us, with plenty of the red meat of anger in the word. He *knew* how to make children listen. 'You aren't coming with us, neither of you. That's if you do what I tell you to. Right?'

Fy swallowed, and jigged her head up and down so strenuously that my sight was full of the path of her red eyes and tear-muddy cheeks.

'Sometimes,' said Mr Oakley, 'I've seen you two and Colly racing along that beach beyond the landing. Now that is very difficult ground. I mean, it's easy to get half a foot sliced off there, isn't it? You know that sure enough, Danny. I can remember they had to sew up your foot six months back.'

'Yes!'

'Fair enough!'

Mr Oakley swallowed. He was enthused and delighted that we would escape. His manner was avidly confidential. Harbouring a secret, and bringing it out at the right time, as if it were bacon or a pair of stockings obtained without coupons, was a joy he rarely had.

'Well, we can't waste time. We might have to go soon. But that young fellow, the one with the gun—don't go staring at him—when we get to the landing, you wait until I tell you to go. When I *do* tell you, you just jump off the landing, run the length of the beach, into the mangroves, on to the road, and straight home.'

He stared at us with a magician's pride, and saw our faces pale with desire.

'Listen, listen!' he insisted. 'You two will have to do the things I tell you, how and when I tell you. That man—and, for the second time, don't look at him!—that man has given his word that he will not shoot when you start to run. He'll pretend that the gun is jammed, that he can't shift the safety lever. He'll lower the gun from eye-level, and tug at it for a long time until he slides the lever back. Then he will put it up to his eye again. If he fires, he'll fire over your heads. But he doesn't want to fire at all, because that'd bring half the town down to the Co-op.'

Fy gazed at Lieutenant Fomaguchi as if he had performed a circus trick, in being able to act by reason and mercy.

'Why don't you come too?' she whispered at the schoolmaster.

'Because, if I try to go with you, he definitely *would* shoot me. If you don't do what I tell you, one of us or all of us, and maybe some of the Cape people, will be killed. But if you follow out what I tell you, you're as good as home.

'Don't both nod!' he went on, seeing that we nodded simultaneously and for all we were worth. 'Don't give a sign that anything's on. Don't say a word about all this after we've finished talking about it. Don't go staring at Lieutenant Fomaguchi. But, most of all, don't run till I tell you. Don't even think about running until we're at the landing. I go down to the landing with you. Now, at the right second, I lean down a bit and say, "Go!" When I say that, don't wait a second. Run together. If you don't run together, if one of you is too impatient and dashes away too early, or too scared and doesn't go when I tell you to, then only one of you will get away. You don't want that, do you?'

Our eyes on the N.C.O.s, we made a tense little shake of our heads.

'You mustn't look back once you start running. They might send a man chasing after you, but these men don't know the beach. They're tired and not properly fed. You'll get away. You're sure to get away.'

He said nothing more. The stillness hung solid purple in the shed. The Japanese whispered, and the lieutenant's fever rattled like wind amongst old newspaper. His head was up. He gazed out of the south-east-facing window, and saw the rain-clouds piled along the horizon. In them was cover for Saito's dash up the coast. Perhaps this consoled him for his decision to save us. Perhaps it was his entire reason for saving us. For although, in view of his sickness, let alone his temperament, he was not the believer Saito was in escape by sea, yet he would be cutting down on a good part of the expedition's slim chances by letting us run away. So he stood by one window, opening and closing his mouth with a pain of which he took little notice, and waited for the man across the room to see the sign from the landing. But all the man across the room did was belch. Fy had retrieved enough of her old temerity to snicker.

When the signal came, we moved in a group across the reserve, and all that was required for concealment was that you kept the bulk of the Co-operative between your path and the dimming town.

The Comrade shuffled like a grandfather. The varied dinginess of life could not be consumed, simply and according to one's bent, in a short blaze of valour. This knowledge oppressed him.

In the something less than half an hour since we had last seen them, Saito and the old priest had fuelled the fishing boat called the *Wanda*. It was moored by the side door of the Co-operative, and both the Co-operative building and the *Gilberta* screened it from the town. Each boat had a long thin jetty running to it from the reserve embankment. Beyond the bank of stone and the slope of Gunulla's beach the creek bottom dipped steeply. But where the *Wanda* stood athwart the tide making furtive sea noises, there was no beach at all. When Fy and I escaped, it would be along the stone bank, then down amongst the clutter of beams and planks, logs and ropes that held *Gilberta*'s landing together, under another such landing, and on to the meagre width of Gunulla's beach. Once there, the confusion of the two intervening piers would give us a sense of definite escape.

As we came near the *Wanda*, you could see Fy tracing our line of flight with her eye, and being pleased with it.

As well as fuelling the boat, the Japanese officer and the priest had seen to its water tanks. Also, Captain Saito had broken the lock on the side door of the Co-op to find it empty of fish, and only one iced bin of prawns in the place—a speciality being kept for an officers' dinner to be held in Gilbert on Friday night. Saito ordered Mr Oakley and the Comrade to carry it aboard with them when the time came.

Fomaguchi limped on to the pier, and leant against a post which creaked. The Japanese ambled silently around the doorway. One of them came out beaming with half a loaf of stale bread. We were lined up against the Co-op wall and the lieutenant faced us. His face was closed up with a very private pain, and I speculated on whether he had lied to Mr Oakley for the strange pleasure of shooting us down. Yet this idea was not half so repugnant as the naked decks of the *Wanda* just on nightfall. There were the wheel-house, the pump, the hatch, a few lengths of rope, a few baskets. On a summer's night, with rain coming up, it all looked as cold as Siberia.

Then Mr Oakley bent to us and hissed, 'Go!' At the word, we cut around the corner, and had vanished instantly from everyone but the lieutenant. We were into the shadows of that first pier. Our sandshoes just kept their grip on the slimy rocks. Under the second landing and on to the beach and, against Mr Oakley's instructions, I looked back to see that Saito had sent off two men after us. I had a glimpse of Saito himself hurrying everyone else aboard the *Wanda*.

Our escape was a scalding series of ten-yard sprints. When I disobeyed a second time and glanced back, all I saw was one of the Japanese sliding down the engine hatchway to the Gray's diesel inside the *Wanda.* But someone was thudding very close on my right, while a veil of mangroves grimaced up and down before us like medicine men. They came no closer, no matter what unknown muscles we brought into the complex of strain and suffocation which was our run down Gunulla's beach. I knew that the pursuers were scarcely twenty yards behind us, but their eyes were on the sand and its complicated hazards. It was nothing but fitting when one of them fell down, screaming as the rocks cut slivers off him.

The other one might have caught us; Fy hurling herself forward with small grunts, and myself quickly losing interest in anything but sitting down, and learning again to breathe. But this one still chasing must have felt doubts about following us into the mangroves, let alone beyond them. It was the sound of the *Wanda*'s motor bubbling over with noise that called him off, and had him staggering back towards the boat.

Within the mangroves, our feet for once not minding their soggy fertility, we waited, and quivered for breath. We could see the Japanese who had chased us helping his comrade along, who held both hands above his head, and watched the blood roll down his wrists. As soon as they fell aboard the *Wanda*, it shuddered into mid-stream, and went grinding towards the thunderheads this side of the horizon.

Memorial Avenue now seemed something sweet and fragile, and joy loosened all the strings of the body when we walked into Finnie's kitchen, to find Finnie himself in a suit and Stell with powder on, glowering at us. Didn't I know the priest was coming? Did I want my mother to be ashamed of me?

Fy chuckled with the irony, but I sat down at the set table and wailed.

26

Father Mullally, since gone, left an account of the voyage of the *Wanda*. It is in a novella-sized letter which he wrote, but neither sealed nor posted, to his brother, a Vicar-General in America. Like many an old priest, he quotes from the Breviary naturally and often.

Heu mihi, he writes at one stage, *woe to me, my habitation here is much prolonged. I have lived with the people of Cedar, and my soul has been very much amongst them.*

What with all the travelling to Pollyanna and the Cape, Emmaville and Mulldera, Mingaratta, Gilbert West and Nebo; what with saying uninspired Masses under tin roofs in all these places; what with being distrusted and victimized in a number of ways by the out-of-work, the leery-eyed abo, the plush good-fellow businessmen of Gilbert; what with the raising of money and the rushing of the Breviary and being more of a Rothschild than an Isaias; what with aridity and accidie and other spiritual ills, I would have been glad to die on the *Wanda*. It's not my world for the running, but I thought my bondage would be dissolved good and proper by those cow-eyed barbarians.

The first night, we must have been nearly ten miles out, and there were plenty of lights on the blacked-out coast to show the little boat its way. A low capping of cloud hung over our heads.

There was no wind until, about seven o'clock, a ferocious southerly came up, and soon after it, rain. All night it rained, and I could imagine the river swelling under the traffic-bridge at Gilbert, the Gilbert being a worse flooder than the Nile.

Saito, I found out much later, was the captain's name. He stayed all night long in the little wheelhouse stuck in the middle of the deck like a glassed-in lavatory. Throughout our journey, he showed himself to be a man of diabolic energy, and I can remember him resting once only.

A soldier kept the gun on us. He stood out in the rain, but he had oilskins on. At the stern or whatever they call it, a tarpaulin awning had been rigged, and beneath it was that young fellow who had insisted on keeping the gun, and thus saved the children. He seemed to be very sick now. Of course, he had pneumonia, or rather, would have it by morning.

As for us, we were in the bows with no cover, and were all seasick during the night. I do not write or preach glibly any more, but I say that in the deserts of night and sea, the deserts of heat and cold, the true God lives. In a way, I was happy there. It is a terrible thing to be a priest in a society which asks little of you except an advertisement of Mass times in the Gilbert *Argus*, and a painless absolution of their petty guilt. It is a terrible thing to be a business-man of God.

Juravit Dominus et non paenitebit eum; Tu es sacerdos in aeternum secundum ordinem Melchisedech. The Lord has sworn, and has not regretted it, that you are a priest forever...

Wet as a lump of sugar, I said by heart the Vespers and Compline of Tuesday. John Oakley scarcely moved or said a word. He was quite brave and hopeless all through. The Madman argued with himself endlessly, mentioning three names over and over, and was arrogant and contrite by turn. He couldn't keep still, but had to wriggle and rant all night.

I still had my watch, and I know that it was after one o'clock that the poor man became ungovernable, and started such a convulsion and screaming that you could hear the sick Japanese calling back to him in delirium, a maniac dialogue between one end of the boat and another. So they kicked the Madman in the stomach and tied him up. I crawled along to him to comfort him, but they kicked me too. It was like Croke Park on All-Ireland Cup Day. I think, incidentally, that Saito was angry because earlier that night, just after darkness had properly clamped down, he had been heading too northerly, and had nearly gone on to the Pollyanna Rocks when he got a glimpse of water breaking on them. The Pacific is full of fizz and phosphorus, and is a fine ocean.

After they had trussed him up, the Madman seemed much quieter, but at some stage or another, he must have struggled like Jacob with those ropes because when morning came, his wrists were galled and bloody.

I crawled back to him once more when his tormentors had gone.

'What's your name?' I asked him for a start.

'Len,' he said.

'Mine's Mullally, by the way. How do you feel, Len?'

'I feel worse at night,' he said, and began to cry and beat his head on the deck. It was a bad mixture of demons and D.T.s this man had.

'How do you feel worse? Does it hurt?' I asked.

'Of course it hurts,' he growled, and he told me about his wife Hilda, whose name I'd heard earlier in the night, and about his sons. All were dead. He moiled with himself on the question of whether he was to blame or not. And he asked me whether I had anything worth drinking on me, and beat his head on the deck again, and screamed. So that one of the Japanese came up and kicked him continuously on the body and in the head, until he was quiet. It was so cold there in the front, with the rain slanting in from the south-east, that I don't think it would have hurt at all if they'd beaten me. Towards morning, I got a fever, very suddenly, and that was a relief, as good as a nip of brandy, from the cold and the sea-sickness. Ugly-looking dawn arrived late at about a quarter to five, and the Madman, with his black mouth open and his leprous face, looked like a drowned man dumped on the deck.

It went on raining all morning. There were no planes beneath the low cloud-wrack, which pleased Saito when he hauled himself, hand over hand and yet regally, along his tossing deck on a rope slung the length of the boat. He surveyed Oakley and me lying sick in the open, the Madman being soundly asleep. Then he went back to the canvas shelter, having shown the new helmsman a course which was, I think, nor'-easterly. We did not see the land that whole day.

Dear God, the thirst of men who have just finished a spasm of sea-sickness. I thought of lime-juice, and Oakley lay with his head back to catch the rain in his open mouth. A lake would be forming over the mudflats in Central Gilbert. There was rain enough to ruin the corn and bog cattle and butt concrete slabs out of the levees up the river. But not enough to satisfy the thirst of an old man of a few poor cubic feet in thickness. I began to covet the condition of the Madman, who had gone on sleeping for hours, an unnatural look of concentration on his blue face.

My sickness left me in the mid-afternoon. A violent sea still sped us on northwards. The rain ran over us in squalls coming from the east. It was sub-monsoon weather at its worst and most persistent. John Oakley said something out of a sick, slack mouth about planes coming to sink us. He spoke of this eventuality as if it were the most desirable of all fates, for he was still feeling very badly and retching green bile.

There was a pleasant, humming fever in all my bones. I was absolutely happy, my stomach luxuriously sedate. It amazes me to remember how content I was with my sodden world, how homely was that befouled deck, how engaging the filthy arc of storm spinning above our heads.

I patted John Oakley on the shoulder, and mumbled as if I had sympathy for him. Sixty-five, in shirt-sleeves and clerical stock, and my old alpaca coat under my head, I could not have been a comfort to anyone, and cannot remember having less sympathy for a living soul. The joy of release from sea-sickness was of opium intensity. I fell asleep.

Hunger woke me. The Madman was screaming with the horrors, but sleep had been deeper than his row, and hunger deeper than sleep. The afternoon had become most sombre. Rain no longer moved in column of march, squall by squall, but came straight down with amazing solidity. I could sometimes see the troughs of high seas swinging upwards on my left or right, pocked with rain, but not tamed down by it. Oakley was asleep now, and I pitied him for this most uncivilized hunger he still had to wake to. In this country, we are badly unschooled in hunger, having only the slightest concept of what it is.

I saw almost immediately that one of the Japanese was stumbling up the deck to silence the Madman, and all I could think to do was recite the Vespers of Wednesday, which day, despite the fever and hunger and wetness, I knew it to be. It all meant nothing to the Madman, and that was just as well. The irony of the first psalm of Wednesday Vespers might have demented him further still.

Your wife is like a luxuriant vine on the walls of your house,

Your sons, as thriving olive vines, sit round about your table.

The wild, gluey eyes turned to mine, and the turnip head. It may have been only curiosity in him, but the flow of the Latin calmed him. The soldier stopped, clung to the rope, and waited for developments. One of which was that Saito came out of the wheelhouse.

'Old man,' he called, to me no doubt. 'You quieten him! Otherwise!' The sou'-easter blew his words into my face. They sounded moist, and the rain that blew in my face was like his spittle. I turned my back on him, and went on mumbling to the Madman.

And you will see your sons' sons, and peace upon Israel.

By now I was quite fevered, almost delirious you could say. The Madman was bound, but his scabrous face yearned up towards me or, more probably, seemed to. It is not the face of Christ, I told myself one second; and the next, it *is* the face of Job. In no time, I had begun translating to him from the first chapters of Job which I knew off by heart from Jerome's Vulgate. I tried to make it impressive, doing perhaps not as well as James I's scholars. But then, I had no time to polish my work.

'When therefore on a certain day, his sons and daughters were dining and wining in the home of their eldest brother, a messenger came to Job and said, "The cattle were ploughing and the asses grazing near them; and the Sabaeans stormed down and bore all away, and slaughtered the herdsmen. And I alone escaped to tell you . . ."

'He was still speaking, and behold another came in, saying, "While your sons and daughters were eating and drinking in the home of their eldest brother, suddenly a mighty wind swept out of the desert, and buffeted the four corners of the house which, toppling down, crushed your children, and they are dead. And I alone got away to tell it to you."

'So Satan left the presence of God and struck Job from head to foot with the worst type of ulcer. And, sitting on a heap of dung, he drained the putrid matter with a fragment of pottery . . .

'And his friends sat with him in the dirt for seven days and nights, and no one said a word to him, for they saw his overpowering grief...

'Let the day perish on which I was born. . . . May that day be turned to darkness. May God not countenance it from above, may it never be brightened with light. . . . May it be swallowed up in bitterness.'

John Oakley sat up suddenly and swore, and I realized what a forced comparison I was pressing. So I quietened down. Of course, as I say, I was a little fevered.

When it got darker, Oakley said, 'There's only one decent way to die. Full of beer and steak, and your heart worn out with active happiness. Notice, I say active...'

His voice trailed off.

'Are you afraid?' I asked him.

'I don't reckon I'll even squeak,' he answered. 'No firing-squad repentances for me.'

This irritated me. The man seemed to be implying that I only spoke to him to take advantage of him, to slip up behind him with a sacramental formula, and tie it round his precious neck.

'I think you'd better wait,' said I, 'till they start shaking their blood-stained clubs under your nose.'

'Hell, but I'd like something to eat,' he murmured.

That night we were not fed. I had not eaten for thirty-six hours, and the other two about the same. Therefore I stood up and approached the wheelhouse on the question of food and water. The Jap guard, unlike Lieutenant Fomaguchi, had no difficulty with the safety slide of his weapon. He could not understand what I was gesturing about, but Saito, who came out of the wheelhouse, understood, and told me that I had now forced him to instruct the men on guard duty to shoot us if we stood up again. I called him a barbarian and even qualified the word with an adjective in common use in this country. In return the guard knocked me off my feet by punching the barrel of his gun into my stomach with all his strength. I writhed for a while, and crawled back to the bows.

Meanwhile, the Japanese blacked out the wheelhouse somehow, and cooked themselves a hot meal on the primus there.

A thunderstorm began about seven. The sky cracked open with a row like the Apocalypse, and every ten or twenty seconds the deck and a few acres of water around would be flooded with a dry, white light. The Madman had cramps in his bound limbs, and I was half the night easing them with rudimentary massage. Oakley neither spoke nor moved. To do so would have been to admit pain, and he was getting too stubborn to do that.

Night lasted, a new sea in which Saito had lost himself. I was becoming used to darkness and the wet, and had got over expecting them to end. But breathing was hard now, and the nausea began to return.

Yet, from perhaps three o'clock, the moon would be revealed for a few seconds at a time as the dome of cloud rolled back from the east.

'The sun will be up today, Len,' I told the Madman, and he groaned, perhaps with the luxury of the thought.

At one time, the *Wanda* slewed madly to the north-west, the port side rose up above our heads. Oakley, the Madman and I shot across the slimy deck. But while Oakley and I were able to protect ourselves, the Madman cracked his head open on a steel rib of the bulwarks. Saito had turned back to the coast, and although I myself knew nothing of boats and knots, I guessed we must now have been very close to the Queensland border, very short of fuel, and open to detection from the sky. With search-planes thrown in and a hostile coast beside him, Saito meant to do what Captain Bligh and the convict woman Mary Bryant had done. Sail to Timor.

Today he would have to hide along some tidal creek, and tidal creeks are desperately tricky. Perhaps he would find himself stranded behind a sand-bank by mid-afternoon.

We must have been fifteen miles out and, as the *Wanda* slid up the flanks of the sea, the commander himself came to see us, using the central rope. He stood a few yards away, his legs far apart, like Henry VIII's in Holbein's picture. His feet wriggled slightly all the time so that he might keep balance and stand with dignity on the unpredictable surface.

'We have no food for you,' he roared in the half-light. 'We shall do the best to get some food for you soon.'

The Madman lay with closed eyes, and blood or shadow occupied his whole blind face. Over and over, he repeated the same obscene word. But fortunately, Saito had never met that curious branch of Anglo-Saxon.

'This man,' he said, indicating the Madman, 'must be kept silent. Lieutenant Fomaguchi is very sick. My men think this is a curse. If it is necessary for our expedition, this man will be shot.'

'He is a civilian,' I rushed in—I couldn't give Oakley a chance for languid heroics—'and if you shoot him, they will hang you.'

It would have been hard for him to deal with me physically and still keep his cherished hauteur. The seas were now steeper, without any rain to damp them down. He glared out across the bows, turned on us, and dragged back to the wheelhouse.

It was light before we were near the coast, but the sky and sea were empty. Behind us, the top of the sun swelled up, the same colour as the sea, dragging the rim of water with it. The sea and it seemed to have the same skin, which explains how the ancients believed that the sun was born of the ocean.

About half-past five, Saito throttled the engine down somehow, and the boat wallowed a few hundred yards out from a tumulus-shaped hill giving into a fine—creek, lagoon, lake?—it had features of all three. Saito edged the *Wanda* into it, with a man hanging over the bows looking for shoals. The Madman, Oakley and I were not interested in this. It was the lick of warmth from that bit of sun, and the promise of further warmth that occupied us wholly, and gave us the energy for talk.

Out of a clear sky, the Madman said, 'They're going to kill me this morning.'

'How do you work that one out?' asked Oakley.

'I've given them a lot of trouble,' he said, 'over the past three or four nights.' It did seem that long, and anyhow, no one knows what hours of daylight and darkness that soggy mind kept.

'Are you a Catholic?' I asked him.

He went a foul red and gave me the same word he'd given Saito.

'All right!' I said. But I didn't have the strength to be the proud priest that day. I did whatever could be done to prepare him for death, throughout which ministrations he gazed avidly at the work being done by Saito and his men to bring the *Wanda* into the creek, and anchor it close in to the shelf of sand across from the mound of sandstone hill. His limbs cramped almost continuously. The face expanded and shrank with his pain. Yet there was a terrible elation about his manner, and his eyes glittered when the engine stopped. I remember that a flock of red and green, blue and yellow rosellas squeaked across the edge of the hill; and I hoped that this was some sort of omen, for I'd never met them close to the sea. Immediately, Saito sent a man forward to cut the Madman's ropes. The released man sat gazing at his untied wrists in wonderment.

Now the captain himself came up to us. He waved his hand before him, as if making a choice from a tray of savouries.

'You,' he said at last, indicating the Madman, 'you are to land with these three men to look for fresh water!'

For a short time, the Madman was terror-stricken and cringed at my legs. While he lay there, I absolved him. John Oakley battled to his feet.

'You can't kill this man,' he said. 'This man is sick. We might be your prisoners, but the land you can see from here is our land. And you're its damned prisoners, and you know you won't get away from it. If you harm any of us, it will punish you.'

The Japanese N.C.O. who had unleashed the Madman nudged Oakley behind the knee, and sprawled him backwards. Now the Madman had calmed himself, and rose to his feet shakily. They fastened a rope around his chest under his armpits. He hobbled down the deck and was pitched over the stern. Three Japanese took to the dinghy, armed with knives, and saplings studded with nails. Then they dragged the poor foundering Madman through the water. Having landed in the dark sand amongst the mangroves, they pulled him the rest of the way. His blunt head bobbed awash and hopeless in the brown water. He came into shore like a despairing fish. At the edge of the mangroves, he half turned and waved or gestured for a moment. That was the last we saw of him.

When the three returned without him, Saito and the other Japanese, disregarding us in view of our debility, lowered over the side to them the skinny corpse of that young Japanese officer I mentioned earlier. It was carried shoulder-high into the low-lying scrub, in a different direction from that they'd taken earlier with the Madman. Saito kept to the gunwales, standing at attention.

It was an hour before the *Wanda*'s engines started again. There was little risk in this place unless a village lay up the creek. The prisoners had varied their uniforms with items of clothing from the wheelhouse and, from the sky, the *Wanda* might have looked like a trawler, honest-working, but at home that day.

Saito moved the boat into the shadow of the hill for the rest of the time. A flying-boat went over very low about midday. In the late afternoon, three of the Japanese came back from a foraging expedition with a loaf of bread and a half-eaten leg of mutton. I hoped that terror had been all they had left at the lonely weather-board farm from which the food must have been taken. I could not clear from my head the image of an emptied meatsafe swinging lazily on a veranda and, beneath it, the body of a middle-aged woman with an apron on.

That night being moonlit, Saito spun the *Wanda* into a wide estuary. My fever was worse by then. I felt unreal to myself and breathing was hellishly hard; but I could see water silvering up against a breakwater. At one time, the captain took our boat too closely around the inside of a river loop and without much jarring we slid on to a mud-flat. High tide, about three o'clock in the morning, lifted us free after a great deal of futile industry by the crew.

A little later still, we came to a fishing fleet moored at a levee close to houses. An oil tank stood at the mooring, a horizontal one on legs. The Japanese were much exercised in gliding the *Wanda* to the side of a trawler, mooring, quietly breaking the oil tank lock. At last, the *Wanda* was replete again. Although there were houses only a road's-width from the mooring, although one of the crew kept tense guard on the landing, no one came near us. Oakley and I could have perhaps slipped over the side at that time; but I was too weak, and Oakley was either too weak or too loyal. On the other hand, Saito had told us that if we made any noise which drew people to the landing, we and they would have been shot down straightaway.

Saito now allowed the boat to be nudged downstream, but failed to start the engines until daybreak. There was something that Saito and that engine didn't understand about each other, and this lapse of time, and the sticking on the mudbank, had destroyed him. Had he got his fuel and negotiated the river earlier in the night, he could have gone a great way north before dawn, and hidden somewhere for the day.

I am sure that he could see his peril and, that morning, protecting his assets for the first time, he fed us. We wolfed down—at any rate, *I* wolfed down—a quarter of a pound of mutton and a bit of bread. I was very unsure of my surroundings by then. The only sound in my ears was the rasp of my own breath. I slept a great deal, and dreamt continuously that I was presenting a paper on some aspect of moral theology to the clergy conference. Heavy, useless phrases of English and Latin slopped about in my chalice of suffering. Oakley held up my shoulders to help the breathing. His Lordship Bishop Joey Kerner insisted on gliding down the deck and congratulating me and, having done so once, would originate once again in the stern, catch my eye, and approach again.

I found it hard to believe, therefore, in the camouflaged and turreted flying-boat which found the *Wanda* and circled it endlessly. When it came down in a low arc over the boat, Saito had Oakley standing in the bows and the gun pointed at his ear. Away flew the flying-boat.

Some time later an armed trawler arrived, slouch hats and rifle barrels sticking up over the gunwales. Somebody with a megaphone hailed Saito over the calm waters, and that I couldn't catch the meaning of what was said worried me immensely, until I understood that it was spoken in Japanese, and made our five boys pensive. Saito stood Oakley up again, and then for our sakes, an English translation came over the sea. It urged on Saito the folly of his case and the necessity of surrender.

'If any of your hostages are harmed,' the voice ended calmly, 'we will attack your boat from the air, and destroy both you and it. Neither will we ever notify your people of your fate.'

The Japanese were gazing at us with lambent fright in their big eyes. Perhaps they suspected that some deadly secret had come to Oakley and me in the English message. They were uncertain now whether to stand or fling themselves to the deck. They were emptied of decision; if someone had nudged them they would have flopped down on the deck. Saito himself became furious. He grabbed the sub-machine-gun out of the limp hands of the guard, and moved towards us hunched like a man in pain. I could see the pupil of his eye, and the flecked brown of the iris blazing through the sights. 'He intends to shoot my head off!' I told myself, and grinned at him.

He let the gun fall out of his hands, and some of the local boys, who are in the army, say that it's a wonder it didn't go off just the same, it being a most dangerous weapon to handle at all.

Running to the wheelhouse, Saito screamed to the others once. They blinked. From then on, we could see his face through the glass of the wheelhouse. A face very white for an Asian, and crumpled with rage. When at last one of the others went to the wheelhouse, it was found that he was propped up impaled on a stake with a blade on the end of it. This weapon had apparently been used in the escape.

The four Japanese sat down on the deck. The armed trawler moved closer to the *Wanda*.

On the day Mr Oakley arrived back in Gilbert, his school was assembled in white shirts and print frocks to greet him. We sang a welcoming song, and then broke ranks and milled around him. Resentment at their grinnings and drawlings drove me through them. I had something necessary to say, and nudged his elbow audaciously, hoping he'd think it was someone of importance beside him.

'Mr Oakley,' I said, 'whatever happened to the Comrade?'

'The Comrade, Danny?'

But then the sub-editor of the *Argus* barged in amongst us, so I went away out of the station, climbed into the empty Cape bus, and flopped down in a seat towards the rear. From the window I could see a Greek café, and two beaten men reading a notice outside the grey employment office.

With a vast surprise which seemed to spill from my body and colour all that I could see from the bus, I found it a grief to be without the Comrade, to be free of his peculiar brand of menace. I was now in the same case as the child who has become accustomed to some form of blindness, deafness, lameness and, having used it as a cover for a number of failures and frailties, is suddenly cured and whole, and judged by the standards which apply to the whole.

I said two *Hail Marys* for the Comrade's soul, though it was hard to think of it as saved or damned or suffering purgation. I said a third one because I was afraid of this deliverance granted me by the Comrade's death.

By then, the others were clumping out of the station entrance. The youngest Saunders sat in the gutter relieving himself of his grubby sandshoes.

Fy and Colly rushed into the bus and towards me, down the aisle.

'Hey, Danny,' Colly said, 'they reckon the fish is really on at Fourteen Mile. You know, after the flood.'

'Coming with us?' said Fy.

Over that week-end, standing half-naked in the surf, the three of us caught nearly forty pounds of fish.

A CHOICE OF ENEMIES
Mordecai Richler

A Choice of Enemies has the highest recommendation: it is a strong, compelling novel by a writer who has produced such bestsellers as *St Urbain's Horseman*, *Cocksure*, *The Street* and *Hunting Tigers Under Glass*. It is a stark tale of two men who are opposites in politics, morality and life-style, and in love with the same girl. Both are refugees from different types of authoritarian regimes, their paths are destined to cross in London – and for neither is life ever the same again.

Fiction 40p

LYDIA
E. V. Cunningham

A $250,000 diamond necklace vanishes. Investigator Harvey Krim's assignment is to find it, with the promise of a big fat pot of gold if he can reach the end of the rainbow before the police. But the going isn't easy when someone else is playing murder, blackmail and fraud – and when in the middle of it all is Lydia, wild, unpredictable and bent on revenge.

Fiction/Crime 35p

THE PERFECT STRANGER

P. F. Kavanagh

This celebrated autobiography, winner of the Richard Hillary Memorial Prize for 1966, is as readable and funny as it is hauntingly tender. It is P. J. Kavanagh's tribute to the memory of his first wife, Sally, the perfect stranger – and it is also the absorbing, amusing tale of his early years, from schooldays and undergraduate life to the time he spent in Korea as a soldier and his happy, but short-lived, marriage to Sally.

'A real book; human, tender, gentle, loving, intelligent' – *Sheffield Morning Telegraph*

'A love story beautifully told' – *Sunday Telegraph*

Autobiography 40p

PROTEST

J. P. Donleavy, Allen Ginsberg, Norman Mailer, Colin Wilson, Jack Kerouac, Kingsley Amis, John Wain and others

One of the most significant developments in post-war literature, on both sides of the Atlantic, was the meteoric rise of the realistic school of writing as practised by the authors of this book. Stripping away all pretention and hypocrisy, they wrote of truth, celebrating man as he is, and in the process brought to bear a powerful social criticism. They were the true spokesman for their age. This is an important source book for all students of modern literature.

Edited by Gene Feldman and Max Gartenberg.

Fiction 60p

VANITY OF DULUOZ

Jack Kerouac

'A dazzling sunburst of white-hot prose' – *Tribune*

The Duluoz saga is known to thousands through such classics as *Desolation Angels* and *On The Road*: *Vanity Of Duluoz* relates the beginning of the whole story from the day Jack Duluoz/Kerouac won an athletic scholarship to university up to his wild time in New York City just as the underground scene there was starting to simmer. In it Kerouac rushes headlong into a frontal assault on life, 'a total abandonment to feeling' (*Guardian*), producing a book that is every bit as brilliant as his modern classic *On the Road*.

Fiction 40p

THE LUCK OF GINGER COFFEY

Brian Moore

The Luck Of Ginger Coffey is a brilliant example of Brian Moore's shrewd observation. Ginger Coffey is a thoroughly likeable failure; his new life in a new land (from Ireland to Canada) is hardly off the ground before it starts to crumble around him. At his lowest ebb, Ginger suddenly decides to fight back against his fate, and armed only with the luck of the Irish and a lot of bravado, he starts running uphill in hope, into a hilarious series of misadventures, disasters – and victories. *The Luck of Ginger Coffey* is a superbly entertaining novel.

Fiction 35p

THE ENGLISH ASSASSIN
Michael Moorcock

The third novel in the Jerry Cornelius tetralogy: in which Cornelius rises from the deep to witness the destruction of the world – and to poop the biggest party ever thrown west of London's Ladbroke Grove.

'The best of the Cornelius novels this far' – *Oxford Mail*

'A master story-teller unwinds a tale which Tennyson would have turned into immortal verse' – *New Statesman*

'Zany, grotesque, fantastical, Gothick, outrageous' – *London Evening News*

Fiction 40p

CAIN'S BOOK
Alexander Trocchi

The darkly brilliant bestselling novel about the twilight world of the junkie.

'An immensely enjoyable book, with all the ego-maniac vitality of the early Henry Miller' – John Pearson, *Sunday Times*

'It is different from other books, it is true, it has art, it is brave' – Norman Mailer

'It has a black icy brilliance . . . a journey to the end of the night by a man who has explored the deepest pot-hole of the human spirit' – Kenneth Allsop, *Daily Mail*

Fiction 45p